The
Shadowmancer
Returns
The Curse of Salamander Street

The Shadowmancer Returns

Returns

The Curse of Salamander Street

G. P. TAYLOR

REALMS
A STRANG COMPANY

Most STRANG COMMUNICATIONS/CHARISMA HOUSE/SILOAM/
FRONTLINE/REALMS products are available at special quantity discounts
for bulk purchase for sales promotions, premiums, fund-raising, and educa-
tional needs. For details, write Strang Communications/Charisma House/
Siloam/FrontLine/Realms, 600 Rinehart Road, Lake Mary, Florida 32746,
or telephone (407) 333-0600.

THE SHADOWMANCER RETURNS by G. P. Taylor
Published by Realms
A Strang Company
600 Rinehart Road
Lake Mary, Florida 32746
www.realmsfiction.com

Cover photographs: Digistock, Goodshoot, and Photodisk
Ship photo © Volvox/Indexstock
Jacket design by Gina DiMassi

This book is being published jointly by Strang Communications Company
and Penguin Group (USA) Inc.

Published in Great Britain in 2006 by Faber and Faber Limited, London.

Library of Congress Cataloging-in-Publication Data

Taylor, G. P.
  The Shadowmancer returns : the curse of Salamander Street / G.P. Taylor.
-- 1st ed.
     p. cm.
  Sequel to: Shadowmancer.
  Summary: Having barely escaped the evil sorcerer Demurral, Kate and
Thomas set sail to London, hoping to make a fresh start, while Raphah, who
has had a narrow escape of his own, begins a terrifying journey to find his
friends.
  ISBN 978-1-59979-084-8 (hardback)
  [1. Magic--Fiction. 2. Voyages and travels--Fiction. 3. England--Fiction. 4.
Fantasy.] I. Title.
  PZ7.T2134Shr 2007
  [Fic]--dc22

                              2007001049

First Edition

07 08 09 10 — 987654321
Printed in the United States of America

To my dear friend
Harmartias—a constant companion

Contents

Prologue

In the year 1752 on the night of All Souls, the forces of darkness pitted themselves against a young boy and his guardian angel. It was a battle so intense that even the devil and all his demons could not overcome the forces of heaven. High on the cliffs above the town of Whitby, the desires of the wicked Obadiah Demurral were brought to nothing. Victory was snatched from his hand by Raphah, Thomas, and Kate, three children caught up in Demurral's mad obsession to not only control the world but also subdue the power of God. Aided by Raphael, the most holy of angels, they fought to the death as the world was spun through the blackness of time, nearly bringing an end to the planet.

With the dawning of the new day, all evil had been cast aside. Demurral and his reluctant servant, Beadle, could not be found. Raphah, Thomas, and Kate escaped the town on the ship of Jacob Crane, a pirate and smuggler. On the journey through the mists of the Oceanus Germanicus, Raphah was dragged from the ship by an army of strange creatures and pulled into the depths of the sea. The ship sailed on to London and an uncertain future, watched from the cliff top by Obadiah Demurral, the vengeful Shadowmancer...

Pergrandis Cetus

It had been three days since the ball of fire had crashed into the earth, somewhere far to the south. The sky had burnt bloodred and made the sea boil. From every tree and every branch came the sound of small birds as they chattered mournfully in the cold evening air. Beadle stumbled as he cupped his bleeding cheek in his torn hands.

"Never mind, Beadle," he said softly to himself as he splashed the cold rain against his face. "On yer own now.... Yer own man, and not a minute too soon." He spoke as if to calm his anger. "Soon be at the sea and then away—never look at Demurral's face again; never hear another lie from his lips."

Beadle had trudged wearily for hours along the twisting path that snaked across the heath and into the forest. Now, as he strode on, Beadle could smell the ocean. It came to him in the fragrance of seaweed and dead fish. He stopped and looked about him. To one side the path fell away into a warren of dark gorse and bramble. Above him, cut into the shale crag, was a stack of narrow treads leading up the cliff. He stopped and looked to the sea below. Then he looked up to the high cliff that seemed to grow above him as if the earth moved upwards minute by minute with his every breath.

Beadle rubbed his chin and panted hard. The thought of climbing the steps onto the high peak daunted him. If he took that way, Demurral might see him from the tower of the vicarage.

"The vicar wouldn't let me go that quick," he said to himself in a croaked voice, as if he was unsure of his own words. "Can't be just running off—don't know which way…" He looked to the path that swept into the arch of gorse and shook his head.

"Never simple, never simple.…Down is so dark—but up?" He paused and sighed.

Beadle took two paces up the flight of steps that led through the trees to the light above. He stopped, listening to the sounds of the forest that rose up before him. From far off came the splintering of wood as if someone or something had taken hold of a small tree and split it in two.

"Down," he commanded himself quickly. The call of his tired bones had won the battle of his will. "And down it will be."

Step by step, Beadle walked on into the gorse tunnel that formed a canopy above his head. Beneath his feet the mud squelched with every fall of his foot. He wrapped his wounded hands in the soft dampness of his neck scarf, muffling them against his worn-out jacket. He smiled to himself as he saw the cut from the dagger that had slivered through the cotton of his frock coat, just missing his skin. The knife had glanced against the unread prayer book that he had carried for years like a talisman.

"He'll never do that again, not to his good servant Beadle," Beadle grunted as he walked, wiping a tear from his eye as he thought of the days before.

Beadle had stood in the remnants of the vicarage high above Baytown. The cannon of the *Magenta* had torn down every ceiling and mantel. When the world began to spin and the sky explode, Beadle had hidden in the cellar and listened as the stones crashed to the ground and what was once such a proud place was shaken to rubble. When he had emerged later that morning, all was in ruins. It was then that he knew his life had gone. What had been a reluctant home was now no more.

Beadle had hidden from his master in the stable and had taken a small knapsack packed with the few items he owned. As the night sky continued to quake, he buried himself in the thick straw and, unable to fight off the hands of sleep, he quickly slumbered.

"*Beadle! Beadle, come out!*" Obadiah Demurral shouted many hours later, the sharp words waking Beadle from his sleep. "*Now!*"

Beadle dug deeper into the straw, hoping not to be found. He listened as Parson Demurral smashed his walking cane against the stones and sobbed.

"Humiliated me, Beadle, humiliated," he squawked, weeping between each word and beating the ground. "They tricked us... a trap... power beyond belief. Imagine, Beadle. They had an angel—and not even Pyratheon could withstand his wonders. It brought the Ethiopian boy back from the dead. I fear he will come for me. I am as good as dead, and for me there will be no everlasting life. This is my curse, my future. I have taken on the powers of heaven and I have been crushed beneath their feet. *He cheated—broke the Commandments and twisted his own magic!* I must leave this place."

Demurral panted pathetically as he wept. "My only consolation is that the Ethiopian boy was snatched from the ship by Seloth and dragged to the depths. Saw it with my own eyes. They came from the sea like a ghostly choir of dead souls and snatched him from the ship. They moaned and cried until it deafened the world to their lament."

Demurral then wailed even louder, "Beadle, come to me..."

Hiding his knapsack, Beadle crawled from the straw, crossed the yard, and warily approached his master.

"Beadle?" Demurral whimpered, looking at him through tearstained eyes. "Is it really you? I thought you were gone—abandoned me like the rest, never to be seen again."

"Still here." Beadle whispered his reply as he held out a hand to Demurral. "Just waiting for you to come back. I hid from the sky-quake and fell asleep."

"*Sleep?*" Demurral raged suddenly as he grabbed Beadle by the arm and pulled him closer. "You slept and I almost died. Stole from me while

I lay in the grave and made your escape. I can see it in your eyes. Shoes for the road and two coats for the night. You weren't waiting, you were going. Weren't you, Beadle?"

Beadle nodded, his arm gripped by fingers that burnt his skin. He pulled to run away as Demurral twisted his cane with one hand and slipped the sheath from a long blade hidden within.

"No, Mr. Demurral. I would have waited. I promise," he wheezed fearfully as Demurral held the blade above his head, ready to strike.

"Why should I believe that? I took you in when no one wanted you. Nursed you, fed you, and this is what you do to me? Was I not kind?" Demurral asked.

"Very kind, sir," Beadle replied as he cowered from the blade.

"Then let this be a sign of my kindness, a cut for the cutting of my heartstrings." Demurral took the sword and slowly pulled it across Beadle's face. "There," he said calmly, stepping back from his servant. "A slice of my benevolence and one you'll never forget."

"Forget?" Beadle screamed as he lashed out in pain, knocking the sword cane from Demurral's hand. "Forget?" he screamed, kicking Demurral in the leg. "No more, Mr. Demurral, no more. This is the last you'll see of me."

Beadle kicked his master again and then scurried from the courtyard. All he could hear were Demurral's curses.

"I will find you, Beadle. You will never be free of me. Remember the blood and the hound of love that pursues you…"

Beadle shook the memory from his head.

"Never did like this place," he said as he hobbled even faster down the path, the drips of rain piercing the thick shelter of the gorse. "Not staying…he'll never see me again. All them years wasted looking after a monster. Sold his soul so many times, he's forgotten who owns it." Beadle rubbed the rain from his brow. "He'll never find me in London. Crane will help me. Three days' journey and I'll be there." He spoke the words as if they were a prayer, knowing that the *Magenta* would have sailed to the south.

Beadle allowed himself a single chuckle. Thoughts of freedom were tinged with sadness. What had been his world had crumbled with the meeting of a boy and the melting of a heart.

Beadle could hear the gentle rolling of the waves upon the rocky beach. In the distance, at the bottom of the slope, he could see a faint patchwork of light as the gorse and brambles thinned and the path ended.

Then the faint scent of decay seeped in from all around him. He could hear the wispy breath and the faint sighs of someone nearby. A yard ahead, just as the gorse tunnel dipped to the beach, was a hole in the tunnel roof. It was as if the gorse had been parted, and when Beadle looked more closely, he could see that each thong of growth had rotted. There at his feet was a pile of bone fragments and strips of skin. Beadle nervously walked two steps and, looking upwards from the shadows, saw the feet of a hanging man.

"Blast, bother, boiling blood," he said in a whisper, and he drew his breath sharply. The body hung from the long branch of an oak tree, the rope so stretched by the dead weight that the man trailed upon the ground. Clinging to him like a heavy knapsack was a gruesome black creature that bit into his shoulder. The beast was the size of a large dog and covered in thick black hair. Upon its back were two thick blades of shoulder bone like gargoyle wings. As Beadle watched, the creature stopped gnawing.

This was the beast that Beadle had often spoken of but never dreamt he would meet.

"Not possible," Beadle said to himself as a quiet breath. "Cannot be…" The fearful words were choked in his mouth as he saw the beast gazing down at him through two red eyes that glowed in the darkness of the wood. It licked its teeth as it sniffed the air, and two black, pointed ears twitched from side to side.

Since he was a boy, Beadle had heard of creatures such as this. From these creatures, the woods below the vicarage took its name—Beastcliff. Mothers would warn their children that if they were not good, then they would be left in the wood for the beast to find. Every cow that disappeared and every slaughtered lamb or fox-snapped gosling was blamed upon the creature.

It was said that the creature would sit upon the milk churns at night and turn them sour, or dance through the corn so it would die of mildew. Its shape was carved and placed upon the high spire of St. Stephen's.

Now the creature was chewing its prey before him. It ripped at the flesh and took another mouthful of meat.

Beadle waited no longer and edged back into the shadows of the gorse tunnel. Soon, he found himself upon the shingle beach of Hayburn Wyke. He looked up and scanned the darkening sky, wary that the creature could be above him.

Walking close to the foot of the cliff, Beadle tottered through the rocks and boulders that littered the cove. Eventually, he came to the waterfall. It gushed from the dark of the wood, falling twenty feet to a large pool gouged from the shale. This was the place where Demurral had conjured the Seloth to attack the ship that had brought Raphah to the shore. This was the place where he had seen the madness take over his master and turn him from man to beast. Beadle slumped wearily on the ancient stone that was cut by the waves to the shape of a human hand. He looked to the sea as he soaked his muddied boots in a pool of water. He stared down at his shimmering reflection in a pool. The wound to his cheek had almost dried. He bathed his face in the cold water and washed away the blood. It burnt bitterly in the salt water. A sudden breeze stirred the pool. Beadle waited until it stilled again, then looked long and hard at the wrinkled face that peered back, half smiling and proud of his escape.

"Getting older and not much wiser," he said as his stare fixed gaze to gaze, looking dreamily into his own eyes. As a warm vapour rose from the pool, the reflection of his face suddenly changed. What was once *his* brow and countenance had in an instant become that of Obadiah Demurral. Gone was the wound to his cheek and blood-covered brow, gone the wrinkled jowls that hung like a mastiff dog. Now, staring back, bold and blue-eyed, was his master. Obadiah had chased him in his imagination and was now before him, a thin smile cast like grim steel across his lips.

Beadle quickly closed his eyes and put his hands across his face for double measure to shield him from what he saw. "*No!*" he shouted.

Slowly he opened his fingers and peered through the cracks. There was Obadiah Demurral glaring up through the water as if he stood on the far side of a glass window.

"You'll not go far, Beadle," the vision said as it looked upon him. "Wherever you go, I will find you."

2

The *Magenta*

K ate looked out at the evening sky from the aft of the ship as the *Magenta* rocked with the incoming tide. The ship creaked and groaned as it was led on by the flood that rolled up the Thames towards the glow of the city of London. High on the stern mast, Thomas rang the fog bell and called out. The trees of Dog Island reached towards him as long, thin fingers, stripped of life. All around the murk grew thicker, and then cleared for a time as the vapours danced upon the water. It would then press in, unexpected and cold, like thick ice against the side of the ship.

Pulling her coat about like a warm mantle, Kate thought of Baytown and her father. She had left without a farewell. She knew he would think she was lost for good. He would fear her gone in the skystorm that had torn through time and spun the sun around the earth, turning day to night and back again as Kate had counted the chimes on the church clock.

All around Kate the crew busied itself. They turned rope, stowed sail, shouted, and hollered from the high mast, but it was as if Kate were all alone.

"Hold her fast," Jacob Crane bellowed. The tide was pushing them on as if the *Magenta* were a bobbing cork. "Take in sail."

Crane bawled to the crew as they scrambled to run the rigging like giants climbing into the clouds. "Keep deep water to the portside and away from the shore."

Kate stared at the black, churning swell that lapped against the ship and searched for some sign of Raphah in the deep and gloomy depths. She couldn't understand why he would have been brought back to life if it were just to meet a watery grave. She ever hoped that he would come from the water, saved, alive.

"Thomas," Crane shouted to the teenage boy, "keep a lookout for ships. Should be all about us. Tide's running fast and we would cut them through if we caught one amidships." He spoke quickly, his words bold and unfaltering as he paced up and down the deck, knowing what each man should do.

Something greater than distance now separated Kate from her friend Thomas Barrick. In the days that had followed their escape from Demurral and the Seloth's attack on Raphah, Thomas had spoken to her less and less. He had sought out a place far away, sleeping in the crow's nest high above the deck. He would wrap himself in an old oil-skin, twist himself around the mast, and sleep on. By day he would search the far horizon.

Neither she nor Thomas had spoken of what had happened to Raphah. It was as if his presence in their lives had been a dream and that in the short time they had known the kind and mysterious African, he had visited them like a ghost and then left for another world.

"Ship ahead!" Thomas hollered, and he rang the fog bell again and again, bringing Kate back from her dream. "Off to the portside, I can see the mast and…" His voice faltered as if he had seen something he couldn't describe.

"What is it, lad?" Crane asked as he held to the rail of the bridge and strained to see what lay ahead in the growing gloom of evening.

There before them, in the mist, was a tall sea-ship. In fine gold letters, painted next to a figurehead of a wolf, was its name: *Lupercal*. It had one mast half-rigged with ropes that hung like tattered hair to the deck.

Crane stood fast and stared as the *Magenta* drew alongside. There, hanging from the yardarm, was the body of a man. In the sullen fog that surrounded the ship he could see that the sails had been torn through. The deck was strewn with smouldering rocks, the remains of the comet that had exploded in the sky. As the ship drew closer, Crane began to smell the scent of death.

"Make to!" Crane shouted as the crew stared on, not wanting to move. "The ship's adrift without a crew and ours for the taking. Salvage, lads, salvage!"

The words brought his men to life. Kate looked at the high yardarm and the dangling corpse on the empty ship that somehow made progress against the tide.

"How can it go the other way against the sea?" Kate asked quickly as Crane drew the cutlass from his belt.

"It can't, lass, and that's what makes it our quest to find out." Crane raised an eyebrow and gave her a thin smile. Then he called to his men: "Heave her to port and tie her on."

From above her head, two men swung from the mast across the open water, landing upon the other ship. Quickly they threw several ropes back to the *Magenta,* and within minutes the two hulks were strapped together.

"Search it from end to end, every door and cabin. If you find anyone, bring them to me." There was the slightest hint of trepidation in his voice, as if even Captain Jacob Crane expected the worst. "And cut that man from the yardarm—dead men often tell the most tales."

Thomas went with the crew, clambering from the *Magenta* over the makeshift ramp that had been strapped across the divide between the two ships.

"Captain," came a voice. "Best be seeing this for yourself."

Crane looked at Kate, sensing she could feel his foreboding. "You better stay here, lass." In three strides he had crossed the bridge and jumped from the steps to the other vessel. Kate could hear their whispers as they glanced this way and that, unsure as to what could be listening.

"Search it well," she heard Crane mutter as he looked back and forth, cutlass in hand. "Go stay with the girl; keep her safe."

Pulling up the collar of her sea coat, she held on to the side rail as Crane's first mate jumped aboard the *Magenta* and sauntered towards her.

"What's the fuss?" Kate asked as he got near, resenting Crane thinking she couldn't take care of herself. "Don't need *you* to nanny me."

"If you'd seen what was over there, you'd be glad of the company," he replied as he took the pistol from his belt and half-cocked the hammer.

"Then let me look—I've seen worse. I once saw a drowned man who'd been dead for a month, crabs had—" She was stopped short as the man quickly put his hand to her mouth.

"You've never seen death like this," he said quickly, in a hushed voice. "Whatever killed him wasn't a man, nor a creature I've ever seen. There's an empty ship in the middle of the Thames, the lamps are lit below, and the captain's table is set for two with not a soul to be found."

"Empty ships don't sail themselves," Kate snapped as she tried to push by him.

"Don't be thinking you're going from here, lass. Crane told me to keep you on the *Magenta*, and that I'll do."

"Then tell me what's going on," Kate protested as she pulled on his coat and kicked her feet against the bulwarks.

"Let her come, Martin," shouted Crane from the deck of the other ship. "If she's a mind to see the state of this man, then let her be. Set three men on watch about the *Magenta*. Tell them to shoot at anything that comes near. Whatever did this might not be far away." His voice echoed through the eerie silence.

With a firm footstep, Kate crossed from the *Magenta*, planted herself upon the deck of the *Lupercal*, and stood beside Crane. She looked for Thomas. Crane saw her glance.

"Thomas is searching the ship," he said in a whisper, without moving his lips. "Whatever did this could still be aboard." He pointed to a bundle of rags that littered the deck just by the forward hatch. "If it's still on the ship, we'll soon find the beast."

Kate glared at what was once a man, lying on the deck empty-eyed and parch dry. He wore a scarlet tunic with gold braids and had a large medal pinned to his chest. She could see that the skin of his face had been burnt so it hung in jowls like an empty sack.

"Captain," came a voice from below, followed by a long groan. "There's one alive."

Crane stepped into the hatch and quickly went below the corked and polished deck. Kate followed, wanting to stay as near as she could, fearing that something stalked the ship and trusting Crane for her protection. A row of fine, neatly trimmed oil lamps lit their way, the likes of which she had never seen before. Small cabins, all neatly trimmed and turned, led off to either side. Kate looked as she passed by; upon every bed was the body of a man. Each was dressed for sea, and all looked the same: faces burnt like the first.

"Here, Jacob," came the shout again from the midst of the gathering that filled the captain's cabin. "He's dying."

Crane barged his way down the long corridor that led from the hatch ladder to the cabin at the back of the ship. It opened into a long galley strung with hammock beds, neatly tied and ready for sea.

"Aside, lads," Crane shouted as he stepped into the room with Kate on his coattails.

The gathering parted. There before Crane was a young man. He was slumped in the captain's chair near to death, his head propped against a large table covered in rolled charts with a ship's clock bolted to the wood. Behind him, two of the cabin's windows had been smashed open.

Kate could see that he was not much older than she was. He was dressed in the coat of a junior officer. He slowly raised his head from the table and tried to smile at them. The skin hung from one side of his face, but the other side appeared quite normal. To Kate, it looked as if he were two men in one, the first young and fresh, the other old and sagged.

"What became of the ship?" Crane asked as the lad appeared to struggle for his breath.

"A comet crashed from the sky. It exploded above us. We had just left the dock. It was as if the world was on fire. I could smell the burning as we were bombarded…" He spoke quietly, then slumped back to the table as if the words had taken from him all his strength.

Crane took hold of him by the mop of thick black hair and held his head to the light. "What did this to you?" Crane asked.

"There was a scream—I came in and…" The lad gulped his breath, his eyes flickering with each relived moment. "It was the dust from the sky. It burnt as it came to earth. Everyone it touched melted; the flesh dripped from them."

Crane stopped and looked at his men. They stared wide-eyed at the lad and then at Crane. "It will kill us too, Captain. The dust is every-where," one said as he stepped back from the door.

"We will not die from this," Crane replied sharply as he raised his cutlass and pulled the pistol from his belt. "Leave him; he's as good as dead. I care for the living, and this is a trick of hell. People don't melt like wax dolls." Above his head the ship creaked as if she would split in two.

"I set a charge in the magazine," the lad moaned. "Strapped it to the gunpowder with a long fuse. It will explode on the hour." He slumped against the table. "I couldn't do anything else. Had to sink her before we reached the sea. I didn't want to die of this. I didn't want to die away from the city. It's always been my home…" He gasped for breath as more of his bile seeped from his skin, soaking through his coat. "I always thought I would die from a Frenchman's bullet and that I would stare into the eyes of the coward as he pulled the trigger. That's how the old sooth said I would see my death: staring into the eyes of a coward."

"What hour was the charge set for?" Crane asked.

"When the hands strike midnight, we will be gone. London will never see such an explosion again, and the name of the *Lupercal* shall live on forever," he whispered. "I thought no one would come for us. We were anchored in the river for three days. I cut the ropes and set us adrift."

"I've heard enough," Crane shouted. "Get every man from the ship—there is but two minutes before this madman has us all in hell."

"Wait! Save the *Lupercal*," said the lad in his last breath. "You could cut the charge."

"And die trying?" Crane shouted as he pushed them all to the door. "To the *Magenta*—we must be free of this place! Run!"

"We've been through this before," Thomas shouted to Kate. He grabbed her hand and they began to run. Kate could hardly swallow—her mouth was dried to a crust, her lips charred by a sudden desire to escape her own pounding heart.

Crane followed and pushed Kate from the galley, his eyes fixed on a square of sky that flooded through the narrow opening onto the deck. He knew that in the hold of the ship, far away in the dark depths, was a charge that would soon explode. "Be off and set the *Magenta* free—save her."

"You can't leave the boy," Kate shouted as Thomas dragged her across the deck.

The chief officer took his sword and cut the ropes that bound the ships together. He jumped the widening gap that swirled with deep black water. Kate was the last to run across the gangway from the *Lupercal* as it fell into the water. Thomas swung the gap on a long rope that stretched from the high rigging.

"Where's Crane?" Kate shouted, unable to see him in the crowd of smugglers who dived from one vessel to the other.

Looking back, Thomas saw Crane coming from the hatch of the ship. He held a pistol in his hand, the hammer fallen and barrel smoking. Thomas realised what Crane had done. The lad would not see his beloved destroyed—he had died close to the city he cherished and, as the seer had foreseen, stared into the eyes of the man who killed him.

"Run, Jacob!" Thomas shouted as the gap between the two ships widened by the second. Crane strode across the deck of the *Lupercal*. The divide was now too wide to jump, and the river was churning beneath.

"If we fail, find *The Prospect of Whitby*, the Devil's Inn—and there we shall meet on the Feast of Saint Sola the Hermit," he shouted from the *Lupercal*.

From the guts of the ship came a sudden boiling sound that began to split the timbers and spit each nail from every wooden board.

Thomas swung from high above and, as the *Magenta* rolled in the tide, swooped to the deck of the *Lupercal*. He screamed to Crane as he sped like a black cormorant towards him.

"Crane, Crane!" he shouted as the rope took him closer.

Jacob Crane looked up as the boy swung near, and grasped the rope as it passed by. Together they swung towards the *Magenta* as the *Lupercal* drifted further away, its boards splitting as from deep within came the sound of the growing explosion.

A ball of fire lit the night sky. The mast fired into the heavens as the rigging exploded across the river. The fire burst from the ship, splitting it in two as it spun on the tide.

Thomas jumped from the rope, falling to the deck of the *Magenta*, and Crane clutched to the side of the ship as a ball of fire billowed above his head. There was yet another explosion. Splinters of wood were blown through the air, and then all was silent. The burning hulk of the *Lupercal* drifted on like a Viking grave ship.

Orcus Gravatus

Beadle stood in the foaming water, the waves washing his feet. On the beach ahead there appeared to be the body of a great fish the size of a small ship. Beadle swallowed hard, fearing the beast above could see him, then ran towards the stranded fish.

"Glory, glory," he said in a daze. "If it isn't a whale! No greater fish have I ever seen. How such a beast should be found in this way—" A sudden wave fell upon the shore, knocking Beadle from his feet. For several moments he lay there silently, his head peering from the surf just above the water like a fat seal pup.

"Bathed," he said to himself and laughed. "First time in a year have I had a bath."

He walked on towards the great fish, soggy-booted and brushing the wet sand from his face.

To his surprise there was a dull groan from the belly of the whale. Beadle listened again, sure he had heard his own name muttered from its bowels.

With an outstretched finger he prodded the whale's thick skin. It was cold, hard, and felt like candle wax. Beadle looked into the creature's glazed grey eye as a large black gull landed upon its back and began to peck at a long tear in its flesh.

The whale writhed slightly and let out another low moan. Beadle placed his head against the side of the whale and listened. Again the groan came from the lifeless creature.

"But you're dead," Beadle said. He opened the whale's mouth with both hands and looked deep inside.

"Hello," he said slowly, rubbing his chin against its large, hairy tongue. "Can't see how you can speak—unless you're a spirit."

Suddenly a dark hand darted from the throat of the whale and grabbed Beadle by the collar. In two tugs, it pulled him headfirst into the creature's mouth. His head was pressed against the inners of the creature's throat, and all was dark.

"Leave me be, spirit," Beadle groaned as the hand pulled tighter.

"Beadle, it is I—Raphah," came the half-drowned voice from the stomach of the whale.

"But you're dead. Demurral told me," Beadle cried as he twisted free and fell back onto the sand. "Said he saw you picked from the *Magenta* by the Seloth, thrown into the sea, and drowned."

"That I was, and if I'm not out of here soon, I'll be drowned again on the next tide and gone for good," Raphah cried, his voice muffled by the tightening inners of the whale.

Beadle stared in through the open mouth of the sea-beast and looked at the glistening black face of a lad he knew well. "It *is* you," he said as he pulled the mouth open wider, tilting his head to one side so he could gain a closer look. "How?"

"Swallowed, completely whole—a miracle of miracles," Raphah replied, forcing a laugh. "Cut me free before I die of the stench."

Beadle reached into his pocket and took out the knife he always carried. With both hands he cut again and again into the side of the whale. Skin and blubber parted as the sharp blade went deeper, until it suddenly spilled open like a broken keg of herring.

Raphah slid like a breech pup into the surf, surrounded by black treacle that oozed from the whale as if it were birthing water. For a moment he covered his eyes as he sat in the waves; then, as the water cleared, he dived beneath the surface and rolled in the gentle swell.

"Free again and by what miracle," he said as he ran his fingers through his long dreadlocks. "Never thought I would see the light of day." He stopped and looked at Beadle as if startled by his presence. "Your master saw me?"

"So he said, but he's not my master. He and I have..." Beadle paused. "Parted company."

Beadle attempted to smile as the sea salt stung the wound across his cheek.

"You're hurt," Raphah said as he saw the man holding his face.

"A mark left so I'll never forget Demurral. Every time I look into a glass, I'll remember the night he gave this to me. A parting gift for all my years of service."

"And your journey now?" Raphah asked.

"London. To find a man who would love a servant like me. Either that or I'll find Jacob Crane and put to sea with him."

"Then I'll walk with you and share the journey. I must search for Kate and Thomas. I know that Demurral will want the youngsters dead," Raphah said.

"Wouldn't be good for you to be yoked to one like me," Beadle replied as he turned to walk away.

"Do you forget what happened, Beadle? A friendship forged in adversity is not to be given away lightly. You helped us escape from Demurral. It was you who saved us." Raphah held out a hand towards him.

"Needs must and I couldn't see you killed. Not another one—there's been too many," Beadle replied. "If you came with me, he would find you easily. And you are the Keruvim.... So I'll be off. Soon be dark and best be out of the woods."

"I know a cave, a Hob-hole," Raphah said hopefully as he followed Beadle. "It's not far. We can have a fire and food. You can tell of your plans, and I'll tell you of mine."

Beadle shook his head. "The further I am away, the better I will be. Demurral has a way of reaching you that grows wicked by night. Don't want to close my eyes again until I am far away. Demurral can see things to which mortal eyes are blind. He can see the future and visions that are beyond the sight of men. Wouldn't be surprised if he happened to be watching us now."

"I'll come with you and watch you whilst you sleep," Raphah insisted.

"No, I walk alone. But perhaps we'll meet in London. Take my advice: head for York. Take a coach to Peveril and there change for London. That's where you'll find the *Magenta*." Beadle spoke urgently and looked nervously about. "Perhaps I'll see you there."

"So mote it be," Raphah said, resigned to Beadle's wishes, "but a handshake for the journey?"

Tentatively, Beadle reached out and took hold of his hand. He looked at Raphah's shining face and his dark hand against his own white palm. He felt its warmth.

"Best be out of the wood before sunset," Beadle repeated. But he held on to Raphah's hand for a few moments and continued to smile, searching his face. "You'd best be getting to that Hob-hole—soon it will be really dark."

"It wasn't by chance you walked this path, Beadle," Raphah said as Beadle turned to walk across the shingle beach. "I asked Riathamus twice for a saviour. Once I was sent a great whale, and then I was sent you. There is a power at work in your life that you will never escape from." But Beadle was walking further away, not turning back. "Nothing happens by chance. There is a plan to prosper and not to harm you…"

Raphah's words faded on the wind as Beadle took the muddied path across the shingle to the shale cliff and into the wood. It rose steeply up a dirt slope and twisted in and out of clumps of trees that gripped the rocks. As he crossed a small mound close to the cliff edge, Beadle turned to look back to the bay. He could make out the shape of the whale on the beach. And there on the beach was Raphah, too, now almost indistinct in the fading light. Beadle stopped and gave a half-wave. Raphah lifted his head and waved back.

"Poppycock and balderdash," Beadle said to himself as his feet squelched through the mud. "I can go alone," he said again and again to mark each step. As he walked on, he thought of what he had become. From somewhere in his head, the memory of a Christmas came to mind. He didn't know where or when. All he could see was a great fire stacked in an old hearth and upon the hearth a weighty stocking that swung in the first light of the morning. Beadle could smell the memory: a burning pine log scented the room, and in the pot that steamed by the fire was brandy and fresh tea. Then, as now, it filled him with great happiness. Joy replaced his desperation and fear. "A merry Christmas," he said out loud as he walked along, "and many of them."

Beadle pressed on as the track climbed towards the high peak that grew from the sea to its stark summit. In his heart he knew that once at the top he would be able to see a castle far to the south and the pasturelands that led to York. Beadle picked up a long staff that lay across the path and peeled the dry bark as he walked, deep in thought.

"Good for villains," he said out loud, dreaming of being attacked by footpads and beating off an attack. "Beadle the Brave—not one left standing, aha!" He laughed as he imagined brave scenes and lashed out at the overhanging branches. "That would be me, given the chance. All would be gone as they saw my shadow, not a single footpad or rogue in the county, and all down to Beadle."

As he walked on, he patted the pocket of his coat and felt for his supply of boiled eggs. "Five guineas in my pocket—enough for bread, beer, and a seat on the roof, with plenty left over for the rest of the way. London calling—to a faraway town, as Uncle Joe would say."

Just ahead, in the dark of the wood, came a sudden cry. The howling of the dog-beast echoed about the rotting tree trunks and moss-covered branches as it ran swift-footed through the forest. Beadle peered into the failing light, wishing he had invited Raphah for the journey after all.

"Nothing to be frightened of. Beast won't come. Not for Beadle, the old feckwhit." He laughed and cast a wary eye behind him with every third step. With a firm arm he planted his staff against the shale path and tottered on, chortling a merry song to try to forget the night-beast. The lane fell away to the undulating vale that continued until it faded into darkness. Scattered across this vale were the lights of farmsteads that glowed like warm candles against the night. A large, solitary oak sprouted from a mound of stones in the centre of a pasture, standing above the terrain like an island. Beadle had come far enough for the night. He pulled his cloak about himself and, turning up the collar of his coat, snuggled down to sleep.

The night was interrupted by the sound of screeching. Beadle woke suddenly and looked about, unsure if he dreamt what he had heard.

"I'm armed!" he shouted, his empty words echoing across the land.

It was then that it came, rising silently from the mist. The beast stood in front of Beadle and raised an eyebrow, staring through glowing eyes that cast a red light upon him. It growled as it slowly chewed the skin of its last prey.

"You'll not get far with me," Beadle shouted nervously as he stood his ground, staff in hand. Every story that he had heard of the creature churned in his head, and he heard voices repeat their warning: "No one can survive the beast."

The beast growled and barked as it stood before him with blazing eyes. Beadle got ready to make one valiant wallop with the stick, knowing he did not want to die without a fight.

"Give me the staff," a soft, dark voice said by his side.

"Raphah?" Beadle asked as the beast growled again.

"You are not a hard man to follow, and I *never* take no for an answer," Raphah replied quietly. "Friends shall always be friends no matter what.... Give me the staff."

Beadle handed him the staff as Raphah stepped before him.

"Go, creature. Leave this world be, and do no more harm."

The beast snarled and bared its teeth like an old dog as it clawed the air, about to attack. "Very well," Raphah said as he held the staff towards the beast. "So be it."

The mound began to shake, and every limb of the oak tree started to tremble. Mud and stone quivered beneath their feet as a power welled up from the earth through Raphah and into the staff. The beast stared at Raphah. In that instant, the staff began to shine and glisten. What bark was left turned quickly into scales as the staff was transformed to a spitting serpent that danced back and forth in Raphah's hands.

"Take him!" Raphah shouted as he threw the serpent towards the beast.

Beadle buried his head in his hands and huddled deeper in his coat as the sound of the attack burst through the night air. The creature shrieked as the snake took it by the throat and pulsed venom into its veins with every bite.

"Is it gone?" Beadle asked when Raphah came and sat by his side.

"Soon," he replied.

There was a final earsplitting howl that shook the trees and swirled the crows from a faraway roost to circle the moon. The wounded beast shook the snake from its neck, turned, and ran into the night. Then all was silent. Raphah stood, picked the staff from the ground, and handed it to Beadle, who cowered by the oak tree. Beadle held it in his hands and looked at the dry wood. A single scale was all that remained of the snake—that, and the faintest outline of a serpent's head in the grain of the wood.

"It has gone," Raphah said.

"What was it?" Beadle asked.

"A Diakka—a creature created through magic, sent by an old friend to haunt me." Raphah smiled.

"My staff—was it transformed by magic?"

"No," Raphah said. "I am no sorcerer. It was by a power that we can all know—the power of Riathamus. This is the power of all goodness."

Raphah sat next to Beadle and held his hand. Together they looked out across the vale towards the lights of the castle and the sea beyond. "Demurral will be wanting us, won't he?" Raphah asked.

"He will," Beadle said. "He will not be content until we are all dead."

"So we find Thomas and Kate and live or die together."

"The *Magenta* will be in Rotherhithe by the morning," Beadle said, as if he knew the lad's thoughts. "It'll take us three or four days if we travel fast enough. We could get to London before Demurral."

"*Us?*" Raphah asked.

"Best we travel together, lad. Can't have *you* coming to any harm." Beadle laughed. "After all, that golden statue you carried must be worth a pretty penny."

"The Keruvim?" Raphah asked.

"The golden creature that Demurral had."

"It's lost," Raphah said as Beadle began to dream by his side. "Dropped from the ship and given to the depths. It was my task to return the Keruvim to my homeland. Now it is gone—but I will wait for a sign. There is a power, Beadle, that speaks through the rising of the sun and the dew upon a blade of grass. Soon it will reveal what I am to do. One thing is certain: as long as Demurral has breath, he will seek us all. His desire is to see me dead and my spirit captured to be used with trinkets of divination. I know it will not be long before I see him again."

The Great Chain of Being

From the bridge of the *Magenta*, Jacob Crane peered into the growing dawn through a long brass telescope. He had not slept but had paced the deck as he had watched the *Lupercal* burn. Crane cast his eye to the entrance of Billingsgate Dock and shouted for the *Magenta* to be turned to starboard and eased slowly into its awaiting berth.

The whole of London appeared to crowd the quayside. Beggars, barons, and mountebanks jostled and tugged as cutpurses snatched moneybags and fob chains and ran into the throng of the morning market. The barking of mad dogs echoed through the lanes as the militia fired musket shot after musket shot, in the way they had done every morning since the coming of the comet, in a vain attempt to quell the madness that gripped every dog in the city.

Looking up at the Custom House, Crane envied the row upon row of silent white statues on the marble façade. There at the height was old greybeard, God Himself, universe in hand and the world as a footstool. To His right was the sun and, stretching into the distance, chiselled and smoothed in stone, was the great chain of being that captured every creature and beast in the order they were created. A week ago, Crane would have scoffed at the mention of such a Creator; now his mind was torn in two with the possibility that such a Being could exist.

As the *Magenta* heaved to and came to rest against the oiled hay bags and fenders that hung from the side of the quay, it creaked and groaned, and the keel shuddered.

From below the mottled deck, Kate and Thomas peered upon the teeming quay. Neither had seen so many people.

"We did it, Kate. We got away from Demurral. I'm sure he won't find us here," Thomas said with an excited smile. "I've never been further than Runswick Bay—and now, Kate, we're in London, the capital of the world."

Kate laughed as she saw the look in his eyes. Gone was the melancholy of the ship, the distant looks and hidden despair. Thomas had returned to her life, and as the sounds of the city filled her ears, she felt that all could be well. With one hand she twisted her hair into a knot and slipped it beneath her triangular hat as she pulled the brim to her ears. "I wish Raphah were here. He'd know what to do. Less than a week since he was taken. Do you ever think of him?" she asked.

"Every minute of every day," Thomas replied softly as they stared from the hatch to the deck. "But now I'm convinced he'll be well. It'll take more than the stopping of the heart to take the life from him. Raphah may be gone to the depths, but it's as if he's not dead. Funny, really. I felt the same when my father drowned. Always thought he'd walk through the door one day, the same as before he'd left. Still…" Thomas paused and looked deep into her eyes. "Maybe not on this earth but one day, I think, we'll see him, face-to-face…"

Without any command being given, a thin gangway was pushed from the quay and down upon the deck. Kate could see three men dressed like clerics waiting for the ship to be tied to the pier. From their garb it was obvious that they were not country parsons but were in the pay of the King. The tallest held a parchment writ wrapped in a red silk ribbon, clutching it as if it contained the secret of life itself.

Crane gave no attention to these men. He motioned for Kate and Thomas to hide from view and checked each line, continuing to shout out a list of commands. When the ship had been finally secured, Crane folded his arms and leant back against the rails, smiling to himself.

It was then that the tallest man, holding the writ, set off at a trot down the gangway and onto the ship. Kate and Thomas watched on as Crane bristled, seeing the men step one by one from land to his ship.

Crane detested most clerics. He had met so many and realised that they were more often than not the third son of a minor aristocrat who could only find them a living in the church. To him, they were men who did not know their Master, nor ever would.

"Is it not the custom to ask for permission to come aboard?" Crane asked as he stepped towards them.

"Depends who owns the ship," chirped the smallest man.

"This vessel is mine, always was and always will be," Crane answered as he took a rope peg from the rail and held it as if he were about to knock an eighth bell from the man and beat him with it. "Anyway, clerks, no matter how holy their orders, are not welcome here."

"Clerks on high orders and not holy ones," replied the writ-carrier caustically as he sidestepped Crane and walked towards the mast. "Give unto Caesar what is Caesar's and whatever is left to whoever you want," he said, and all three started to giggle and laugh like cackling children.

"I'll have no games here," Crane shouted, holding the rope peg like a club. "Tell me what tax you enforce and then be gone."

"*Militia!*" shouted the cleric as he took a hammer from his robes and nailed the parchment to the mast.

Above Crane's head, the crowd parted as a row of brightly clad militia stepped forward and lined the quayside. Each man pointed his musket towards Crane's head and took aim. "I advise you, Captain Jacob Crane, not to resist what we do," said the tallest cleric. "We have it on the highest authority that you are remiss in your duties."

"In fact, you are found out by sin," chivvied another as he turned his hat rim with long bony fingers.

"What have I done that brings a legion of redcoats and three half-wits to my cabin door?" Crane asked quietly as he nodded to Kate and Thomas to keep under cover.

"Payments and debts for docking in the port of Whitby, leaving without the payment of the aforesaid monies, the carrying of goods without a certificate, and…the abduction of children." The tall cleric spoke smugly.

"For any writ you need a complainant. I know no one who would complain against me in those parts," Crane replied.

"The Crown is your accuser and Parson Demurral is our witness. Are you acquainted with him of whom we speak?"

Crane shuddered at the words. "Dogs, rats, slugs, and priests— I know them all in the order of their creation, and you take his word over mine?" He walked to the mast and read the charges nailed upon it.

"See for yourself, my dear unfortunate fellow," the cleric said through pinched cheeks as he tapped the writ with his finger. "You have twenty-one days to pay the Crown the sum of *two thousand guineas* and return the children you took from Demurral's care, or the ship will be lost." The cleric spoke in one breath and then paused. "In the meantime, I would be grateful if you'd take your belongings and vacate the ship." He paused momentarily and looked about him as if he had just remembered something important. "We also seek a thief, Mr. Crane—an Ethiopian who has stolen an item of great value. For him and the gold we will search your—or should I say, *our*—ship. Guards, see that Crane and his men are gone this day, and if they refuse, I give you permission to kill them where they stand."

The cleric wrung his hands together, then wiped them on the front of his long black cassock. It was as if he tried to brush away the grime of what he did. Crane eyed the militia as one by one they marched onto the *Magenta* until they outnumbered the crew.

"Two thousand guineas?" he asked. "What makes you think I can't just pay you now and have you off the ship?"

"What makes me think?" the cleric asked, half laughing. "I know Parson Demurral and on his word have it that you are a villain, a scullion beyond scullions, and penniless to boot, and that if I were the last man alive and you the richest, it would break your soul to give the money to a mere priest. Am I not right?"

Crane shrugged his shoulders. "So it is not just for the money that you are here. I know of no children taken from Demurral, and as for the African, what is your real interest?"

"It is more what he has taken. The item he stole is of great value."

"Do you have long arms? For where you will have to search, you'll be wet up to your elbows. The boy's dead. Went overboard in a storm. Took all he had with him, and it was his to take—not Demurral's, the pope's, or the King's, but his."

"Do you have proof of this?" the cleric asked as his companions clustered around him and grumbled like foxes.

"Proof? What is proof? Tell Demurral that all he seeks lies twenty leagues beneath the waves and will never be seen again."

"That, my dear friend, is not the news I would wish to convey," the cleric said. "Read the writ and bring all I have demanded in twenty-one days, or else your precious *Magenta* and everything in her rotting hull will be taken to Dog Island and scrapped. Is that clear enough for you to understand, *Captain* Crane?"

The cleric nodded to his companions, and together they filed from the ship as if they followed a funeral procession, heads bowed and hands grasped in pious prayer.

"Search the ship," the cleric shouted to the militia as he walked the gangway and stepped onto land, followed by his two assistants. "You know of what we search: an item of gold that could be hidden anywhere. Search the ship, I say. And when you are done, cast Crane and his vile friends to the dock. Remember, Crane—two thousand guineas and the children, or the *Magenta* will be matchwood."

Crane didn't grace him with a reply. He urged Kate and Thomas to go deeper into the darkness and then slowly followed them as the militia set about the search. He had known such times before; riches and poverty had always slept in the same bed.

"The day is lost. Remember, go to *The Prospect of Whitby* on the Feast of Saint Sola the Hermit," Crane said to the chief officer as his crew gathered what they could and left the ship. He turned to Thomas and Kate and spoke quietly. "I know a place where we can go until this *temporary* setback is taken care of. There is a street not far away from here. I have a friend who lives there called Pallium. He'll look after us."

"Demurral got here before us," Thomas said as Crane pushed them into the ship's store and a guard stomped upon the deck above them.

"Faster for the old goat to get a message to London than for us to sail here," Crane replied under his breath. "Thought we were done with him. But don't fear." Crane smiled. "Can't say I have ever wanted children, but now I appear to be stuck with you."

"If the militia are looking for us, how do we get from the ship?" Kate asked.

"Powder monkeys and sewer rats never get stopped leaving the ship," Crane said as he reached to a shelf at the back of the store and pulled the stopper from a wooden barrel. "Smother your face with this grease and take a handful of black powder and do the same. You'll stink and look as if you've come from the bowels of hell. If anyone should speak to you, mumble a reply and keep walking. I'll talk for you. Carry a sack on your shoulders, and we'll be from this place without an issue. Stay here and I'll be back for you, and don't move until then."

When Crane returned, he nodded without speaking, bidding them to follow. He pulled a sea-sack to his shoulder and buried his face in the side. Kate and Thomas did the same, then went ahead of him from the darkness of the ship into the light of the London morn.

On the deck of the *Magenta* there was no sign of the militia. "Below deck," Crane muttered as he urged them on towards the gangway. "Looking for the Keruvim."

"*You!*" shouted the officer of the guard as he stepped from the bridge. "Where are you off to?"

"Doing as the writ commands—leaving my ship to the care and providence of the militia," Crane replied as he pushed Kate in the back to walk on.

"But you will not leave this ship without being searched," said the officer of the guard.

"I would prefer to die with a sword in my hand than a rope around my neck. You'll not search me."

"Very well. Then you die on your ship. Smithson," he shouted high into the ropes and furled sails.

From the rigging above they heard the long slow click of a musket ratchet. Thomas, who had reached the dock, turned and looked up and in the crow's nest saw a rifleman.

"*Rats! Plague!*" Thomas screamed the distraction over and over, his words echoing around Billingsgate Dock, and every mouth took up the cry. Fear of the plague had hung over London since the coming of the comet. Now it was as if God Himself shouted it from the echoing stone of the Custom House, and panic swelled the multitude. Thomas pushed Kate and set off to run.

"Run!" shouted Crane as a musket shot rang out from the rigging, missing Kate by an inch and splintering the plank beneath her feet. The sound of the musket rolled from building to building, growing in anger like distant thunder and sending people running for cover as the panic spread.

"Quickly, every man for himself—remember, go to *The Prospect of Whitby* on the Feast of Saint Sola the Hermit!" Crane shouted to his men as he pushed them towards the quayside.

Thomas sprinted along the plank as Kate panicked, threw her sack into the water, and frantically gave chase. The three ran from the ship as the rifleman madly reloaded his musket.

The three ran panting along the muddied, cobbled streets, their hearts bursting as catcalls and shrieks bit at their heels. It was as if the whole of the city had taken up the cry of the plague.

"Quite a storyteller," Crane said when they finally slowed to a quick march and looked back to see if they were still being followed. "Thought I would have to kill him until you came to my rescue."

"First thing that came to mind," Thomas said as they rested in a doorway of a narrow street. Even in the morning light, it felt as if it was well before the dawn. "How will you get the ship back?"

"Steal it from under their noses," Crane said as they walked on.

"Will Demurral come looking for us?" Kate asked anxiously.

"As sure as night follows day. Demurral has unfinished business with us all," Crane said as they escaped along the narrow marketplace.

They trekked through the narrow streets and alleyways by the river. Crane led them past the same place several times, as if the street for which he searched didn't exist. There was no one to ask the way. All the roads were empty of life, and as they went on, the streets became narrower and darker.

"Here," said Crane abruptly after they had walked the hour through a maze of alleyways. Above what looked like a small doorway was a sign cut into a wooden plate. Crane read the words: "Salamander Street."

The Glory Hand

The crowing of a pheasant called the dawn as Beadle woke from his sleep. He was alone, nesting in a pile of dry bracken that kept him warm.

"Raphah," he called out.

There was a cough from the branches of the mighty oak. Beadle looked up, and there in the heights of the tree was his companion staring down at him.

"Can see the castle and the sea, ships at harbour," Raphah said with a smile etched on his face. "And the road to the west."

"Then we best be following your eyes," Beadle replied as he stood up and brushed the dirt from his coat.

Raphah dropped from the tree and cartwheeled across the grass.

"A stroll to London?" he asked. He strode on, expecting Beadle to pick up the pace and follow.

"If you keep striding that fast, you'll be dead before we get across the field," Beadle panted, and Raphah slowed his pace.

In the distance they could see the spire of the great Minster Cathedral that hung grey against the bright blue of the November sky. They saw no one; it was as if the land had been emptied of all life.

The dirt track they followed through the day opened out into a winding lane and then to a narrow, muddy road. For several miles they followed in the wheel ruts of a heavy carriage that was some way ahead. Occasionally, they could hear the baying of the coach hounds and the call of the horn carried on the breeze. Then it would be gone far into the distance as it rattled against the thick cobbles that stuck out of the ground like so many dead men's skulls.

It mattered not to Beadle how far he would have to walk. The journey was an opening to a new life. As he marched on, he listened to Raphah's stories of Riathamus, and the thoughts of Whitby and fear of Demurral faded.

With every word that Raphah spoke of Riathamus, Beadle was taken to a new world. "Allow Riathamus to touch your heart and you will find peace," Raphah told Beadle, and the words brought him hope and comfort.

The low sun that had followed their day began to set and shimmer against the sky. As night drew closer like a blanket, the sound of the coach hounds came again.

"There's an inn down the road," Beadle said, suddenly remembering the purpose of their journey. "We can get a coach from there to Peveril and then to London—that's if…" He stopped and looked to the ground, the joy gone from his face.

"If what?" Raphah asked.

"They may not let you travel inside the carriage. I have the money for two of the best seats. All I have is here, honestly, and I will gladly pay, but…" He gabbled the words faster and faster, not wanting to get to the truth behind what he spoke of.

"Because of my skin?" Raphah asked with a smile.

"Not used to it…different…I know, but they might not…" Beadle choked on his words, knowing what he meant to say but fearing speaking what was so obvious.

"Then I will travel on the roof, as I have done before," Raphah said.

"And I with you…and they will not say a word against you. I will stand for you and speak my mind no matter how gigantic they may be."

"Brave words, my fellow traveller," said a steel-bright voice from behind an upturned cart that lay at the side of the road. "I am glad you would stand and be so bold. Who is this knight of the road to whom I now speak?" the man said as he wrapped a black cloak around his shoulders and stepped towards them.

Beadle eyed him up and down. He was tall, half a man higher than even Raphah. He was incredibly thin, as if a layer of translucent skin had been draped across his bones. He had eyes of the deepest blue.

"And you are?" Raphah asked as he took a step back from the man, uneasy at his presence.

"Barghast—if a name should matter at all," the man replied.

"We are—" Beadle said, only to be interrupted by the man.

"Beadle and Raphah. I am well acquainted with you both, having listened to your ramblings for these last few miles as we travelled together along the highway," said the man. "Come.... It is a mile to the inn, and we should walk together. The sun has departed the world yet again and darkness reigns. It is a dangerous place since the coming of the comet and the sky-quake. Many people lost their lives, and so will many more." Barghast waved his cape back and forth like the wing of a huge bird trying to scoop its prey beneath.

"Then we are pleased with your company," Raphah said. "To the inn," he continued, hoping not to give the slightest glimpse of the suspicion that filled his heart.

Barghast walked slightly before them, his head bowed low as if to stoop to their height. "From your accent, Mr. Beadle," he said, "I would say that you come from Baytown?"

"Nearby," said Beadle with a nod.

"I once passed through—had business with the parson. Demurral...have you heard of him?"

"And you, sir, from where do you hail?" Raphah asked, ignoring the man's question.

"I am a wanderer, always have been and always will be. Never will I rest until I have travelled every road that man has made." He paused and gazed sadly at the stars as he rubbed his long nose with the tip of his finger. "If I had only given *him* rest, then life would have been so different."

Up ahead, by the crossroads, the sound of the inn grew closer.

"You will want a room for the night?" Barghast asked his companions.

"Barn will be good for us," Beadle replied. "Plenty of straw for a night's sleep, and why spoil yourself for a fleapit of a coaching inn?"

As they approached, they could see a pack of coach hounds sleeping by the stable door. The beasts crowded together to keep out the night cold. Behind them was a smouldering forge from which hot embers were lifted upwards by the breeze like fly-sparks. A few men sat on stools near the doorway with the innkeeper. For the travellers, the scene murmured contentment and peace.

"We would like some rooms," Barghast enquired of the innkeeper. "Do you have rooms?"

"Full," said the man pointedly. "To the brim. Three coaches from York and one from Peveril. Can't fit 'em all in."

"Then I suggest you go inside and turf someone from their bed so that I can have a night's sleep," Barghast growled at the man, dropping his bag to the floor and taking off his cape.

"Tell 'em yourself. Not one will budge, not even for the devil himself," the man replied, awash with ale and ready to fight.

Barghast knelt over the man and for several moments whispered in his ear as he held him by the scruff of his collar.

"Very well," the man said feebly as Barghast lifted him to his feet. "That'll be done."

It was as if the drink had suddenly left the man. He sucked in his gut and tightened his belt as he stepped across the threshold and into the inn. Barghast followed on, dragging his cape and leather bag behind him.

"We have rooms—at my expense. You will be my guests," the man said as he waved for them to follow.

"I have money for the both of us," Beadle protested.

"But not enough when there is no room at the inn," Barghast insisted.

Raphah nodded to go along with the man as he pushed Beadle forward. "Don't worry, Beadle. This is no chance meeting. For now, we do what he desires," Raphah whispered, stepping over the threshold.

As they walked into the hallway, they could hear the frantic conversations that filled the downstairs rooms. From the large front parlour with its raging fire came the hubble-bubble of a gathering of men. They stilled their chatter to hushed voices as Barghast led Beadle and Raphah onwards. To one side of the hallway was a large kitchen; the door was open and a black oven range steamed in the candlelight. Beadle looked in and saw a maid, who gave him a soft smile.

They tramped up two flights of stairs and along another dark hallway until the man took a key from his belt and opened a door for Barghast.

"Hope this'll do, sir. I'll have someone come and take the things away. I'll double this man up in another room. Don't think he'll mind—not if he knows it's you who has taken his room."

Barghast didn't reply. His eyes scanned the room, and then he turned to Raphah and Beadle. "Only one bed, sadly. I am sure our host will find you a soft resting place?"

The man nodded. "Yes. And Mr. Barghast, we tend to turn in early. If it's a coach for Peveril you want, then it leaves at six. Breakfast at four. Three tickets?"

Barghast nodded and smiled as he slid into the room and quickly shut the door.

"Important friends," said the innkeeper as he hurried Beadle and Raphah along the way they had come. "Without him *you'd* be in the barn, *if* you were lucky, *and* you'd be walking to Peveril." His mood had changed, and he glared at Raphah.

The innkeeper pushed them along the landing and down the stairs until they came to the kitchen door. Once again the gathering in the parlour hushed their voices to a mutter as Raphah and Beadle went by the open door.

He took them into the kitchen. "In here and up there," he said, pointing to a double bed in a loft just below the roof. "It's warm and too high for fleas, so think yourselves lucky. Eat, drink, sleep, and make it quick—not good to be awake when it's dark. Too much goes on that's not the doing of men." The man gestured for the maid to leave the room. "All you can eat on the table. The oven's stacked, so it will keep you warm. *Important friends*...huh!"

"What did he mean, Raphah?" Beadle asked when he was certain they were alone.

"He meant we take some bread and cheese and drink some ale and fall asleep."

"No, about the darkness and the goings-on....And what about Barghast? Why did he follow us?"

"It was only when I saw him in the light that I realised who he was. I have heard of him. Mr. Barghast is a collector of antiquities. He searches for that which he thinks has special powers. I was once told that he carried the finger of a saint and that he desires to find the Grail Cup," Raphah said. He picked at the meat that had been left on the table and pulled a chunk of bread from the loaf.

"The Grail Cup? Demurral spoke of it often. So what's Barghast doing here, and why does he travel with us?" Beadle asked.

"That we will discover, my friend, that we will discover," Raphah said as he climbed the ladder to the high bed and looked down at Beadle from the ceiling. "If Barghast is the one I was told of when I sailed to this land, then he will soon reveal himself and his purpose. Until then, let us keep close counsel." Raphah rolled himself into the blanket. "This is a good place. A warm night's sleep and then on to Peveril. Soon I'll find Thomas and Kate."

The heat from the oven had warmed the bed. Raphah smiled to himself as he looked down at Beadle. "Beadle, sleep."

"*Sleep?*" Beadle asked as he stepped too close to the oven and singed his rear upon the scalding door. "Sleep? How can I sleep when we have trouble with us? That's what Barghast is—*trouble*. I can smell it a mile off, and it'll follow us all the way to London."

"And all I can smell is a burning Beadle." Raphah laughed as Beadle wafted the smoke from his burnt trousers. "Whatever Barghast may be will not concern us. In the morning we will be gone to Peveril."

Beadle reluctantly began to climb the ladder to the bed. Lying next to Raphah, he gazed down to the wooden floor far below. With the coming of night it was as if the house began to yawn and tremble.

The sound of footsteps could be heard on the landing and then got closer. From beneath the scullery door, Beadle could see the flickering of a shadowy light.

"There's someone coming," Beadle whispered to Raphah. But Raphah didn't stir.

The large brass door handle began to slowly turn. Beadle pulled the covers up about him and peered quietly from the bed as he pretended to sleep. He could feel a rising sense of panic as the door slowly opened.

From his vantage point, Beadle could see a bright glow. When the door was opened wide, he was surprised to see a Glory Hand. Beadle knew the likes of it well. It was like the one that his master Demurral had used several times before—the hand of a hanged man, severed at the wrist, dipped in saltpetre and wax, dried, and charmed by a magical incantation. Once a Glory Hand was lit, all who slept could not wake; to put out the flame would take blood or the milk of a mothering cat.

A cloaked figure held the lit Glory Hand. With a clank of bagged coins, the figure placed it on the table and emptied the moneybag beside it, counting the money coin by coin. The figure stacked the coins in neat piles, gold to the left and silver to the right, but seemed to be searching the bag for something more.

Beadle could not see the figure clearly, but he was certain it was neither Barghast nor Demurral. The figure was far too small and its hand far too delicate.

"Money and nothing more," the soft voice said.

The coins were placed back in the bag and the Glory Hand removed from the table. Without any backwards glance, the figure left the room.

Beadle counted the footsteps back up the stairs and along the corridor. Again, at every room they stopped until their sound faded into the still night. In the kitchen, Beadle sniffed the air that hung heavy with the fragrance of wild jasmine.

Salamander Street

Salamander Street was dark and muddy. There was little light from the sun; even on this bright morning the oil lamps burnt as Thomas, Kate, and Jacob Crane walked slowly on through the shadows.

"Good place to stay," Crane joked as he pulled the scarf around his face like a mask. "I know a man here called Pallium. He's a banker. He'll give us a room and see what is to be done."

Crane stopped by a wooden door that had once been painted white and had now dulled to a mouldy yellow. Nailed into the broad oak panel was a lion's head that had once heralded the call of visitors, but now its jaws were rusted shut.

"This must be the place," Crane said as he rapped his fingers against the wood. "I hope Gimcrack Pallium is here." There was unexpected warmth in Crane's voice. His eyes glinted, suggesting he had shared much with Pallium and remembered him as an old friend.

"The most generous man in the kingdom—he came here but a year ago, and never a nicer man would you want to meet. If it is within Pallium's power, he will get it, and if it's in his benefit, he will give it to you. But beware—he is the fattest and most gluttonous man in the kingdom. Eats like several horses and will pinch the food from your plate."

Crane banged on the door again as he leant against the wall and looked back and forth along the empty street.

"No people," Kate said as she followed his eyes. "Strange for the time of day. It's morning, and every house looks as if it still sleeps."

Crane rapped again upon the door and shouted, "*Pallium! Pallium!*"

From the dark bowels of the house came the babbling of what sounded like a madman.

"Who wants me?" asked the croaking voice from within. "It's the middle of the night, and I am one for sleep."

"Pallium?" Crane asked, scarcely believing the frailness of his friend's voice. "Is that you?"

"Who should want to know such a thing?" came the reply. A small wooden slat was slid open, and two feeble silver eyes stared out into the gloom. "Crane—Jacob Crane? *He* said you'd be coming. All's made ready, all ready. What an amazing thing…"

The bolts were pulled and the door slowly opened. A frail hand came from within and was held out towards Crane in greeting.

"Pallium," said Crane softly in greeting to his friend, looking at the shrivelled body that wore the clothes of a man thrice its size. "You have changed, my friend. I was telling my companions—"

"Changed?" argued the voice as he snapped back his hand. "I am as I have always have been. Never in finer health, and a more robust creature in London will you never find. I didn't expect such an argument in the middle of the night."

"We seek rest and not discontent, Pallium. My friends and I are in need of a bed. I am without a ship, and I do not wish to be without a friend. This is Kate and Thomas, and we have travelled from Whitby." Crane smiled as he spoke, hoping to calm his friend.

Pallium rolled a worn gold coin in his hand as he looked at Thomas and Kate and gave them a slight grin.

"*Suppose* we could find you a straw mattress…somewhere. Things are not as easy as they once were, Jacob. Money doesn't grow on trees, and I am sure someone has been helping themselves to mine. You never know when you will need all you have. Always death and always taxes— nothing so certain as those two creatures."

"Since when has concern for the future been a thought for Gim-crack Pallium?" Crane asked as he looked about the cobwebbed hall-way with its rotting drapes and tattered rugs. "The man I once knew wouldn't give a thought for the morrow. Weren't you the one who would tell me never to worry for the morrow, as this day has enough troubles of its own?"

"That was then," snapped Pallium, pulling his baggy coat about himself as if it were a blanket. "A year ago I would have agreed, but things change, people change, lives change, and with each day in Sala-mander Street..." Pallium stopped short and looked at them all through a screwed-up eye. "Not short of money, are you? Not here to take what I have, are you, Jacob?"

"If it's money you want, I have plenty for us all," Crane bellowed, his temper growing shorter. "I may be a thief, but I have honour for my friends, and from you I would take nothing. If you want me to pay for our lodging, then very well, but don't think I'm a thief."

Pallium shook his head, as if he tried to rouse himself from a dream only to be sucked back into his waking slumber. "A shilling for the lodge and find your own food?" he offered, slobbering over the amount. "Each?"

Crane looked at the dust-covered panelling and smiled. "It would be a pleasure, Pallium. I take it you would then burn some wood to warm this place through?"

"Only enough to take the chill from your breath. Can't have Gal-phus thinking I am being wasteful."

"Galphus?" Crane asked as Pallium led them through the long hall and into the scullery. "I have not heard his name before."

"A fine man," Pallium said. "And my landlord. He has a word for every season, and if I'll be blown, it is as if he knows everything. Owns the whole street and deserves every glorious brick and beam. This is the finest place to live in the whole of the city. Never been happier, and it's such a place. I'm honoured to live here, honoured, Jacob, and you will be, too, when you meet Galphus."

"Where do we eat?" Kate asked, looking around with eyes that spoke of her discontent.

"The inn, of course," replied Pallium. "The Salamander by Potter's Yard. No finer place to eat in London, and Galphus dines there."

"Then that will suit us well, for we could eat a whole ox," Crane said as he stepped into the scullery. "In fact, you will join us and we will all eat together."

"Can't leave Pallium's Palace," Pallium sniggered as he held out his arms as if to show them the finery of the scullery. "Well, that's what I like to call it. Never know when someone will come. There's always work to do and so little time and so much to count."

The three looked about the room. Its cold stone floor echoed the sound of their steps. In the centre of the room was a long candlelit table that was stacked with neat piles of gold and silver coins. By the table was a solitary chair.

"Don't get out much," Pallium said wearily as he looked at the coins. "*They* need so much work, so much consideration. Just like children, they have to be kept safe. I know each one as if it were my own. I look after them for Galphus, and he would not be best pleased if I were to lose a farthing or halfpenny."

"We'll need a bed, Pallium. Sleep has been a stranger to us these last days," Crane said as he eyed the sparseness of the room.

"You'll have to share," Pallium said briskly to Thomas and Kate as they looked nervously about them. "I have a room for you, Jacob, all ready. Fit for a king, and some would say an emperor, with a sea hammock and not a bed. Was told you'd want it like that. Prepared it all yesterday when I knew you were coming." Pallium rolled the coin in his hands as he spoke.

"*Knew* we were coming?" Crane asked, his sharp eyes searching Pallium's face.

"Yes, Galphus told me yesterday," Pallium said in a matter-of-fact way as he edged his way closer to his precious coins. "Came especially. Said he had heard that Jacob Crane would come and stay at Pallium's Palace. Never thought he'd be right, but as with everything, Galphus is astounding."

"I would love to meet a man who knows my thoughts a day before they come to mind," Crane said suspiciously.

"Galphus is a seer and prophet beyond doubt. He has made me a happy man since I came here. For years I had a melancholy that would never leave me. Galphus soon fixed that—for not only is he a seer, but also a physician. When Galphus said you were coming, I didn't question his word. I made up the beds and strung up the hammock." Pallium spoke quickly, pulling on his long brown whiskers and frowning. "But he didn't tell me *why* you were coming…and I don't want any trouble, Jacob. Can't be having any trouble…"

"The last thing I would want," Crane said as he eyed Kate and Thomas to be silent on all that had happened. "Just a few days' rest until I get the *Magenta* back, and then we'll be to sea."

"Then," Pallium grumbled reluctantly, "my home is your home." His eyes flickered from one to the other and back again as if he were a cornered animal.

As they stood in a long and uncomfortable silence, Thomas looked Pallium up and down. His jacket and waistcoat hung from his body like a horse blanket, and his breeches sagged like sash curtains about his spindly legs.

The one thing that gave Pallium an ounce of glory was his shoes. Thomas widened his eyes as he stared at their beauty—never had he seen foot coverings so fine. In the dust and the murk they glimmered and shone like burnished jet stones. Large silver clasps held them to his sullied, socked feet. Thomas could not help but gasp as they glinted in the candlelight.

"A lad who appreciates the finer things?" Pallium asked, breaking the long silence.

Thomas nodded, then glanced to Kate and then to Crane and back to Pallium's feet.

"Made by Galphus and never taken from my feet in the last year. Prosperous shoes, boots of providence, and a charm against the world," Pallium said, suddenly sparked to life. "Blessed me with them, he did— the finest, most assiduous shoemaker in the country. Italian leather, fine silver, and Mandarin cloth. Warm and soft, lad. Restful for the feet."

Pallium sighed and sat at the chair by the table as he raised a foot in the air for all to see.

"You speak of them as if they have a life of their own." Crane laughed. "Does this hammock have a life of its own? Will it be decked in finest Mandarin cloth?"

"No—hemp, and found in the room above," Pallium snapped as a cloud of gloom enfolded him again. Slowly, his thin smile slipped from his face. "If you follow the stairs, you'll find where you sleep. I won't walk with you. I have to be about my counting. All these interruptions keep taking my mind from the task. If I were lonesome for a year and a day, it wouldn't be long enough." With that, Pallium turned from them and looked to the table and the neatly stacked piles of coins. Ignoring Crane, he picked a stack and began to count each coin slowly and precisely.

Taking a candle from the side table, Crane nodded for Kate and Thomas to follow him up the stairway.

Crane brought them to a large room that overlooked the dismal street. He lit the two candle stubs that were on the narrow table by the window.

"I'll leave you to it." He smiled and stepped into the passageway that ran the length of the house. He stopped abruptly in front of a black door that was double-bolted. "Sleep, and then we'll eat," Crane said as he took the light.

Kate and Thomas stared at each other for a moment and then looked about them. In the corner of the room was a *Fortbien* magichord. It was propped against the wall like a gigantic flat pyramid with four octaves of ivory keys that were discoloured with age. The magichord looked like a grand piano stood on its end. Above it, an elaborate candelabrum hung, webbed and wax-dripped, like the tangled roost of a dawn rook. By the narrow window was a small bed, neatly made with fresh but tattered linen, whilst at the fireplace was a daybed that had been turned down, ready for sleep, and an old leather chair.

Kate smiled as she saw a neat bundle of fire sticks and a tinderbox. "He made ready for us," she said in a whisper as she tiptoed across the wooden floor and sat upon the bed. "Do you really think he knew we were all coming?" she asked.

"He's mad," Thomas said quietly as he looked at the magichord, eager to press the keys. "Did you see him? Looked as if he'd shrunk away to almost nothing, and all that money hanging about—just asking to be robbed, if you ask me."

"Thomas…" Kate said as she sat on the daybed in front of the fireplace. "I keep thinking of going back. I can't get the thought from my head. It's like something's pulling at my insides and telling me to go home."

"Back? Not now. It's all changed, Kate. Have you forgotten what we saw at home? The creatures in the wood? I've seen too much to go *back*. My life is away from that place. Anyway—we are villains. Go back now and Demurral would have us dead. Wouldn't be surprised if he wasn't planning to come and find us as we speak."

"What about your mother?" Kate asked as she lay back on the bed.

"You saw what I saw. That creature in my mother was a monster; it tried to kill us. Whatever it was is now long gone, and my mother with it. That's all I could think of on the ship. All I could see was my mother's face and then that demon coming from her mouth. I couldn't rid my wits of the vision."

Thomas knelt by the fire. He angrily snapped the kindling and placed the broken sticks in the hearth. He felt as if he were breaking up every memory of his life. With one hand he reached into his coat pocket and pulled out the torn handkersniff given to him by his mother. For three years he had carried it with him every day, always the ever-present memory of one close by. Thomas thumbed the darned initials before he screwed it up in his hand. He pushed it quickly into the grate and in his heart whispered good-bye to her. Taking the tinderbox, he sparked the fire and watched it take hold. It burnt brightly and quickly, crackling from stick to stick as the flames lit the room and warmed his face.

"The room's not too bad with the fire lit," he said, wiping his face with the cuff of his jacket to take the fresh glint from his eye.

48

"If we stick with Crane, things will be right, Kate. What else have we got?"

Kate had been smiling as she watched him light the fire. As the flames took hold, she remembered another room only days before where she had slept in a deep dream and been woken with joyful laughter and the calling of children. There had been warmth, comfort and an open hearth in that place. It had proclaimed hope and love and was something she had wanted all of her life.

"Do you think we'll see Rueben Wayfoot and our friends again?" Kate asked, remembering his bright whiskered chin and the warm fire of Boggle Mill.

"Only when I hear that Demurral is dead, then will I return, and not until," Thomas said, his words determined and edged with hate.

"On that day, will you take me back?" Kate asked. The thought of again seeing Boggle Mill with its smoking pots and glistening windows was fixed in her mind.

"On that day, I will take you. And I will dance on Demurral's grave," Thomas said as he stood and looked at her shadow-flecked face. "I have you, Kate, and no other. I realised when we sailed from Whitby that I had no more family. No father, mother…but I have you."

"Then we'll stay together till death parts us," Kate said sleepily. She leant against the pillow, closed her eyes, and smiled as the room warmed them.

"Do you mean that?" Thomas asked. He turned to her and in disappointment realised she had slipped into sleep. "*Do* you mean that?" he asked again in a voice lower than a breath, hoping she would hear him in her dreaming.

Taking more logs from the firebox, Thomas stacked the grate and then leant back against the lounge chair. The fire crackled in the hearth, and the flames danced. Pulling the old blanket up to his neck, he rested against the back of the chair. A growing sense of unease kept him from sleep, even though his eyes sagged with bleary tiredness. As Thomas drifted from the world, he tried to keep an open eye, fearful that Demurral stalked his dreams.

Suddenly the flames flickered and then faded. Thomas blinked hard to rid his mind of what he now saw. It was as if every strand of fire had come together and just for a moment were frozen in time, and there looking at him from within the flames was the outline of a gaunt, twisted face. Then, as quickly as it appeared, it was gone.

Ord Vackan's Chair

Beadle was shaken from his sleep as Raphah leapt hurriedly from the bed to the floor of the kitchen below. As Beadle had dreamt fitfully of the sea, so the house had been whipped into a storm. The clock had struck the fourth hour; every traveller had been pulled from their beds and now clustered by the fire in search of enough food to break the night fast.

From outside came the jangling of a horse harness and the clatter of hooves. It was like the preparation for war as the carriages were made ready and wicker baskets stacked with journey food and wire-corked beer in pot jars.

Every corner of the inn shuddered with the sounds of making ready. Coats were warmed by the kitchen fire, and hot stones were rag-wrapped for the coachman's feet. Men shouted a morning's welcome as maids bustled back and forth from hearth to table. Laughter echoed along the passageway as the joy and trepidation of the coming journey filled all with its excitement.

Standing in the shadows, Raphah listened enviously for a moment. He had not been a part of such homeliness since leaving his family in Africa. He stepped from the kitchen unnoticed and walked the three paces across the passageway and into the parlour.

A long oak table was stretched across the room and covered with pewter serving plates and jugs of warmed beer. Quickly the room filled with people. No one looked at Raphah or bade him any welcome—it was as if he could not be seen. They gave their welcomes to one another, but none spoke to him. Everyone had a place but him. A china plate of rich cooked meat was handed along, and as Raphah reached forth his hand, the plate was pulled away by the innkeeper.

"Good breakfast," snorted a rotund man with a tight golden waist-coat. "The journey will be fine to Peveril. Heard they have hanged the highwayman—now we have nothing to fear."

There was a rumble of approval as heads nodded on both sides of the table. Raphah leant against the fireplace as the conversation gathered pace, looking for a place to sit at the table.

The fat man caught his eye and gave him a slight smile, curling the corner of his lip and allowing a dribble of meat juice to scurry across his chin.

"Where are our manners?" he said mockingly as he saw Raphah looking for a place to eat. "The Ethiopian has travelled a long way to eat with us, and we have not made him welcome."

The gathering bristled silently, spreading out along the benches so there was no room for Raphah to sit.

"Gentlemen, we have a foreign guest who would like to sit with us. How can we make him welcome? Surely there must be one seat in which he can take his meal in such pleasant company?"

Raphah edged his way towards the gap on the long bench between the coachman and the bugler, who was dressed in a leather apron and heavy tunic. As he approached, they snuggled together so he could not be seated.

"I know, gentlemen," the fat man said quietly. "There is always Vackan's chair by the fire..."

The bugler shook his head in deep disapproval and whispered to the fat man, "That would not be a good thing, Mr. Bragg, not a good thing."

"But we could test the chair, see if what is said about it is true," Mr. Bragg replied.

Raphah noticed the large dusty oak chair at the far side of the brazier. It was unlike any chair he had seen before. Two spindly front legs were turned in dark wood and capped with lion's claws. A large third leg the width of a man's arm followed the line of the chair back to the floor.

"Would you like to seat yourself there?" Mr. Bragg asked as he filled his mouth again with food. "Ord Vackan loved to sit in that place—was taken from it on the last night of his life. Loved it, he did, loved it."

"And all who—" The bugler tried to speak.

"Reserved for special guests—that's what he would like to say. Special like you—a friend from far away," Bragg said, sipping his wine from the flask. "Please be seated, and we will serve you. It is tradition to eat a hearty breakfast before..."

Raphah slipped quietly into the chair, and all was suddenly silent. Words stopped half-spoken as every head turned and stared. Raphah became aware that all who were gathered were glaring at him. Everyone glanced at each other, urging with sharp eyes for someone to speak.

With a ruffle of his long black cloak, Barghast walked through the doorway and saw Raphah sat in the Ord Vackan's oak chair.

"Did no one tell him?" he shouted loudly.

"What?" Raphah asked as his eyes went to the faces of the gathering.

"You let him sit in the chair and not one of you came to the lad's aid?" Barghast bellowed again, his white face reddening for a moment.

"We never saw," muttered a small, shrewlike man with a thin face and jagged front teeth sticking from his mouth.

"Rumour, legend. Nothing is for certain—they could have all died by coincidence," said Mr. Bragg feebly.

"What do they speak of?" Raphah asked, unsure as to what he had done and why it should cause such a commotion.

"Vackan's chair," said Barghast solemnly. "There is a legend that it is cursed. Whoever sits upon it meets an untimely death. Vackan was a villain of these parts, a cutthroat and a murderer. On the night that Ord Vackan was dragged from here and hanged, he cursed the chair on which he had sat and said that whoever rested in it would come to an end worse than his."

"A curse upon a chair? Should I be worried by that?" Raphah laughed.

"Such a thing cannot be shaken from you by laughter. It is well known in these parts and has become more than legend. Too many coincidences have taken place, and I am saddened that your fellow travellers should play such a trick," Barghast said.

Bragg snorted as if pleased with himself. "I never thought for a moment he would actually take the seat."

"Perhaps Raphah offended you in some way?" Barghast asked of him.

"I have a spell that will break the curse on you, lad," the shrew-man said above the babble of voices, and he held out his hand clutching a folded piece of linen. "Take it, and it will stop the evil befalling you."

"I need no magic to break the curse, for that was done for me in ages past—I fear not wooden chairs nor the curse of those who sat in them, nor what lies in a man's heart." Raphah stood from the chair and brushed the dust from his breeches. "I will eat my vittles with those who are not afraid of my company and can understand I am a free man."

"Then sit with me," said a soft voice in the darkened corner of the room by a far-off window. "I travel alone and have no concern for curses or Ord Vackan."

Raphah looked across the room to where the voice had heralded a welcome. In the shadows by the shuttered window, he saw the outline of a figure edged in a dark cloak, the hood shrouding about the head as if to keep the wearer from the draught.

"And I, too," said Barghast as he snatched bread and meat from the table and followed Raphah across the room.

Together they sat in the half-light. Raphah saw that his welcomer was a young woman of his own age. She smiled at him as he sat in a high-backed chair and then nodded politely as Barghast joined them.

Barghast extended his hand. "The esteemed Mr. Barghast at your service," he said with a flourish. "And you are?"

"Lady Tanville Chilnam," the young woman replied.

"A delight to meet you, madam. A great delight, indeed."

"Do you travel together?" Lady Tanville asked as Barghast offered Raphah some meat and then poured some beer from the table jug.

"As of last night, this fine fellow is my companion upon the road," Barghast boasted as he peered at the girl. "Are you going far?"

"Does not everyone travel to London?" she asked as she looked at Raphah. "But such a journey will be a trifle to you. For what reason do you travel—friendship or skirmish?"

"Or just the joy of the wayfarer?" interrupted Barghast. "We could ask the same of you and our enquiry could be unwelcome."

"That you could, Mr. Barghast, and it most probably would."

Raphah smiled as the candlelight flickered upon her face. "I travel to London with Beadle," he said quietly. "I search for some other friends who have gone ahead of me."

"Then we share the same journey. I too search for someone. My sister went to the city on business and has not been heard of since." Her voice trembled slightly. "Some with whom I have shared the journey have not been the politest of company." She nodded towards Bragg, who continued to fill his face as if the meal would be his last.

"Then I will make you my ward on the coach and tell you of the world and all of its complications," Barghast jested as he held out his hand and smiled benignly.

"That would be a fine thing, Mr. Barghast, at least to Peveril. They say that since the sky-quake the coach to London has been stopped, as the horses all went mad in the city and had to be shot. I don't know if we shall have a coach to take us on from there."

"Then I will walk with you all the way and my cloak shall be a bridge to whatever we have to cross." Barghast smiled again.

"Mr. Barghast, I wonder if you would be kind enough to bring me some milk?" Lady Tanville asked.

"My pleasure," he replied as he stood from the table and walked to the kitchen, scowling at Bragg as he went by.

The woman leant forward and spoke quickly to Raphah. "Be careful with this man; he may not be what he appears to be."

With that, Beadle appeared, muttering to himself. "*He* sent me with some milk. *He* said I had to bring it. Beadle, do this now, *he* said. Take it to Raphah, *he* said. I'm off to pack, *he* said." Beadle scoffed loudly as he came to the table clutching a pot jug of steaming milk. "Gone off to pack, *he* said, and thrusts this in my hand for the *lady*." Beadle stopped and stared, his eyes darting back and forth from the cloaked figure to Raphah. "It's you," he said without thinking, believing her to be the nocturnal visitor to the kitchen.

"Yes, it is I....Have we met before?" Lady Tanville asked as she smiled. "Perhaps you were asleep and you dreamt of me. It would not be the first time that such a thing has happened. When I was a child, I once dreamt that my great-aunt leapt from her painting upon the wall and her ghost gamed with us all night. I awoke in the morning to find my room was strewn with everything from the cupboards and her picture upon the floor. Was it a ghost or just a dream? Do you believe in such things?"

Beadle was silent. He looked at Lady Tanville's hands and the soft black cotton shroud in which she was wrapped.

"Perhaps it was a dream and one in which I thought I was awake," Beadle said slowly as he stepped away from the table. "Coach is ready, my friend. Barghast has booked us a seat on top with a double rug and an oiled skin. We'll be snug all the way to Peveril. Barghast travels inside *and* he's booked on to London. From what I've heard, we'll have to wait a night at Peveril before we can go on. Word is that all the horses went mad when the comet struck. Only five carriages left in the whole of the country." Beadle turned from the table and walked away, giving neither Raphah nor Tanville any courtesy of his going. He seemed to be in another world, his mind weighted down with concerns for the morrow as he pulled nervously upon the hairs of his brow.

"Your companion thinks much of you," Tanville said as she poured herself a tip of milk and sipped it slowly.

"Much...and much more as each day passes," Raphah said cautiously.

"Always a good judge of character and always remembers a face."

"Tell me, Raphah. Do you really not fear Ord Vackan's curse?" she asked.

"I fear not curse, spell, or spirit."

"Then by what magic are you protected?" Tanville asked.

"Not magic, Lady Tanville. Something far more powerful."

Sudden shouting in the hallway broke into the eating room. A sharp draught of cold breeze rushed through the doorway. Ord Vackan's chair tumbled to one side and fell onto the charring embers of the fire.

"It's the Ethiopian, I tell you. Who else would steal my money?" shouted Mr. Bragg as he leant against the doorway. "Robbed as I slept—could have cut my throat, to boot!"

"How do you know?" argued the innkeeper. "Could have been his companion as well."

"Then bring them both here and we can speak to them directly. Two hundred pounds have gone, and he will have it," wheezed Bragg, red-faced and stricken with anger.

"I am here of my own accord," Raphah said as he got up from the table.

"Thief, laggard, and footpad!" yelled Mr. Bragg. "Give me the money and let's hang him now!"

Raphah was grabbed by the arms and dragged before the fire by the coachman and the bugler of hounds.

"It has to be him—who else could be a thief amongst us?"

"Guilty? Of what am I guilty?" Raphah protested.

"Theft, housebreaking, robbery," slobbered the man as he lunged towards him, then held on to the mantelpiece to steady his frame from falling over. "Take him and hang him, and the dwarf as well."

"Dwarf?" protested Beadle as he ran from the hallway to kick Bragg in the shin. "Call me a dwarf and a thief? At least my stomach tells my mouth when to stop."

"What is he accused of now?" shouted Barghast, arriving in the hallway holding his bag as the room filled with travellers.

"Your companion is a thief. Last night as we slept, he made into my room and stole my purse. Let him be searched and all will be found."

"I have nothing and would not steal," Raphah protested.

"Is this what you search for?" Lady Tanville asked, holding out a leather purse and jangling the coins within.

Bragg looked for a moment. "The very same. See, we have found the evidence. Take him and string him to the oak. He can dance from the same tree as Ord Vackan's ghost—what did I tell you? The curse comes true."

Raphah looked into her eyes as she held the money before him and smiled. "I'm sorry.... It was where you left it," she said, looking back at Raphah.

"And Lady Tanville Chilnam as a witness," Bragg gloated, almost choking on his own spittle with excitement.

"No—where *you* left it, Mr. Bragg. This morning at breakfast before you went about your business. I have just found it upon the bench warmed by your weighty posterior."

"The case is altered, Mr. Bragg. Is my companion is free to go?" Barghast asked as the coachman let go of his grip.

"This is not to my liking, Mr. Barghast, not to my liking. I smell conspiracy, and my eyes will not leave you all for the journey."

Digitalis

Kate woke to the sound of Thomas snoring. The fire still crackled and gave off a warm glow. In her sleeping she had heard music from the magichord by her side. In the opening of her eyes, it had ceased to be, and it was as if she had been cheated of something wonderful. The music had danced through her thoughts. Every note had been like the chiming of a summer bell, and it reminded her of all that was good.

Kate rested upon the bed and stared through the darkness at Thomas. It was then that she heard the jingle of the magichord again. The room was filled with the scent of a woodsy perfume.

There was a sudden and shrill icy blast that took the flame from the candle by her bed and dimmed the light in the room to a soft gloom, lit only by the flames of the fire. From under the bed came the rustle of dried winter leaves that scraped the wood like dead fingers, tapping a tale of grief. From all around, the odour of the murky, deep wood grew stronger as the room was transformed into a dark woodland glade. Kate thought she saw the magichord grow into an old oak, gnarled and knotted. The firelight faded, dimming to a meager glow. The leaves swirled about themselves, spiralling higher and higher.

From somewhere far away she heard laughter. She dared not look right nor left, but kept her sight fixed upon the trunk of the oak that now grew about her. What had once been the ceiling of the room had been replaced with a canopy of dead branches. There was no sky, just a grave thick mist that hovered above them.

The music played gently, a flowing hand tracing over the keys like a butterfly breath, and Kate became aware of someone standing near to her. A warm voice began to sing the melody, and Kate pulled the covers close about her neck. The singing quickly turned to a child's laughter as a cold hand touched her face. Kate turned—the room was empty. The forest had gone in the instant. Looking to the magichord, she saw the ivory pegs moving on their own, each one tapped out in succeeding notes by an invisible hand. She watched, unsure what to do, more intrigued than frightened as the keys danced back and forth along the octaves. Kate gulped, unable to find her voice.

The laughter came again, this time from the window, as suddenly the music stopped and the lid of the magichord slammed shut. The notes jarred loudly. A swirl of dust twisted by the bed as a jagged and unseen finger prodded Kate sharply in the chest. Again she heard laughter, deeper, and groans as if tinged with pain. A shadow crossed the candlelight, and for the briefest of moments Kate saw the dim outline of a girl.

"Thomas," Kate said shakily, "are you still sleeping?" She hoped he would hear her voice. Thomas moaned in his slumber and returned to his snoring by the fire.

"Look at me..." came a whisper from the direction of the magichord.

Kate turned and stared.

"No...here..." The voice came again from the window.

Kate turned again.

"Or here..." whispered the unseen voice from next to her.

Then, inch by inch, a figure began to become visible. First the tips of her fine silver shoes, then the white leg stockings, then the bottom of a pink crinoline dress embroidered with a thousand foxgloves. It was an experience that was stranger than strange, to watch someone appear from thin air. Kate gulped and held her breath as the smell of perfume grew stronger and stronger. Finally, like a Cheshire cat, the face of a girl materialised at Kate's side. She smiled and looked to be quite human, solid and very real.

"I was watching you sleep," the spectre whispered. "Wanted to wake you up but waited until *he* was away." She gestured towards Thomas, who slept soundly on. "When did *you* die?"

"I didn't—well, not that I know," Kate replied, unsure what to say.

"I thought the same. Didn't realise I was dead for a week. Kept trying to speak to everyone and no one was listening. I even followed my coffin to the funeral and thought someone else had died. Mother crying, Father crying, all of them sobbing. It was only when the priest said my name that I realised that all those morbid tears were over little me." The ghost paused as if to take a breath, her dark eyes searching the room as she continued to speak. "Strange thing, death. It's when you find out what people *really* think of you. All those salutations of how sweet, what a pretty face, and how charming. If only they had said them to me when I was alive. Even if they were insincere, life could have been so much cheerier."

"So you are dead?" Kate asked.

"Buried and resurrected." The girl laughed as she pulled on her skirt and smiled. "You shine too much for someone who's alive—sure you're not dead?"

"Alive…I hope." Kate shuddered as a shiver ran down her spine. "How can I see you?"

"Because I want you to—well, for now anyway."

"I've never seen a ghost before. You're not how I expected," Kate said anxiously as she looked the girl up and down.

"Neither are you," the spirit said, then paused and looked at Kate quite strangely, as if she attempted to peer inside her head. "I knew you were coming. I listened to old Pallium as he made the bed and stacked the fireplace. It was him who brought me here." The girl pointed to a portrait in an old gilt frame that hung on the wall next to the magi-chord. "That's me."

Kate hadn't noticed the picture before. It was blackened by fire soot, the face nearly invisible in the dark sky against which it was set. Rusted spikes jutted out from the frame as if the portrait had once been imprisoned with bars.

The ghost caught Kate's stare and knew her thoughts. Kate turned quickly to look at her.

"They thought it would keep me in, said I was a nuisance in my walking. Got a priest to pray upon the portrait—that it would lock my spirit away. *Somehow* I found it easier to escape." The spectre looked at Kate and smiled as Kate touched the painting. "Zurburan was a master painter—so my mother said. Painted me when I was sick, and caught me in the moments of death."

"Nice," Kate replied slowly, unsure what to say in conversation with a chattering spectre as she peered at the dim image that hung on the wall. "Did you live here?"

The spirit glimmered as if angered. Her face changed colour as she searched for the words in which to reply, and she spoke quickly, trying to tell all before she vanished completely. "That picture is my dwelling place, no paradise for me. I live within the picture. It is my prison, and wherever the portrait shall go, so will I be. Some say it's cursed. I listen to them, hear them screaming when I walk from it. Then it's quickly sold and I go to yet another keeper. I'm a long way from home and wish to return. It has been so...so...long."

The ghost looked no more at Kate but gazed at her own deathly portrait.

"So where are you from? What's your name?" Kate asked, her lips trembling as the ghost walked from her towards the wall as if drawn back to the picture. "Come back...speak to me..."

"*Again...sometime soon...tell no one...*" The words were spoken without a movement of the lips, and then she blew a kiss.

"Now," said Kate, trying to seize her before she disappeared. With one hand she grabbed at the pink dress and for a brief moment took hold by her fingertips. Her words were of no use. There was a swish of crinoline and a twirl of dust. The magichord shook momentarily as if it, too, was bewitched, and the ghost began to fragment. As if made of melting ice, all her form subsided to nought. With a sudden gasp, the girl was gone.

"*Tell no one…*" came the voice again from all around her.

Kate lay back on the bed, staring at the portrait. The dark eyes of the girl stared back at her.

Kate heard a sudden rush of footsteps outside the room and the voice of Jacob Crane. Thomas stirred from his sleep.

"Did you say something, Kate?" he asked.

"It's just Jacob Crane," Kate said, wanting to keep the ghostly visit a secret for fear of not being believed. Crane tapped on the door and walked into the room.

"Thought I heard you playing that old magichord," Crane said as he smiled at them both. In his hands he carried a large bowl of steaming water and two folded towels. "Quite a talented lass when you want to be, eh, Kate? Get washed, and I'll see you both in the scullery."

"I don't like this place, Kate. I saw a face in the fire last night. It was Demurral," Thomas said.

"It was a dream; nothing more," she replied. "He'll never find us here."

In a short while, Thomas and Kate stepped into the scullery. All had changed. Pallium sat at the table, the money gone and the floor swept. A fire burnt brightly in the hearth, and the room smelt of fresh lavender.

"My dear friends, you look so clean—and hungry, too," Pallium said as he sipped from the glass in his hand. "I decided—er, *we* decided—that I had worked for too long and had neglected many things. It was Jacob who reminded me that there was more to life than counting coins."

Pallium looked disheartened, as if something had been taken from him. His fingers twitched without the coins to count. The half-smile broke at the edges of his mouth, and his lip quivered slightly.

"Fine thing you've done, Pallium. A very fine thing. Can't be spending all your life locked in here counting money," Crane said.

"Good to have you here, Jacob, and I'm sure that Galphus will agree."

Pallium coughed the words as he pulled his coat about him.

"Where can we meet this great Galphus?" Crane asked.

"The Salamander Inn would be a place to start. He will be taking breakfast there. I will introduce you." Pallium looked at them one by one and smiled again.

"Such a seer of the future would not need to be introduced to the likes of us. He should know our very thoughts before they trip from our tongues," Crane said.

"That he will, I am sure, for he is not just a mender of soles, but a maker of them."

Pallium waved his arms excitedly as he blurted the words. "Galphus is a man of business transactions and has the desire to prosper. He is cordial, jovial, and greatly avuncular. To be in his presence is something beyond the imagination."

"Then we must meet him," Crane said, wiping the dust from his hands and slipping on his frock coat. "I have always wished for an uncle, especially one who is jovial! Perhaps he will take me under his wing, as he has you, and I too may prosper. The Salamander Inn shall be visited with haste, and we all shall eat merrily."

Thomas grinned at the thought of food.

Kate held her place, unwilling to move. It was as if she wanted to speak, to hold Pallium in conversation for a moment longer. Her eyes glanced quickly from Crane to Pallium and then to Thomas, betraying her agitation.

"Mr. Pallium," she said, her voice croaking with indecision. "There's a picture in my room—where did it come from?" She asked the question quickly, wanting to rid her lips of the words before she could think of their consequences.

Pallium nodded his head slowly up and down. He began to speak like an excited child. "Wonderful picture. Galphus bought the portrait for me, and as soon as I saw the girl's face, I fell in love. Never was there one so pretty, but beauty like that comes at a great price." Pallium stopped for a moment and thought, his eyes withering within their frames. "Not a question I would have expected. If you had asked about the magichord

I could understand, for it is a fine piano, but the picture?"

"It was that she looked so young…and the bars across the frame. I have never seen the likes before." Kate stumbled in her answering.

"Nor will you again. The portrait is unique. An ageless painting of that which will age no more."

"Did you know the girl?" Kate asked.

"Not for even a minute of a day. Galphus had the picture delivered. She looked so lost, and I wanted to give her a home. I find her entertaining."

"And I find my stomach screaming to my wits," Crane interrupted. "Kate loves to talk, Mr. Pallium. It is the finest thing she does."

The Delightful Mr. Ergott

Beadle pulled the blanket about him and wrapped the oilskin around his and Raphah's shoulders. The first shards of hail began to fall like teeth of ice, clattering upon the stacked baggage that was strapped to the roof and protected Raphah and Beadle from the biting wind. They perched high above the ground in their one-guinea seats outside the coach. To the front the driver cracked the whip above the horses' heads, and the bugler called the hounds to his side.

Beadle could feel a tingle of excitement growing within as the carriage sped onwards. His heart leapt in his chest, and he smiled. Faster and faster they went, gaining speed with each yard. The hail beat down as the squall from the fell burst like a dam above them. All was glistening white as the hounds wailed and cried, struck by stones of ice, and the horses snorted steaming breath as they lathered on.

"Do you think *he* will follow?" Beadle asked Raphah as they were beaten against the baggage and twisted in the oilskin by the rocking of the carriage. "I keep thinking I've got away. That now I'm on the coach to Peveril, I am free. With every yard of every mile, another step away from Demurral." He tried to smile, but the happiness of his escape suddenly faded. "But I never thought I'd ever, ever see you—and look at us now."

Raphah didn't speak. He clutched the oilskin over their heads and braced himself for the journey. All his mind could dwell upon was his birthright to serve Riathamus, to follow him always. Raphah could think of nothing else but his task to come to this strange land with its primitive people and find the Keruvim that had been taken from the temple. Something, some strange thought, nagged his mind, telling him that this would be his chance to overcome the powers and principalities once more. That lurking in the shadows were the works of darkness and that soon he would come face-to-face with evil yet again.

Above the sound of the rumbling wheels and the snorting horses, Raphah could hear snippets of the conversation through the leather hatch by his feet. Bragg shouted with moans of complaint with every stone and rut that jolted him from his seat.

Within the darkness of the carriage the five passengers sat in a haze of thick smoke. In one corner, snuggled in the leather seat and wrapped in a velvet scarf, was a young man. In his hand he held a large wooden pipe, filled to the brim with roasting tobacco.

The man listened to Bragg's complaints but never spoke. He puffed on his pipe, his wide, owl-like eyes surveying each person. To his right was a weasel-faced man named Mr. Shrume, and then Barghast. Bragg filled half of the seat opposite with his fat rump. By his side and pressed into the corner so she could not move was Lady Tanville. Her face was lit by a tallow lamp that jarred back and forth with each roll of the carriage.

"Do you never stop complaining?" Barghast quizzed Bragg as he moaned yet again.

"If only they would slow down and transport us in sedation," Bragg complained bitterly.

"Then we would never get to Peveril and never get to London," Lady Tanville said quickly.

"I find it delightful, quite delightful," said the young man as he slurped upon the pipe. "It's as if we are at sea and tossed upon a storm."

"If I had wanted to be at sea, then I would have travelled by ship and not by coach," spluttered Bragg as he coughed. "Do you seek the pleasures of London, too?"

"I travel on business, and that business takes me to many places," the man said as he tapped the pipe upon his boot, then stomped on the burning embers with his foot.

"What is that business, Mister...?" Lady Tanville asked.

"Ergott. Vitus Ergott. I am a dowser."

Barghast leant forward and smiled. "Interesting," he said above the rattle of the wheels. "And for what do you search?"

"Whatever my wand and I are paid to enquire for. Some would have us look for gold, others water, and still more a precious item they have lost. All I need is my clear seeing and divining wand. I express the intention in my mind and allow the spirits to take me to that place. Simple, really, and quite delightful."

"Do you always find what you seek?" Lady Tanville asked.

"Is that a request for my services?" Ergott replied with a raised eyebrow as he puffed on his pipe.

"Peradventure, Mr. Ergott," Barghast interrupted as he leant across Mr. Shrume and tapped Ergott on the arm. "Does your divination take you to the city?"

"Delightfully, yes. All paid for and a first-class seat. Apparently I am highly recommended."

"And will you tell us of your quest, or does it have to be a secret?" Tanville asked as she smiled at him.

"I search for stolen children. My employer has given me an element of each child, and therefore I know I will be drawn to them." Ergott spoke in a matter-of-fact way as he looked at Barghast and then to Lady Tanville. The coach fell silent, and even Bragg stopped his moaning as all the inhabitants thought on what Ergott had said.

"And when you find them?" Lady Tanville asked.

"They will be liberated from their captor and he will be put before the Crown."

"You speak as if you know who has them," Barghast said.

"That is my only clue. I only know the name of the man for whom

I search. A man so vile and sinister that I would not mention his name in such company. When I took on the adventure, I sealed myself never to speak his name until he was fettered and being dragged to Tyburn." The look on Ergott's face changed suddenly, as if the quarrelsomeness of his thoughts marred his youthfulness.

"I have met many wicked men, Mr. Ergott. Perhaps I could help you in your task?" Barghast asked.

"Delightful, and kind. But I work alone. In all my investigations I find it better to keep close counsel. I even try to hide the conclusions from my own thoughts as there are creatures that can listen to whispering wits as if they were shouted from the rooftops."

"How childish," Lady Tanville said, her voice cold.

"Far from it. Who is to say that all we have not said has been eavesdropped by some creature right now," Ergott said.

"With the noise of this troublesome carriage they would be driven deaf, Ergott," Bragg replied.

"Tell me, Bragg, what is it that takes you to London?" Ergott said, returning comfortably to his pipe as he pulled his velvet scarf about his neck.

"I am a collector of fine art and ancient artifacts," Bragg replied.

"And you, Barghast?"

"I am just a traveller. Always have been."

Within the hour the storm had given way and the clouds parted. Beadle peeked from beneath the oilskin where he had slept. From his pocket he took a boiled egg and cracked the shell. Breaking it in half, he shared it with Raphah as they sat upon the high bench.

In the midmorning they stopped at an inn and changed the horses, and then for the rest of the day they travelled. By late afternoon the hills to the south loomed above them.

"Are we nearly there yet?" Beadle shouted to the driver.

"Three hours to Peveril," he shouted above the rattle of the carriage. "Two before we get to …" The driver stopped as if he didn't want to say the name of the place. The bugler elbowed him in the ribs and shook his head to tell him to say no more.

"To where?" Beadle pressed.

"To a place where we might need this," the bugler said, pulling the butt of a blunderbuss from its long leather sleeve and showing it to Beadle and Raphah. "The Galilee Rocks. Not a place to be as darkness falls."

"What about the militia—won't they protect us?" asked Raphah.

The bugler laughed. "The militia are more frightened than we are—see the madman once and you'll know why."

"See him?" asked the driver without turning his face from the road. "You'll hear him from three miles. Screams like a dying dog. Why do you think we run with hounds? Only thing that'll keep him away."

"But he's never stopped you?" asked Beadle as he pulled the oilskin about him.

"Not us, but some have gone to Galilee Rocks and never come back."

"Can't you rush the horses through and out the other side?" Raphah asked.

"Only if you could fly. Imagine a hill that stands before the entrance of a deep valley. There you'll find Galilee Rocks. The road takes you to Peveril, but it twists down the side so steep that the brakes will hardly keep the carriage from rolling on. Trouble is, we have to stop the carriage and all walk down the rise as we hand brake the wheels. Far too dangerous to drive down with passengers. Too steep. That's where we'll take our chances." The driver tapped the large wooden hand brake on his left.

"And the madman?" Beadle enquired nervously.

"Will be somewhere waiting for us. Thinks he owns the place and doesn't like visitors. Would take an extra day if we went by Casterton. So we face the madman and hope for the best."

Beadle watched the sun as it tarried towards the west.

The hours passed slowly. Beadle was cramped and stiff, and there was no conversation from the carriage for him to be distracted by. Finally, far in the distance, Beadle could see Galilee Rocks—mounds of outcropped limestone jutting across the horizon. The vast upturned boulders gnarled from the earth like dragon's teeth. In amongst the stones grazed a herd of pigs that squealed upon the approach of the hounds.

Raphah woke from his slumbering to the sound of Bragg shouting in discontent.

"I'm frightened," whispered Beadle as he shuffled closer to his friend. "What will become of us?"

"They're pigs, Beadle, not monsters from hell," Raphah joked.

"What of the madman? We have to get from the carriage and walk. What if he attacks?" he asked, his voice quaking with fear.

"Then the bugler will use the blunderbuss and the hounds will see him off. Fear not," Raphah said.

"But we are on the outside," he protested.

"So will be Barghast and the others—we will walk together."

The carriage slowed to a crawl as the shadows grew longer. The horses' pace slowed even further as they pulled the carriage higher towards the peak.

Then it came—first as a distant sound like the call of a buzzard, then again like the screaming of a child. The bugler slipped the blunderbuss from its case and rested it across his knees as the horses twitched and danced nervously.

"Peveril within the hour," said the driver hopefully.

"When do we walk?" Beadle asked as the wailing came again from the high tor.

"As soon as we've gone through Galilee Rocks," said the bugler, pulling the hammer upon the gun.

"Why Galilee?" Raphah asked as he pushed the oilskin from his knees and looked towards the craggy outcrop that appeared from the gloom.

"On the morrow you'll see the lake. A man once said it was like the Holy Land. Built his house up there. Nothing but ruins now. Crusader, they said he was. A knight of knights. Carsington's his name. He brought the sickness."

"Cursed as a misguided fool," Raphah muttered quietly to himself. "A war for God and the murder of innocents."

"Does no one seek to help him?" Beadle asked as the coach reached the top of the road.

"It carries on from generation to generation," the bugler said. "Every male descendant of the first Carsington is stricken with madness within an hour of the birth of his son. All of them follow the same pattern. One moment they are about their business, the next they are ranting and eating grass. They leave Peveril and come and live amongst the rocks. They can look upon their town but never return."

"Enough of your legends," said the driver as he pushed the braking handle. "Time to walk."

Beadle looked nervously at Raphah. The sound of screeching and clattering iron fetters came again from beyond the marsh grass. "He's out there—the madman."

"And that's all he is, nothing more," Raphah said as they stepped to the road.

"If only it were true, my friend," said the bugler as he gathered the hounds about him, feeding them with dried meat. "If he were just a madman, then we wouldn't need the hounds. Some say the madness makes him change into a beast. Saw him once upon the rocks, and it was no man that I saw."

It was then that the screams came again. They echoed from all around as if a legion of creatures joined in the baiting of the travellers.

The Salamander Inn

Jacob Crane had to drag Pallium from the house. "This is the first time in the year you have left the place, and it shall not be your last. You need to eat and eat you will," Crane insisted.

"I need to eat," said Thomas. "Beef, bread, and gravy."

Pallium protested loudly that the walk to the Salamander Inn would dirty his shoes and that they were not to be sullied. He jumped from toe to toe as he tried to keep his precious shoes from the mud.

Thomas tried to hold back his laughter as Crane lifted Mr. Pallium from the cobbles and carried his meagre frame along the street, tucking him neatly under his arm like a roll of French carpet. With every step Pallium would kick and protest and shout so loudly that his words echoed far into the distance, but there was no one to hear. The street was empty. The clock of a far church chimed the hour.

The closer they got to the inn, the more respectable Salamander Street became. Walls were newly painted, timbers oiled, and doors garlanded with wreaths of holly and mistletoe. The sound of music came from behind several of the doors. High above, the roofs of the tall houses met to form a continuous arch that blocked out the sky. From each window, lamps like tiny stars flickered and lit the street below.

Kate could only think of what she wanted to eat. She was sure that she could smell the faint aroma of milk pudding, melted cheese, and roast apple. It hung about her like a garland and rumbled her guts with longing.

"We shall eat, drink, and then carry Mr. Pallium back to his abode so he doesn't dirty his prize shoes," Crane said. "Tonight will be a good time to decide how to get the *Magenta* back and find the crew. But first, breakfast."

"And you're paying?" Thomas asked.

"Payment for your sailing, boy. Your life belongs to me," Crane replied with a smile and a wink, the light from the door reflecting from his face. "Onwards—the Salamander awaits. I shall have two herrings and a boiled egg."

The inn was a place of warmth and light. Music played loudly, and people sang and danced on the polished wooden floors. It was packed with tables, and at each sat four or five people. Kate was aware of Crane, Pallium, and Thomas following on, but her mind was taken up by something more incredible. For the first time that she could ever remember, Kate suddenly felt totally happy. It was as if every care in her life had gone, forgotten in the bewitchment of the Salamander Inn.

A gigantic fireplace warmed the room, and everywhere she looked there were happy, shining faces. People of all sizes and ages talked merrily. This was not the discord of the gin house but the open conversation of friendliness. It was not like the dirty drinking houses that lined the quayside at Whitby. The hosteller looked over the crowded, noisy room and gave his welcome, nodding his whiskered face to four seats in the corner by the fire.

Pallium led them on, shrugging his shoulders as he looked back to the door. "Shouldn't be here," he mumbled to himself. "Should be at home with the money."

"Nonsense," came the loud voice from a table by the lighted window. "This is the place you should be, Mr. Pallium. See, I have saved you a table and a seat for each of your guests."

Mr. Pallium suddenly changed. He quickly stood upright and puffed out what chest he had left. His hand speedily smoothed his hair and rubbed his cheeks, and then, spinning on his fine shoes, he turned in the direction of the voice. "*Mr. Galphus!*" he exclaimed as he threw open his arms as if to welcome a long-lost friend. "It is you…"

"Of course, dear Pallium, it is me. What a pleasure to see you here again." The man stopped speaking for a moment and stared at Jacob Crane and then at Thomas.

"Jacob, Kate, Thomas, come and be seated, and we shall drink together," Galphus said. He raised his hand to signal to the hosteller, who immediately arrived at the table, followed in turn by two servants who carried large trays with silver warming tops.

Kate looked at Galphus sitting serenely in a high-backed oak chair by the window. He wore a small green felt cap upon a bed of neatly cropped hair and the suit of a trader with a thick green tweed coat that came to his knees.

"Kate," Galphus said softly as he noticed her staring at him. "Tell me—what brings you to Salamander Street?"

"Our mutual friend, Mr. Pallium," Crane interrupted. "I have known him awhile, and he said that should I be in London then I was to call." He looked at Galphus. "Then again, from what he has said to us, you already knew we were on our way."

"Another cruel joke of a cruel creator." Galphus laughed. "I have been dogged with seeing what is to come. I dream. Practically live in the sleeping world, and whilst there I experience what is to come. That, and a device which helps me to focus my dreams so that everyone I choose can see them also."

"How can you do that?" Kate asked, forgetting that Crane had told them to be silent.

"Kate, it is a great mystery. Mankind can travel to the farthest-out places of the world and discover whole continents. Yet within us all there is a galaxy just waiting to be explored. It is an inner universe." He looked at the food that had been placed upon the table under the silver warmers. "If I am correct in my assumptions, then what is on each of your plates is what you all really desire to eat at this very moment."

"Then you would not be a man to gamble with," Crane said as he lifted the silver lid from his dish. There on a white china plate were two perfect fried herrings. By the side of each had been placed a fresh soft-boiled egg that had been meticulously peeled.

Kate gasped as she lifted the lid upon her breakfast. There was a bowl of steaming milk, curdling cheese, and roast apple. The smell of nutmeg swelled from within and brought to her the memory of her mother and the coming of Christmas.

Thomas laughed as the eyes of the gathering fell upon him. There was great expectation, as if he were the last piece of a puzzle about to be placed. "You could never guess what I desire," Thomas said as he slowly lifted the lid, his eyes widening in disbelief.

"Beef slices upon crusted bread and smothered in gravy?" Galphus asked.

"'Tis true," Thomas replied as he cut the meat with his knife and then ate it with dramatic celerity.

"Very good, dear Galphus," Crane said, looking at Pallium as if he had somehow informed upon them. "Not only did you herald our arrival, but you know what we would eat. Is there any point in conversation? For you will know what we are to say before the words appear upon our lips."

"Party tricks, Jacob, party tricks. I know nothing of your thoughts and am but shown portions of the future. I dreamt of the ship coming and of your food. What good is that in telling the future? That in itself will not change the course of history."

"No food for you, Pallium," Crane said. "Galphus must know you have lost your appetite."

"But I do know where the *Magenta* is berthed," Galphus said quietly.

"By another dream?" Crane asked.

"By street gossips," Galphus replied. "It will be taken to Dog Island, the rigging chained, and a charge of gunpowder placed in its belly. It is the news of London. A plague ship full of rats—that's what they say. It is also said that two children were stolen from their master in Whitby." Galphus spoke quickly. He looked directly at Crane. "If you were to be caught, they would hang you for kidnapping, Captain Jacob Crane. Think on that as you swallow your herring."

"Then you'll turn us in?" Crane asked.

"Luckily for you it was made very clear in my dream that you were to be protected at all costs. Whatever you are running from is coming to find you. At least in Salamander Street you will be safe."

"Even with a price on our heads?" Thomas asked.

"There would not be enough money in the world to make me give you up." Galphus spoke quietly, his words stern. "This is not by chance that you are here, not by chance." Galphus smiled as he picked a fish-bone from Crane's plate and began to clean his teeth. "I would betray a friendship. Someone whom you have met. I too have the acquaintance of Abram Rickards. I believe he was known to you in Whitby and helped in your escape."

Kate and Thomas could not contain their exhilaration, but all Crane said was, "You're well connected, Galphus. News travels fast."

"Have you heard from Abram?" Kate asked Galphus.

"Not in a long while. But I hear he is in London. He was seen some nights ago by London Bridge just before the sky-quake." Galphus became sullen and drew them close as he leant towards them and hushed his voice. "I have known him many, many years, and I know he will be very surprised to see me again."

"So, Galphus," Crane said. "You say we are safe. I say I'll wake up and find a militiaman standing at the end of my bed if I stay here."

"Still don't trust me?" he replied. "Look about you, Jacob. Everyone here is just like you. They have run from their past, left families and fortunes so they can be free. Yet to a man they all trust and believe in Mr. Galphus."

"Never trust anyone until they prove it."

"Perhaps I can do just that," Galphus said as he picked up a long thin silver cane from the side of the chair and twizzled it in his hands. "I have a party trick, a way of entertaining my guests," he said jokingly. "Gather round and see what is to come." With that, Galphus took the cane and held it before them all. It looked to be made of solid silver and was tipped with a round glass globe that shone milky white. Galphus looked solemnly at each one of them before he spoke.

"Wonderful, amazing, marvelous…" he said as he looked into the crystal ball and then tutted as if he saw something unexpected. Kate stared into the crystal; she saw nothing but the reflection of the fire and the people who were gathered around.

"There is a rumour that someone close to you will be seen again. Someone you thought to be lost and long gone—do you know of whom I speak?" Galphus asked with a dramatic smile. "I can see him travelling, walking across the windy moors."

Kate cast a glance at Thomas, daring not to say the name. He stared back at her and then at Galphus, his look urging him to speak.

"I have lost many people in my time and can't recall…" Crane said, his face telling the children to be silent.

"You are wise not to mention his name or where he is from. But I can tell you he is alive. He searches for you with a desire that can overcome death."

Kate felt as if she would explode if she didn't say his name. She had to know the truth from Galphus. "Do I know the one of whom you speak?" she asked, talking as she ate.

"Not only do you know him, but you have spent much time with him. From what I can see in the crystal, he is on his way to London." Galphus touched the tip of her nose with his finger. A spark cracked from the tip as if a minuscule bolt of lightning had jumped through the ether towards her.

"Don't give them great expectations, Galphus. These kids are in my care, and I don't take lightly to them being made fools of."

"I tease not, Jacob. Within the crystal, news travels faster than the horse and outruns the mortal messenger. These matters are of heavenly importance. For as your friend seeks you, so does another—an adversary. I can see him in the stone; he hides his face like a spectre in the candlelight. You all know his name, and it doesn't need to be repeated," Galphus rambled as he stared at the walking stick. "You are being hunted by your friend, and news is but two days away."

"So what is your place in all of this?" Crane asked. "You speak as if we were brought here for this very purpose."

"Believe me, Jacob. This is the safest place for you to be…for the time being. All I can say is that Salamander Street will grow upon you. It will become like a haven of rest. Stay in Salamander Street and all will be made clear. Kate and Thomas, you will find your friend, and you, Jacob, will be on your ship again."

Galphus turned to Thomas and held out his hand. "I see you're the son of a fisherman. How would you like to make shoes? I could teach you myself this very day. You could be my apprentice. Jacob and Kate can take old Mr. Pallium back to count his money, and you and I can make shoes. Whatever you make you can keep. How does that sound?"

Thomas nodded, his mouth filled with food. "Can I go?" he asked Crane as he swallowed quickly.

Crane smiled and gestured for him to go. "Go and make some seaboots. If Galphus is right, then we will soon be sailing again."

Galphus got to his feet. Kate hadn't noticed before how tall the man was. As he stood, he seemed to tower above them. Crane stood with him and held out his hand.

"Come, come, Thomas," Galphus said slowly as he made to walk to the door. Then he stopped and turned. "I'll bring him back tonight. We can talk again, Jacob. Perhaps I can help you free your ship."

With that Galphus stepped from the Salamander Inn and disappeared into the street with Thomas following like an obedient dog. Kate shrugged to herself, not wanting Crane to see her anger at being left behind.

"Do you believe him?" she asked Crane.

"Of course he believes him," said the silent Mr. Pallium as if suddenly stirred from a trance. "That is Galphus you speak of. Didn't he amaze you with what he knows of your lives?" he asked.

"We've seen much in the past days. Enough to last a lifetime, Pallium. It's only right she should ask," Crane replied.

"But it's Galphus. He's a seer and knows the future. The man has the finest leather factory in London—some say he has a thousand silver guineas. Imagine all that wealth, and he ate with *us*."

The Rocks of Galilee

ithin the minute the travellers were all on the road and walking
with the carriage as it began to descend the steep and winding
hill. The bugler walked ahead, his faithful hounds close to his feet. He
carried his blunderbuss at the ready as he looked about him.

"How far do we keep this up?" puffed Bragg discontentedly. "The
hill can't go on forever, and I paid to be carried, not to walk."

"Just a mile, sir," muttered the coachman, pulling the brake even
tighter as the carriage pressed hard against the horses.

They quickly descended into what was a vast open cavern with
steep sides, littered with dark, jagged boulders. Pigs grazed on the
sparse grass between the rocks.

"I prefer the inside of a hostelry, with a warm fire and hot food,"
Bragg continued.

"Then you better keep walking or else we shall never see such a
place again," said Barghast, his long cloak flapping like a bat's wing.

For a while the road became steeper. The horses slipped their
footings and the carriage rocked back and forth. The light of the
carriage gave a meagre glow that surrounded the travellers. Not one
would step away from the glow of its paltry flame. Like moths they
were drawn closer to it step by step, as if it would provide them with

some protection. Outside the rim of its defence, the blackness was so intense that the travellers could not see a hand's breadth in front of their faces.

"We're like sheep," Beadle said as they shuffled even closer together, as if herded by an unseen shepherd. "Ready for slaughter."

"The hounds say we are alone. They show no fear," the bugler said as he cocked the blunderbuss.

"They're dogs. What do they know?" Bragg argued again.

"They can see and hear that which we cannot," the bugler replied. Suddenly one of his beasts began to growl.

From the outer darkness came the babbling cry of a young child.

"There's someone out there," Beadle said as they walked slowly on.

"Not for long," said the bugler as he aimed the blunderbuss into the darkness.

The screaming came again. It echoed around the walls of the valley.

The bugler fired his gun. The shot rang out just as lightning cracked over the moors. Falling to his knees, he reloaded the weapon.

The carriage horses reared up in panic. Lady Tanville screamed, and from somewhere near came a loud growl as if from a tiger. The lightning flashed again, and a creature leapt from the road and disappeared into the night.

"It's taken Barghast—he's gone!" Lady Tanville screamed. She held his cloak in her hands. "He was here and then the creature took him."

"Then we are at war," Ergott shouted as he pulled his divining wand from his jacket and held it like a short sword.

The hounds hollered, sensing that a chase was about to take place.

As the night sky lit up with a crack of lightning, the shape of a man could be seen upon the moor. For the briefest moments he was clearly visible. His hair blew in the wind; a beard covered his face. He raised his hands to the sky as if he wanted to catch a lightning bolt as it crashed to earth. His arms were bare and about his shoulders was tied a tattered cloak. From each arm dangled a short, broken chain of iron fetters, manacled to his wrist.

"*Mad Cassy!*" screamed the coachman as he fought to control the horses and battle with the brake.

The bugler took aim and fired into the night. The barrel of the blunderbuss exploded with a flash of double-charge so bright that it dazed and blinded the travellers. In the darkness there was a long moan.

"You got him!" shouted the coachman as the hounds barked.

"And I'll have him dead," shouted the bugler, double-charging the gun yet again.

"He's wounded," Raphah called as the moaning turned into a scream. It was shrill and harsh and pierced them to the bone. From peak to peak it sounded like the dying of a mad dog. "You've got to help him."

"Kill him, lad. That's the only thing good for him," the bugler said as he rallied the hounds to set off on the chase.

"But what of the creature that has taken Barghast?" Ergott asked.

"Your duty is to protect *us!*" screamed Bragg as he desperately tried to mount the carriage and hide within.

"Can't let a chance like this go by," the bugler replied. "Could be my making."

"Could be your death. What if the madman takes you like he has taken Barghast?" Ergott asked. He waved his wand frantically.

"Then it'll get some lead as well," the bugler said excitedly as he stepped from the toll road and began to slowly make his way upwards through the steep rocks.

"We can't let him kill the man," Raphah said quietly to Beadle.

"Oh yes we can," Beadle replied, burying his face in his hands. "The man's got a gun and can do what he likes."

"Then I'll go with him," Raphah said, breaking rank from the gathering and jumping from the road. He ran through the stones and into the darkness. In the blink of an eye he was gone.

Beadle ran up and down the road shouting for Raphah to return as the carriage came to a halt. Bragg screamed in protest from inside the coach. He locked the doors and slid the window shut.

Mr. Shrume, fearful of the night, took up a place under the coach. Holding the axle in both hands, he hung on from beneath so that he could not be seen by whatever had taken Barghast.

"Let us in," screamed Lady Tanville, banging on the carriage door. Reluctantly, Bragg slipped the lock and edged it open to allow her to enter. The travellers ushered each other inside as Shrume appeared from his hiding place, quivering with fear. Beadle took hold of the handle and stepped upon the mounting plate. The door was pulled tightly shut and locked before him.

"You paid for the roof," Bragg said. "And the roof it'll be."

There came a shuddering howl from the ridge above them as if one of the coach hounds was being torn to pieces in the darkness. Beadle jumped quickly from the road and pulled himself to the driver's seat.

"Take this, and use it if you must," the driver said, handing Beadle a small flintlock pistol. "It's not right here. They should never have gone."

On the far side of the valley, they could hear the hounds making their way up through the rocks. With every flash of the storm they could see the bugler followed by Raphah, both clawing their way higher.

"What took Barghast?" Beadle asked the coachman anxiously as he pointed the pistol into the blackness.

"There's talk of a hound, a hellhound. Comes from the fell and uses a storm to take its victims. They say that the madman feeds the beast and in return it keeps him safe. The Ethiopian is a brave fool."

"Do we stay?" Beadle asked.

The driver stared him in the face and wiped the sweat from his brow. "I'll be gone before they come back. Peveril in the mile. I'll run this coach down the hill and take my chance."

"Give them time," Beadle insisted. The horses jerked upon their hooves and danced upon the road as if it were hot coals.

"I can't hold them much longer," the driver said, holding the reins tightly in his gloved hand. "There's something that they can see and we can't. If it comes closer, they shall be from this place like the devil were chasing them."

"Just a time longer," Beadle pleaded.

"Go on, man, go on—think of your passengers," screamed Bragg from within.

"You can't leave them," shouted Lady Tanville. She tried to open the door, only to be pushed back by Mr. Shrume, who now quivered violently as if he would fall apart at that very moment.

There was a crash of glass from the far side of the coach as something smashed the window. The carriage swung to the side as if the weight of a beast fell upon it.

For a moment, in the flash of lightning, Beadle thought he saw a beast. Full of fear and trembling, he tried to aim the pistol. He closed his eyes as he squeezed the stiff trigger. The hammer fell suddenly, and the plate ignited. But there was silence. "No!" he screamed as he realised that it had no charge.

"Not loaded?" shouted the driver. "I never thought..."

And then the lead stallion bolted, its black mane streaming like silk fingers as it took off from the road. The other horses gave chase, and the carriage was dragged at speed down the hill. The driver held them fast with one hand as with the other he pulled the screaming brake. But the carriage got faster and faster, the wheels clattering ever quicker.

Beadle gripped the iron rail that ran the width of the carriage seat as he was pounded up and down. Inside, Ergott and Shrume were buffeted from their seats and heaped upon the unconscious Bragg. Lady Tanville held tightly to the fading lamp, her hands burning upon the metal.

From the darkness the roar of the beast came again as if it gave chase. The horses were spurred faster, not caring that they raced to death.

"I can't hold it!" screamed the driver as the reins began to slip from his gloves.

Lightning flashed again. For a moment Beadle could see the road ahead. It twisted and turned, flattening out as they approached Peveril. At the turn in the road he saw a vast expanse of water.

"Galilee!" shouted the driver as he battled to pull the sweat-lathered horses to a halt. "We'll never make the corner."

Beadle let go of the rail and grabbed the driver's hand.

"By Riathamus, we will not die!" He gripped the reins for all his life, desperately trying to pull the horses back.

A shard of bright blue lightning hit the lake and appeared to jump from the water, hitting the clouds and then in the blink of an eye firing to earth. The explosion was so intense, so loud and powerful that the sound knocked the wind from Beadle's chest. It was like the final note to some great concerto. All fell silent. The storm was over.

Beadle gripped the horses' reins with both hands, knowing his life depended on it. They began to slow. The driver leant upon the brake, holding it fast as the leather and wood braced the wheels and squealed.

Far ahead, Beadle could see the lights of Peveril and the mouth of the cavern in which it was built. Upon the hill was the dark outline of a large castle. Scattered all around were the smoking chimneys of the houses. To the west was the vast entrance to a large cave.

"You did it," said the driver, panting hard and drawing his tight breath. Beadle turned his head and looked away. "I'd lost my strength, couldn't find it in me to hold on—but you did it."

"I fear it was not I but the lightning that saved us," Beadle said, his teeth still chattering with fear. "What of the bugler and Raphah?"

"Pray they are not lost to the madman," the driver said.

The lights of Peveril beckoned them onwards.

The Mender of Bad Soles

Galphus walked nimbly along Salamander Street and Thomas followed. Without saying a word, he turned into a long, narrow alleyway.

"Mister...Mr. Galphus," Thomas said as he attempted to catch the man, nearly breaking into a trot to keep pace with his steps. "Where do we go?"

"Onwards, ever onwards. Questions, always questions," Galphus barked with a swagger and a clatter of his cane as his coat appeared to sparkle in the lamplight.

The passage made a sudden turn and opened out into a neat and well-lit yard.

Galphus led the way to a large green wooden door. It had an ornate handle and a knocking plate moulded in the shape of a lion's head. Above the door was a large carved shoe. Thomas wondered how this place could be chanced upon or how it could bring any trade.

With his left hand, Galphus raised his cane and struck the door three times. He turned to Thomas and tried to smile. "We are not but a minute from where we started, Thomas. This is the Salamander Factory," he said proudly, nodding with contentment and rubbing his angular chin.

"Factory?" Thomas asked, unsure what he meant.

"A place of business—a building containing equipment for manufacture. Have you never been to a factory?" he asked. Thomas looked even more puzzled. "Then you shall have a great delight. I see factories as the palaces of the future. The people shall live at the place they work. Their beds can be next to their anvils. Gone the squalor and the roughness of life. This is fair trade. Mankind shall do what it was meant for—work and sleep, Thomas. Work and sleep."

Galphus looked proud. The door to the factory opened, and he stepped inside.

Thomas followed. He turned to see who had let them in, and there in the shadow of the door was a young child barely five years old. Thomas did not know if it was a boy or a girl. The child, wearing a regimental suit of grey wool with a jacket of the same cloth over a clean white shirt, had short-cropped hair. Upon its head a neat round skullcap gripped tightly to its forehead.

Thomas smiled at the child, who neither spoke nor acknowledged that he was there. Galphus pressed on and entered a busy hallway with a spiral staircase of rough wood that spun upwards out of sight. On every side of the hallway, people all wearing the same clothes busied themselves. From every corner came the sound of hammering and industry. An overpowering smell of tanning leather burnt Thomas's nose and caused him to cough with the fumes.

"This way," Galphus said, leading Thomas up the staircase to a higher floor.

"Before we go another step, let us sign the contract of employment." Galphus laughed, and then, as if he were a fairground magician, a quill pen and piece of parchment appeared in his hand. "Here. This is for you. A job for life and your life for the job. All will be found and you will be found wanting...nothing. I even have something that will make you smile with merriment. Sign, and we will be friends, and then the teaching will begin."

"But..."

"There are no *buts* in life, Thomas. Do you think I would have got to my station in life if I had said *but* all the time? Seize the moment and every opportunity that comes your way. Say a brilliant *yes* to everything and the world will open like a clamshell, nay, an oyster, and there inside you will find the most precious thing of all: the pearl. Sign. Quickly."

They stood upon the landing in front of another large door and Thomas felt a compulsion to run. But Galphus grabbed his hand, and in the flick of the wrist, Thomas saw his name scrawled in black upon the paper. He read his name clearly printed upon the contract and then fine large letters that he could easily see. As he read on, they grew smaller and smaller, until by halfway down the page they were like tiny dots that looked as though they moved across the parchment of their own volition.

"*Done!*" Galphus shouted as the door in front of them opened. "See, Thomas. When you say *yes* to something, doors will open."

"I would like to go back and see Captain Crane," Thomas demanded. He had seen that what he had put his name to was an indenture of employment. "He will want to know where I am if I do not return. This is *not* why I am here. I came for a day, not a lifetime."

"Thomas, Thomas, Thomas—ever doubtful and kept in the dark." Galphus stooped to him, took a hankersniff from his pocket and put it into Thomas's hand. "I am sorry, lad. I now realise he didn't tell you. I knew you were coming because Crane told me. He sent word days ago, before he left Whitby. Crane said he would bring two young people who were without work or family. I paid him his usual fee as agreed and met him in the Salamander Inn as requested. We couldn't say so at the inn, but our meeting was arranged. All has been pretence—Crane could neither care for you nor help you in your future. You are every bit the young man he said you would be. You will be happier here than in Whitby, and safe from Obadiah Demurral."

"Demurral? How did you know?" Thomas asked.

"My old friend Jacob Crane. He told me everything, everything. Don't worry; Kate will be here within the day."

"Crane would never do this to us. He never mentioned a factory or work. He told us we would have a new life with him, and that he'd look after us," Thomas protested as he looked about for a means of escape.

"And that he has. Crane has looked after you in the best way he could by bringing you here. I in turn will keep my bargain and give you an apprenticeship. From now until you are twenty-one I will encourage you as a craftsman, and then on that day you will be free to leave and set up for yourself."

Thomas could hardly take a breath for the panic that filled his chest. Somehow it had all been a misunderstanding. "I can't stay that long—I'll be old."

"Old, but wise," Galphus said as he took him by the arm and led him onwards.

They stood on a large gantry overlooking a vast factory floor. Each anvil was the same. By each one stood a worker dressed in grey with a white shirt. As if keeping time, they all hammered the leather and smoothed it flat. On the far side, lit by strong lamplight, were row upon row of sewing lads who needled the threads through the leather to form the shoes. They moved as in a dance, the thread slipping through with a twist of the elbow and wrist and back, again and again.

"Look, Thomas. This is the future. One day the entire world shall be like this. Gone the squalor and the hunger. A worker is worth his keep, and whilst he shall work, he shall live." Galphus pulled a fine timepiece from his pocket and looked upon it. "Did you know that a lad of your age need only work for ten hours a day to be profitable? Think of it, Thomas. That gives you fourteen hours of your own time."

"Then I can see Crane, once I have worked?" Thomas asked.

"Crane has gone by now. I paid him the money he needed for his ship and now he is gone. Kate will stay the night with Mr. Pallium, and then she too will come and be indentured."

"Tomorrow?" Thomas asked, as what Galphus had said began to take hold.

"And you will stay?" Galphus asked, placing a warm hand on his shoulder. "And not try to run away?"

Thomas nodded in a daze as he stared at the factory workers. It all began to take shape. *Crane had been so adamant to come to this place,* Thomas thought. Of all the inns and lodging houses in London, Crane had brought them to Salamander Street and had given him to Galphus.

"How much did you pay Crane?" Thomas asked.

"Not as much as you are really worth as an apprentice. I know someone who would give far more for you than I ever would," Galphus replied sweetly. "Then again, I shall have each day's work from you. And Thomas, with my help, all this could one day be yours. I have been looking for an heir. Marriage is beyond me, and I would like to hand all this to someone I can trust. Could you be that man, I ask myself?"

Thomas didn't reply. He still couldn't think; his wits were screaming to him whilst he tried to control his body and not let it shake.

"I will take you to your room. Every new boy has a companion, and he will teach you all that you need to know. Remember, Thomas, I am always here. Look upon me as a...father."

Galphus led Thomas down the stairs and across the factory floor. He could see that here all the workers were about his age. None of them looked at him, spoke, or even smiled. All of their concentration appeared to be upon the anvils and the leather that they pounded and softened with what looked like felt hammers.

Together they crossed the room. Galphus marched at his usual pace, pounding his cane to the time of the hammers. It was as if they were inside some gigantic clock and the hammering was the signal for time to move on another second. Eventually they left the factory floor and stood in the entrance to a large room with rows of neat, clean beds. Each bed had a small locker by its side with a new candle in a pot holder. At the far end a lad swept the floor with a brush that rasped against the wood with its thick bristles.

The lad turned, put down the brush, and stood to attention. He appeared to be the same age as Thomas but was of an incredible size. His face was that of a beaten stick, battered with a broken nose that made him look like a pug dog. The lad looked to the floor as Galphus approached and said nothing.

"Aha!" Galphus said brightly as if he had seen the lad for the first time. "Thomas, meet Smothergig." The lad nodded as Galphus spoke again. "We only know his last name. Tattooed upon his back by a caring blood relation. I think his friends call him Smutt. Doesn't speak much, but sweeps well. He'll be your companion."

Smutt nodded again and looked Thomas straight in the eye. His own were dark and edged with black. Galphus looked at them both, slapping them on their shoulders. He turned to Thomas, took the contract of indenture, and tore it in two. "This is for you. I will keep my half until you are twenty-one. Then you will be free to do as you wish. Smutt—Thomas is in your care. Do well for him, and you will do well for me." He spoke the last words very slowly as he stared at the lad. Smutt nodded, picked up the brush, and continued to sweep, saying nothing to Thomas.

"And I stay here?" Thomas asked Galphus as he began to walk off the way he came.

"No. Smutt will take you to your room and you will be given all you need. It should be there, waiting for you." With those last words Galphus walked away. He whistled as he went, tapping his cane against the floor merrily.

Once he was out of sight, Smutt put down the brush and looked at Thomas. He stared at him eye to eye, then began to take off his grey jacket and roll up the sleeves of his shirt. The boy made a fist and Thomas could see the broken knuckles and scars upon the skin. Smutt nodded slowly, as if to invite Thomas to do the same.

"I'll not fight you, Smutt," Thomas said as he stepped back. "Solves nothing. I would be your friend."

"What do you need friends for?" Smutt asked through clenched teeth. "These is me friends," he said, holding up both his fists and jabbing the air. "So do you fight or do you give in to me?" Smutt growled.

"Neither," Thomas said as he walked away and looked about the room as if he didn't care.

"Brave talk or just a fool?" the boy asked.

"I want no fighting. I just want to go from this place to my friends," he said.

"I can make that happen," said Smutt. "Step onto the punch and you'll see more than your friends."

"Don't make me fight you," Thomas said. "I've had enough fighting to last me all the days of my life."

"Then you'll have one more," Smutt screamed as he lashed out at Thomas, missing him by a hair's breadth. The lad danced from toe to toe, jabbing the air and snorting like a bull. Thomas looked at the dance and slowly put his hand behind his back.

Smutt jabbed again and Thomas moved his head to the side. The blow glanced against his cheek and snapped in the air like a thunderclap.

"I don't want to fight," Thomas said.

"This is my way, my rules, and my workhouse. I fight everyone, and when I win, you'll do what I say." Smutt screamed like a madman as he lashed out again at Thomas's face.

The blow, when it came, knocked him from his feet and sent him spinning to the floor. Blood splattered the boards. He lay in a crumpled mass, unable to move.

Black Shuck Inn

"No bugler and no hounds?" asked the hosteller as the carriage pulled up in the yard of the inn at Peveril.

"Gone after the madman at Galilee Rocks," the driver said. He climbed from the seat and opened the door to the coach. "There's been trouble—more than we expected. Could have been a wild boar or a wolf."

"A Shuck?" the hosteller asked, his eyes raised in alarm.

"Don't go saying the likes of that," said the driver as Beadle got down from the coach. "No one will ride with us if they thought that Ord Shuck was out."

"It was a vicious beast. If we had not fought it off, then we would have all died," Bragg boasted.

"Are the militia here?" the driver asked. "I have need of them. We lost a passenger—well, two passengers. One went after the madman; the other has disappeared."

"In front of our very eyes," Bragg said loudly as he stepped down from the coach and pulled his coat about himself. "Give me your best room. I was injured when I fought off the beast. I need to sleep." The hosteller took Bragg by the arm and led him away as Ergott and the others stepped to the ground.

Ergott followed on as the coachman set about loosening the horses and fixing the broken door. The inn loomed above them like an old castle keep. It was made of ancient stone with a small bridge that went over a deep moat. On all sides were high stone walls that surrounded the brightly lit courtyard. Two large oak doors kept out the night.

Above the door was the sign of the inn that swung with the wind. Upon it was painted the head of a man with the face of a dog, and underneath were the words: The Black Shuck Inn.

Throughout his years Beadle had heard stories of Peveril and the beast that had come from the night and killed a priest. The marks of his death could still be seen upon the church door. It was a beast that would howl as it ran and then would snatch its victim without a sound, so quickly that they couldn't even scream. Beadle would always listen, intrigued by the treachery of the place. He never thought he would ever stand in the courtyard of the Black Shuck. He had been told that it had once been a castle that had stood over the town and governed Peveril, and that now within its walls was the only safe place a traveller could stay.

"We owe you our lives," Ergott said to the driver.

"Not I, but your companion: Mr. Beadle. If it were not for him, we would have perished," the driver said as he pulled Beadle forward.

"Then, little Beadle, I will buy you dinner," Ergott insisted. "In fact, I think we should all eat together and talk of what is to be done."

"Kind sir," said Shrume as he stumbled across the cobbles, "I will be away to my bed. It is late, and the things of the night do not concern me."

"Then that leaves Lady Tanville and Mr. Beadle, or will you both be running away from me?" Ergott asked.

"I cannot eat, Mr. Ergott. I will drink with you, but until I know what has happened to Raphah and Barghast, my stomach will be empty," Beadle said.

"I too, Mr. Ergott," said Lady Tanville as she walked towards the door of the inn.

"Then it will be drink and nothing more, and in the morning we shall find out what has driven this world to madness."

Stepping over the threshold, Beadle saw Bragg and Mr. Shrume walking up the long staircase that led to the rooms.

The inn was empty, and Ergott sat as close as he could to the fireplace. Lady Tanville warmed her cloak by the fire as servants brought them food and drink.

Beadle felt uncomfortable. He hoped that someone would point him to the barn.

Ergott looked up and smiled. "Mr. Beadle, our saviour," he said as he laughed and held out a hand in welcome. "To this fire and to my company you are very welcome."

"And I to my sleep," Lady Tanville said as she bowed to Beadle and went the way of Bragg and the others.

"Then it is you and I," Ergott said as he poured Beadle a drink. "We shall toast the night and the finding of your friend. Tell me, Beadle. Do you know Whitby?"

For the next hour, Ergott talked of nothing but the town. Beadle watched the longcase clock by the staircase.

"I hear that Whitby was ravaged by a smuggler. Jacob Crane, I believe?"

Beadle spat the beer from his mouth as he choked on hearing the words. "I believe also," Beadle said.

"Then you know him well?"

"I have had acquaintance...once or twice," he muttered. "Everyman jack knows of Crane. The King and Crane: one king of the land, the other of the sea."

"I would like to meet him, talk with him," Ergott said.

"He's gone. Left Whitby by sea. Bad business."

"That I know," Ergott replied cautiously. He took a small cloth from the table and wiped the beer from the corner of his mouth. His face was sullen and gone was the smile of a fellow well met. "I saw the madman, Beadle. In the darkness on the moor. I have seen many things and never had that experience before. These are strange times. Let us hope that in the morning we will have an end to all this and be away from Peveril."

"I'll stay until they find Raphah, or what's left of him," Beadle answered.

"Raphah—the Ethiopian. Doesn't he do *healings*? Isn't he accused of witchcraft—healed a blind boy, or was he deaf? Stole Bragg's money and then put it back, by magic..." Ergott took a long splinter from the fire and lit his freshly stoked pipe. With each inhalation, Ergott began to snigger. His eyes glazed and reddened as he stared at Beadle.

Like a small child, Ergott jumped up, spun on his feet, and danced across the wooden floor. He took the stairs two by two, and upon the landing he turned and looked angrily at Beadle before retiring for the night.

"I am an eagle, swooping down upon my wings to pick you from the ground like a hare, Mr. Beadle. Never forget that, an eagle, always watching. Even when you can't see me." Ergott slobbered his words and stared at him in a drunken fashion. "Do you know...do you know you are the ugliest man I have ever seen? If I were you, I would wear a bag upon my head or cut off my face." Ergott sniggered as he clutched his pipe and vanished along the landing.

Beadle counted Ergott's footsteps as he staggered along the corridor above him. He listened to the creaking of the door and then the clumsy turning of a lock as Ergott took to his bed.

Beadle stacked the fire, piling the logs as high as they would go, and nestled himself upon the hearth. No one came to show him a room, and very quickly the house fell silent. He dozed, half-dreaming, half-waking. In the distance he heard the innkeeper locking the doors and sliding the bolts to keep out the night. The cold wind whistled outside. Beadle felt safe, knowing that upon the walls an armed guard waited.

No matter how hard he tried to dream, his mind was brought back to Raphah. All he could see was the lad's face as he went off into the night. Beadle found himself doting on the lad, fretting as to what had become of him.

There was an unexpected and sharp footfall from the gallery. Beadle pulled the cloak tightly about him and hid himself, pretending to sleep. The footsteps came closer, walking across the landing of the gallery and then onto the staircase. One by one and step by step they drew near. Beadle held his breath as he tried to peer out through his half-closed eyes.

A dark figure was coming towards him carrying the lit Glory Hand. Upon the stairs it was held aloft and then motioned in the sign of a star as the words were chanted again: "*Sleep one, sleep all.... As the night shall fall.... Sleep once, sleep twice.... Bedbug, lark, and mice.... And all shall dream, and all sleep well.... Until the dawn shall break the spell...*"

The hand spluttered and winced and let off a swirl of blue light. Beadle pretended to snore, hoping that he would be left alone.

Beadle knew that the Glory Hand was not a commonplace object. Whoever had it in their possession was not to be trusted, and it was only by chance that he too had not been controlled by its charm.

With one eye he followed the figure and suddenly recognized it as Lady Tanville. He watched her walk towards the far end of the room. By the side of a large oak panel, Lady Tanville stopped and from a small bag unfolded a piece of paper. She studied this map for some time and then pressed the wooden panel in front of her face. The oak panel parted, and she stepped inside.

Beadle waited, then got to his feet and followed. Something inside, a cold dark voice that defied reason, told him to go onwards. He reached the open panel, and just as he stepped across it, the panel slammed shut, pinning him to the wall with the force of a landslide.

He squealed momentarily as he tried to grasp his breath. Then he heard the footsteps coming back out of the darkness towards him. Beadle was trapped, his head in the hall of the inn and his body inside the passageway. The footsteps came even closer. There was a click of the secret lock and the panel slid open. He breathed a sigh and slid down to his knees. It was then he found a knife at his throat.

"You're supposed to be asleep," Tanville said as she pressed the blade against his flesh.

"So are you," Beadle grumbled as he tried to speak without opening his mouth.

"How long have you known about the Glory Hand, Beadle?" she asked quietly.

"Since the night before. I saw you counting the money—Bragg's money."

"And you said nothing?"

"You helped Raphah. I know not why. It would have been easy for you just to let him hang and you would have the money still. No one would suspect you," Beadle said.

"He was innocent. I wouldn't let him hang for me." She took the knife from him and pulled him within the passageway, shutting the oak panel behind them.

"What are you searching for?" Beadle asked, looking around the dark passageway that was illuminated by the Glory Hand.

"Bragg is an art dealer, an expert on all things literary and artistic. He collects books, pictures, anything of beauty. He took a picture from my family, and now I want it back. He sold it to a merchant in London. It was Bragg who sold the Glory Hand to my uncle, exchanged it for a piece of the true Cross. It's what he does best: magical artifacts."

"Can't you just buy the picture from him?" Beadle enquired as he rubbed his neck and stared into the flames of the Glory Hand.

"I am following Bragg to London. He takes something to the merchant, something that I believe to be hidden in the cave beneath us. Bragg will take me to the portrait, and then I will kill him so that he can't stand in my way of returning Isabella to her home. Now, Beadle, tell me secrets of yourself or I'll have to kill you." Tanville put the knife to his nose.

"I am Beadle. I have no secrets," he said nervously.

"Then how do you know of the power of the Hand?" she asked.

"My master ... he used the Glory Hand many times."

"And who is that?"

"Obadiah Demurral. But I have run from his service," Beadle muttered, hoping that he would never have to say the words again.

"And you say you have no secrets? Demurral is a warlock and knows

99

Bragg well. I would say we are equal in our skulduggery. Swear an oath on this knife that you will say nothing."

"Swear," said Beadle.

"Then follow me. You are now in *my* service. Bragg hid an item here the last time he travelled. It will tell me all that I need to know." Tanville led Beadle down the passageway and over the rock steps to a cavern below.

14

Uninvited Guests

"Smutt, Smutt, wake up," Thomas said urgently as he began to lift Smutt from the floor.

"Never before," Smutt moaned and tried to focus his bleary eyes on Thomas's face.

"I tried to tell you. It could have been different," Thomas said quietly.

"You hit me so hard. I never saw you."

"You'd have hit me, if I'd given you a chance." Thomas looked at the lad. "Why do you fight everyone?"

"Always have. It's what I do best," Smutt said cautiously as he held his face. "It's my job: keep the lads in order. Top dog—that's what Galphus says. He always brings them to me and leaves me alone with them, and I give them a good beating and tell them the rules of the place." Smutt swallowed hard and looked at Thomas. "It'll be your job now— best bed, best food, and all that goes with it. Here," he said, pulling a bunch of keys on a brass ring from his pocket. "You'd better 'ave these. I was on lockup. No one would ever argue with me. When they find out you beat me, they'll all wanna 'ave a go."

"Keep your keys," Thomas said as he helped Smutt to his feet. "Show me my bed and keep yours. I'm not planning on staying here.

I was tricked into this place, signed against my will, and I'll be off by the morning."

"They all say that, every one of them. But those that try to escape get *shoed*, and then they can never leave," Smutt said as he wiped the blood from his nose.

"Shoed or barefoot, I'll still be going, every day. Even if I was caught a hundred times I won't be staying. I've a score to settle, and my blood boils." Thomas spat the words as he thought of Crane's betrayal for selling him to Galphus.

"If you get shoed, you can't leave. Once they're on your feet, Galphus will know where you are every minute of the day. If you ever did get out, they'd come alive and stop you. If you run, they trip you up, and if you hide, they shout out. No one has ever got from this place. Once you hear the bell, you'll know what I talk of."

"Who's heard of shoes that do that?" Thomas said. He suddenly remembered Pallium's magnificent shoes.

"I've seen them. Galphus makes them. They stick to your feet, become a part of you, and you can never take them off. Does it to people he wants to *control*. Seen it with my own eyes."

"Then you'll see me jump from them and from this place."

Smutt hit the wall with his fist. "Been here three years and hate every minute. Said those words myself. All I know now is fighting. Fought the lad who had this job before me and will fight everyone who comes to keep it. A hundred kids look to me as boss—all this landing and half the one above. The only people I answer to are Galphus and his Druggles." Smutt dropped his head. "You were the first to beat me. It's yours now—them's the rules: get beat, get lost. That's what Galphus said."

Thomas noticed the chequerboard of cuts upon the lad's arms. They crisscrossed back and forth across his skin in ribbons of cut flesh. Smutt saw him looking and quickly rolled down his sleeve to hide the marks.

"Who did them to you?" Thomas asked.

"No one. Did 'em meself. What else is there to do?" He spoke half-proud, half-ashamed, his eyes cast to the floor.

"What for?" Thomas pressed him.

"When you've been here three years, let me see *your* skin. It's what we all does...part of the apprenticeship—cut yourself, cut out the pain and the misery."

"Then I'll be gone by the night—coming?" Thomas asked.

"What makes you think I won't tell Galphus?" Smutt asked.

"Because I would beat you every day to within an inch of your life and enjoy doing it," Thomas said. "You can keep your job and your keys. If anyone asks, I'll say you beat me. Treat me like you would a new lad. Treat me bad. Do that, and I'll be gone and no one will ever know different."

Smutt paused for a moment. It was as if you could see his mind whirring as he thought out the consequences. Slowly a smile came to his face. "I could help you get out. You could go now. Galphus would never think you'd make a break straightaway." He kicked the heels of his boots as he sprung to life. Thomas didn't notice the glistening leather and the golden soles that shimmered radiantly as Smutt walked on.

"We go now?" asked Thomas.

"Right now, before anyone suspects. Galphus will think I am showing you the room where you'll live. I know a place where there is an open window. From it you can get onto the roof, and from there into a courtyard and across the city. It's the only way. Every door is guarded, and the only things that leave this place are Galphus's shoes." Smutt seemed excited as he spoke. "It won't be easy—if we get stopped, tell 'em I'm showing you the place. We won't get far until you get out of them clothes and into your kit. This way."

Smutt led Thomas down a narrow flight of stairs and stopped by an open door with a warm light that bled into the passageway.

"Here," he said. "You can get fixed up. If we get caught, you'll get banged up for a week, and then Galphus will have you shoed, no questions asked. Them's the rules, so let's not get caught." Smutt's eyes darted around the narrow room. "Get garbed and make it quick." Smutt pointed to a rack of clothes hanging from a rail. White shirts hung next to grey jackets with dull trousers, drabber socks, and black, dowdy boots.

Thomas changed and in an instant looked just like the rest. Smutt laughed to himself, already knowing what was to come. Thomas reached for a pair of fine black shoes that looked to be his size. They were different from the others and looked inviting. He hesitated before picking them up, then made move to take them.

"No," said Smutt as Thomas was about to slip his foot into the shoe. "Them's the ones I told you about. One toe in that and he'll have you for life. Take these." He handed Thomas an ordinary pair of black lace-up boots. "I've changed my mind," he said capriciously as he took Thomas by the hand. "I'll come with you. Had enough of life here, going nowhere. Might as well get out of the place."

Thomas paused before slipping his feet into these shoes, suddenly unsure whether Smutt spoke true to him. He decided finally to trust him; the shoes looked plain enough to be safe. "Then we'll flee together. I have one thing to do when we escape, and then I'm heading for France—come with me if you want. I could use a mate like you."

"That's right—I'm your *mate*, and always will be. Right to the end." Smutt rubbed his fist in his hand as the bruise to his face began to ache. "Ten floors higher and then we can get out of this place. There's a window in the tower."

They set off together, Smutt slightly ahead and walking at the same pace as everyone else. The factory seemed endless, as if it was built like a city within a city. They walked for several minutes, Smutt stopping to point out the workstations, water butts, and the feeding hall. Each doorway was guarded by a boy not much older than themselves. They all held thick cudgels behind their backs. They stood deathly still, faces cast like stone, eyes dead to the world. Smutt smiled at each one in turn, and they duly nodded and let him by.

"They're the Druggles," Smutt whispered. "Get picked by Galphus to keep an eye on us. None of them is any good—keep 'em sweet by giving them your food."

"Do you not get paid for what you do?" Thomas asked.

"Galphus keeps it until you're twenty-one. What do you need money for in here? You can't spend it. Sixpence a week and all found.

Free boots and a shirt for your back. 'Tis luxury beyond dreams," Smutt said sarcastically.

Upon the seventh landing they were stopped by a guard who asked Smutt his business. He explained that he was under Galphus's orders to show the new lad the factory, and they were let by without further question. They walked through another workshop that appeared smaller than the rest. In its centre was a large platform, and upon the platform was a metal sphere encrusted in gold and hanging from a wooden frame. In the centre of the sphere was a hand-painted dragon with an eye that seemed to follow Thomas wherever he stood.

Thomas stopped and stared.

"It's a gong," Smutt said, as if he knew what it was. "Only heard it once—they use it when someone gets shoed. Dragon's Heart, Galphus calls it. No one gets out if they hear the Dragon's Heart."

Thomas stared at the Dragon's Heart and wondered what power it contained and how the beating of the gong would stop anyone from escaping from Galphus.

Smutt took Thomas higher and higher. Each floor was identical: on each level a Druggle, each Druggle staring in the same manner. All wore the same boots that looked as if they were a part of their bodies. They were made of thick black leather with deep wooden soles. Thomas noticed that the colour of the bootlaces changed. "Why are they different?" he asked Smutt as they walked by another Druggle.

"Red for the Druggles and black for the interns—Galphus calls us apprentices. Indentured for life and only leave when you die."

"But you can go when you get to twenty-one," Thomas said. "It's in the contract. Galphus showed me."

"Galphus lied. Look around you—you won't find a man of that age here. Come eighteen, they all vanish and no one knows what happens to them."

"And you would have stayed?" Thomas asked.

"I wouldn't live that long. Not here. After a while you give up caring. Living or dead—what's the difference?"

Two Druggles approached as they walked the corridor. Smutt

looked swiftly to the floor, his face coloured to glowing scarlet. Thomas stared straight ahead as if they weren't there.

"Sweeper boy," one said, taking hold of Smutt by the collar. "What you doing here?"

"New lad," Smutt said, his voice wavering as he spoke. "Galphus told me to show him the factory—top to bottom." Smutt put his hand to his face to hide the bruise.

"Someone smack you, did they?" asked the Druggle mockingly.

"He fell—a brush hit him in the face," Thomas said as he stepped towards the Druggle and held out his hand. "I'm Thomas, a new apprentice. Mr. Galphus picked me himself."

The Druggle stepped back and looked at him. He was older than Thomas and taller, with the first fledge of hair growing on his face. His chin was blistered with a deep red pox.

"New apprentice, eh? What would you like to apprentice for, my lad?" the Druggle asked. "Sweeping, like young Smutty?"

"To be a Druggle, that's all I want, for that's the best there is," Thomas replied mellifluously.

"So it is, so it is," said the young Druggle as he stared at Thomas. "Shall we let them pass?" he asked his companion, who smiled a toothless smile but had not the wits to answer such a complicated question. The Druggle waited for a moment. His eyes fixed sharply on Thomas. He looked him up and down slowly, as if he took in everything about the lad. "On your way—I'll see you later."

"They know," Thomas said as they walked off as calmly as they could, fearing to look back. "I could tell by how he stared at me so."

"He does it to us all—it's in his nature. A dangerous creature and a vile bully. His family fell on hard times. Father lost all their money—a gambler, so I hear. Galphus paid five pounds for him, cheap at the price," Smutt scoffed in a low voice for fear the words would carry far.

"And how much did Galphus pay for you?" Thomas asked.

"I was given to him. Not worth a penny. Hate it here, but it's home. One day want to run, another want to stay, and another wish myself dead. Better here than on the outside, some would say. All them wars and fighting, things falling from the sky, earthquakes and misery. Galphus tells us at prayers. I saw the sun once. It burnt my eyes. Prefer the dark; it's better for you. Hides many things."

Eventually they came to the top of the tower. Here was a room with no doors. To one side was a tall window that nearly came to the floor. Like a door, it was locked with a bolt and bracket. The glass was blackened, all except for a small square which had been etched away by eager hands seeking the outside world.

"Some come here to see the world. Makes 'em sick for it. A bad thing, I says—best forget and just work until the day you move on."

"How do we get out?" Thomas asked as he looked for a way of escape.

"The key. Simple, really—had it with me all the time, but didn't know until last week," Smutt replied.

Thomas peered through the scraping. It was a black, dark night.

"There," Smutt said, opening the window. "A few feet below is a roof, beyond that the alley, and further still the river. Freedom, Thomas."

"How do we get down?" Thomas asked.

"Just hang from the ledge and let yourself drop. I'll keep watch, then follow on." Smutt tried to be convincing, looking Thomas in the eyes for the briefest of glances. "Do it quickly—the Druggles will come and check this place, and we have to be gone."

Smutt seemed agitated and his voice trembled. Thomas looked from the open window into the pitch night. He could hear the distant cries of the town. Far to the east a ship's bell rang out. Thomas looked below. It was as if he stared into nothing.

"You sure about the roof?" he asked.

"Sure. Trust me, it's just a short drop—you won't feel a thing," muttered Smutt as he looked away.

"Then you go first. I'll follow you," Thomas said, and he pushed Smutt towards the window.

Smutt panicked, his eyes flashing to the lamp and then to the stairs.

Thomas could see he had set his mind to run.

"Give me the key," Thomas demanded. He snatched it from the lock and threw it through the open window. There was no sound of it clattering to the roof. "One…two…three…four…five…six…seven," he counted, and just as the last word left his lips, the faint sound of metal dashing against stone echoed through the mist.

"It was a way out of this place," Smutt snapped in panic as he saw the look of anger upon Thomas's face.

"It was a way to my death—you tricked me, Smutt."

"Tricked yourself—should have let me beat you. Things would've been different. Never be beaten, that's what Galphus says. You knocked me to the ground once, but *I* would have listened as the ground swallowed you up." Smutt spoke like a resentful old man, his face contorted with bitterness. "Let me pass, boy. I've shown you the way out—now go. If you dare," he taunted.

"Then I go alone." There was a crack of the wrist as all that burnt in Thomas's heart exploded through his fist, knocking Smutt from his feet yet again. Thomas stood over him and kicked him in the chest with the tip of his boot. Smutt moaned, not knowing where he was or what had happened. "Could have been so different, Smutt," Thomas said as he snatched the brass ring and keys from his belt and ran off down the stairs, hoping to find a way to escape.

Vere-Adeptus

Beadle followed Lady Tanville Chilnam as she ran up the steps from the cave, along the passageway and through the oak panel to the inn. There was a sound of barking hounds and a frantic pounding at the great door. Beadle and Lady Tanville hid quickly beneath the stairway as he slid the panel back into place to seal their escape from the passageway. With long, nimble fingers she took a vial of milk from her bag and extinguished the flames of the Glory Hand. She looked at Beadle with his ruffled hair and wild eyes that spoke of years of misery and gave him a half-smile.

"The spell is gone. They will soon hear," she said as the sound of the banging grew louder and the dogs' barking more insistent.

"Coming," screamed a voice from above as the barefoot innkeeper ran the length of the corridor and stumbled down the stairs. As he fumbled with the lock, Tanville hid the Glory Hand within the folds of her cloak.

The door opened and in spilled the night mists. Hounds leapt into the hall, looking for food and a place by the fire. The bugler stepped within and grabbed the innkeeper by the shoulders, shaking him as if he were a rag doll.

"To see it, to see it!" he screamed as he shook the man even more.

"Carsington is made well. The madness...gone..."

The innkeeper dropped his arms to his side and took a step back as if he had been given dire news. "Carsington—well?"

"Tonight on Galilee Rocks—I saw it with my own eyes. They are coming now, here," he said quickly.

"Who comes here?" the innkeeper asked as the hall filled with the barking of hounds.

"Carsington and the Ethiopian that was with me." The bugler stared with his wide eyes as if he couldn't believe his own words. "It's true, they follow on. I shot Mad Cassy in the leg as he screamed from the rocks. I went to finish him off but the lad got there first. He took the madness away, and if I dare to speak, he's as sane as you..."

"But what of the inn? I took it from him. It belongs to Carsington," said the innkeeper.

The man had just finished his words when the doors opened. Raphah stood before them, drenched with the storm, his hair dripping. He smiled when he saw Beadle by the fire. "All is well," he said as he pulled Carsington in from the night and walked him to the fireside. A second dark figure followed on, skulking into the room like a scolded dog that edged the walls and kept out of sight. Barghast held his hand tightly to his side as blood trickled from his fingers. "Bring sage, water, and cloth—he is injured," Raphah shouted to the innkeeper.

Soon the Black Shuck had come to life, as from every corner of the inn came people to stare at Carsington. Raphah sat the man by the fire and pulled the rotting fabric from his leg. It covered the wound of a musket ball that had split the skin. The man didn't speak, his eyes glaring at the fireplace and looking about the room. He hunched himself, as if he were unsure of his surroundings and the people who stared at him.

The innkeeper brought Raphah all he had asked for and sat and stared at the man. Taking a pair of shears, Raphah began to trim back the hair from the man's face. It hung in thick clumps, matted by dirt. From its midst stared two bright eyes. Slowly his face began to appear.

Soon Carsington looked like a man and not the beast that had plagued the moors.

"So long," he said, breathing the words. "So different."

"What did he do to you?" the innkeeper asked.

"The Ethiopian spoke words and held the madman by the throat. I saw it all, everything," said the bugler as he enacted the deliverance. "Raving one minute, and like a lamb the next. The sky burst open and it was gone."

"Truly healed?" the innkeeper asked as he wiped his hands upon his nightshirt.

"Truly," said Carsington.

"Then you know this house."

"Well, I know it is mine." Carsington stopped and looked at the innkeeper. "From the look of the place, you have kept a better house than I."

"Then it shall be yours again, for I took it in your madness and gave you nothing," said the innkeeper.

"We were once friends and will be again," said Carsington as he held out his hand. "I have back my wits and the Shuck."

"And what of Barghast?" Lady Tanville asked.

Barghast sat against the far wall, clutching his hand. The innkeeper took Carsington up the stairs and smiled at Raphah. "We have a lot to be thankful for," he said as they went.

Barghast sniffed and gave a sly look as they went. He wanted not to talk and held his gaze to the distant fire.

"We thought you to be dead," Lady Tanville said as she saw his wounded hand. "There was a madness in the storm—we all saw it."

"I saw nothing—fell in the dark, that is all. Woke in the ditch and then heard the hounds coming from the hills. There was no beast, only dogs and pigs."

"And your hand—it's damaged?" she asked.

"A slight wound from the fall. A night's sleep and it will be gone," Barghast mumbled.

There was a clatter of fat feet from above as Bragg and Ergott came along the corridor.

"What is this? What is this?" Bragg shouted as if to wake the dead. "Barghast alive?"

"Very much so," echoed Ergott, wand in hand. "Survived the moor and only a scratch, the maid has just left my room and…"

They stopped at the landing and looked down at Barghast.

"Never thought…never thought I'd see him again," wailed Bragg. "To think, Mr. Ergott, we worried ourselves to sleep over Barghast. I thought you had been taken by a beast on the moor, Barghast—the least you could have done was to be eaten by it."

"There was no beast. Your eyes cheated you," Barghast growled. "I was the one lost, not you. Remember that."

"And I was the one who nearly lost my life in that carriage."

"All is well and everyone is safe," Raphah shouted. "Is it not time for you all to go back to sleep?"

"The Ethiopian has elected himself our leader. One miracle and he becomes the saviour. Whatever next, Mr. Ergott?" Bragg said as he pulled the cord of his coat even tighter.

"The boy's right. Best we all sleep. Good night, Mr. Bragg, and may your money be as comfortable to sleep on as the fat on your backside," Barghast said as he got up from his seat and crossed the room to sit by the fire. "Sleeping here, Beadle?"

Beadle looked at Raphah. "They have nowhere for us to sleep, so I pitched myself here," he said.

"I'll bring you blankets and some food," Lady Tanville said, and she followed Ergott and Bragg up the stairs.

Barghast and Beadle dozed while Raphah stared into the fire. He thought of Africa, and his heart called him home. *Fulfil your desires,* his father had said the night he left the village. Raphah searched his heart, knowing no more what he really wanted. The night he had set off, he had known so clearly what he had to do. He had touched the golden Keruvim with his fingertips and felt its power filling his bones. It was as if it spoke to him, gave him strength and made straight every path.

Now he sat alone. He was tired, empty, and far away. All he knew was that he wanted to see the faces of Thomas and Kate.

"Here," said Lady Tanville as she carried a bundle of thick woollen blankets and dumped them on the floor by the fire. "I'll leave you to the night. The driver said there will be little chance of comfort on the roads, so sleep well."

"That's if we sleep at all," Barghast replied as she walked away. "There's more to her than can be seen at night," he said in a whisper as she turned upon the landing of the stairs. "She seeks something. I knew her grandfather well."

"For a man so young, you have lived such a long time," Raphah said.

"Is this the time for honesty, or does the game continue?" Barghast asked.

"My father told me to be honest, but only trust a man when he had saved your life. I trust no living thing. We are all fallen from goodness and our hearts can turn on a silver coin."

"So when will you trust me to tell you a story?" Barghast asked.

"It is the night and a time for stories. Beadle sleeps and I have no need for that distraction. I would be cheered by a lullaby," said Raphah.

Barghast moved closer and wrapped himself in a blanket as he threw another log onto the fire. He looked to Raphah and hesitated before he spoke. There was something about Raphah that intrigued him. It lay deeper than his broad smile and bright eyes. Something shone from within him, something Barghast desired, a look he had seen once before.

"There's an old legend of a man who is cursed to live forever," Barghast said slowly. He stooped towards Raphah, drawing him closer with each word. "He was once a wealthy man who in the eyes of the world had everything. On a dark Friday on the way to a hill of execution, soldiers were dragging a beggar to his death. In his poverty the beggar asked the man for water. The man had the chance to help the beggar, but turned his face. All that was asked of him was one sip. Instead, he tipped the water to the ground at his feet. All the beggar said to the wealthy man was, '*I will go now, but you shall wait until I return and walk every path until you find me.*' Little did the man know that the beggar was a king in disguise. On that day, at the time of the execution, the beggar cried out, and then as the thunder roared, he died. In his dying, he took away the power of death.

"From the wealthy man, the beggar took the gift of dying. Years passed by, and his family grew old and died; yet the wealthy man stayed the same. In anguish, he threw himself from a high cliff. Instead of finding death, his broken body healed itself. He threw himself into the sea and the water cast him to the shore, even though he had given up the will to live. Neither flame nor frost nor fire of hell could take his life."

"And what of the man now?" Raphah asked.

"Upon every road he walks until he has trod all the paths of the earth...until the day the beggar returns and he can ask his forgiveness and be set free. Every road he has walked has led to despair and loneliness. The beggar is not to be found."

"Is not the beggar already here with us?" Raphah asked.

"You speak as if you know him."

"I think I have met the foolish man," Raphah said as he took hold of Barghast's hand. The skin was newly formed over the wound as if no injury had befallen him. "Your prophecy about your healing was truthful, though several hours too soon and before a night's sleep."

"Had I slept and not entered into foolish stories, you would never have known," he replied.

"So was meeting us a coincidence?" Raphah asked.

"Like a moth to a flame, I seek the beggar and his people. I could feel it in my bones. Something stirred within the earth. I knew that Riathamus had returned, but was too late. The night of the sky-quake and then the comet—all were signs of his return, and the world saw them not. I followed my heart and upon a barren road found you." Barghast spoke quietly as if the walls listened to them. "Tonight you showed yourself on the moor—powerful, healing a madman. I quite expected the pigs to rush into the lake and drown themselves...then again, you are not the beggar, only his lackey."

"And you're the carcass that can never die," Raphah said as he gripped Barghast's hand until he called out in pain. "I would not expect a man who can cheat death to cry like a dog."

"Nor a prophet who heals to bring pain," Barghast said as he snatched away his hand.

"So you follow us?" Raphah asked.

"Don't flatter yourself. News of your arrival spread amongst my associates. Soon everyone was talking about the healer. If Demurral hadn't caught you, there would have been others far more powerful than that meddler. I searched you out for selfish reasons." Barghast moved closer to the fire. "I hunt for the last road on which my earthly feet will walk. I have looked for it many times, but it can't be found. It's as if it only appears to invited guests, those whose fate it holds in its hands. You are the key I have been looking for." He leant closer to Raphah as if to bring him in to a deeper secret. "There is another who travels with us who seeks the place also. Somewhere in the city is—"

From the room above, Lady Tanville screamed in horror. It pierced the silence of the dark night. Beadle jumped from his sleep as Raphah and Barghast ran to the stairway, and he followed, not knowing why he was running towards the screams when his wits told him to flee.

The landing quickly filled with the guests at the inn. Barghast kicked open the door. In the centre of the room was a large black dog the size of a man. Lady Tanville cowered against the end of the bed, candlestick in hand as she screamed.

The dog turned and looked at Barghast and growled. Barghast stepped forward into the room. The dog snarled and stood its ground.

"Stay away," Barghast said to Carsington as he attempted to push by.

"It's Black Shuck—he's returned," Carsington cried as he caught a glimpse of the dog. It bristled with fear and repugnance at the smell of humankind.

Slowly, inch by inch, Barghast moved closer, his eyes fixed upon the beast. Its red eyes glared at him as it bared its teeth. There was a sudden cry from the passageway as fearful voices spread the word of Black Shuck.

Without warning, Carsington ran into the room and dived upon the beast, grabbing it by its throat and attempting to wrestle it to the floor. Lady Tanville ran from the bedroom as Black Shuck twisted and spun with Carsington gripped in its jaws.

Barghast slammed the door behind Lady Tanville and locked it from within.

Raphah banged against the door, shouting to be let in. From inside came the screams of Carsington and the howling of the beast. Raphah and Beadle kicked and punched the wooden slats. The door held fast as the pandemonium within grew louder. It was as if two beasts pitched themselves to the death. The floor trembled like the opening of hell's gates. The sound of the howling dog filled the inn and shook the windows, and all who heard it trembled.

There was then complete silence. With one hand Raphah turned the handle and pushed against the door. It opened slowly. He looked into the room. Gone was the beast. Carsington lay like a cloth doll in a pool of blood. Raphah took a pace inside. He listened for any sound of the animal. All was still.

Inside the chamber was the heavy smell of blood. By the window lay Barghast, his face looking as though a wild animal had attacked it.

As he looked on, Raphah saw what should have been Barghast's hand. The flesh was pulled from the bone.

"Let no one see," Barghast said as he laboured to speak. "I thought that it would kill me and for a moment saw death. How cruel this curse," he whispered. "There is a changeling in our midst, a beast of hell that wants to see us all dead."

Quondam Discomfit

The moment Thomas stepped upon the factory floor, the sound
of screaming rang out.

"He's escaped!" Smutt screamed loudly. "A killer—he's escaped..."

"Rooms—back to your rooms!" a voice repeated through the loud-
speakers.

Footsteps clattered on wooden boards as hundreds of feet dashed
to their lodgings. Thomas hid in the shadows, wondering what to do
next. Two Druggles ran by, each with a cudgel and red-laced boots.
They dashed up the stairs of the tower, following the sound of Smutt's
cries for help.

Thomas knew that somehow he would have to retrace his steps
through the countless passages and workshops until he found the doorway out of Galphus's workhouse. For the moment, he hid himself in a
dark corner of the stairwell and tried to think. Smutt's screaming grew
louder and closer by the minute as the boy yelled out how Thomas had
tried to kill him by throwing him from the tower.

Thomas could wait no longer—he would have to run. Darting from
the blackness, he made for the workshop. All was still.

He crouched behind a rack of heavy overcoats, moments before a
Druggle appeared. He held his breath, hoping that the Druggle would

turn and go back the way he had come. But footstep after footstep, the Druggle came closer to his hiding place.

If it was just one boy, Thomas thought, *maybe I could take a chance and take him by surprise.* He waited until the Druggle came to within an arm's length. In an instant Thomas thrust the coat rack upon the lad. Its wooden spikes cracked against the Druggle's skull. Thomas kicked out with his boots as he grabbed the Druggle's cudgel. The fearless lad seized Thomas's leg and held fast with brawny hands.

Without thinking, Thomas lashed out with the cudgel as hard as he could. There was a head-bending scream as the lad's arm snapped. Thomas ran. On and on he blindly stormed through the building.

Then the gong of the Dragon's Heart beat out and echoed from hall to hall, shaking the building with each beat.

Thomas ran as fast as he could to get away, but upon his feet the boots came to life. They seized his ankles, squeezing his feet to bursting and stopping him dead. The louder the Dragon's Heart rang, the greater the pain. It was as if the shoes had been brought to life and fought against him. He dragged his feet clumsily across the wooden boards and, hiding in a dark shadow, tried to untie the laces. They became like tiny snakes in his fingers, snapping at him to leave them be as they coiled about his ankles.

The boots twisted and pulled, turning his feet until he fell to the floor. Thomas dragged himself across the workhouse to the stairs and slid facedown. The demon boots gripped him until tears came from his eyes and blood flowed from his ankles.

Pulling himself into a tight ball, Thomas attempted to roll from flight to flight. The treads of each stair bit at his back as he fell downwards. High above him the beat of the Dragon's Heart went on.

Ahead of him was a light. He could see the lanterns that had welcomed him to the factory. There was the green door, its paint flaked from the wood like dead skin. The Druggles had gone. Thomas was alone. He got to his feet, dragging them as if he pulled the world behind him. He screamed with pain as he reached out. His boots were rooting him to the wooden floorboards as he clutched the brass handle.

Incredibly, the door fell open as the beating footsteps of the Druggles thundered down the stairs. Thomas fell into the dimly lit yard. The sound of the Dragon's Heart faded. He was free.

The boots loosened their grip as he got to his feet and began to run. He ran towards the blackness of the alleyway and then—a cane snapped across his legs, knocking him to the ground. Within two paces, Galphus's hand gripped him by the throat and held him to the floor. As he looked up, he saw that Druggles surrounded him.

"Take him to the cell and teach him a lesson," Galphus said eagerly as Smutt appeared in the doorway. "You did well, Smutt. For this you will be rewarded."

Smutt bowed, grinning as Thomas was dragged past him. Smutt cracked him one to the face and then the chest as quickly as he could and laughed out loud.

"Even," Smutt said as he spat in Thomas's face. "Pray they keep you in prison, for I'll be waiting."

Thomas was pulled back inside the factory and pushed down a flight of stone steps to a basement room. It smelt like a converted sewer with iron bars across the grates. In the corner was a wooden bed held against the wall by two iron chains. He sat upon the bed in complete darkness and was able to take off the boots. This time there were no snakes to bite at his fingers, and they slipped easily from his bruised feet. The power of the Dragon's Heart was finished when the gong ceased its ringing.

Above him, Thomas could hear Galphus barking angrily at Smutt for allowing Thomas to get that far. There was a sudden crack of a cane and a shriek of pain. Thus, Smutt was given his reward. He could hear the lad's tears as he cried over his treachery.

"Take him away from me forever," Galphus said to the Druggles. "Do unto him what he would have done to another."

Thomas waited in the dark. The green door slammed shut and footsteps echoed along the alley above. The sound of Galphus's footsteps filtered through the drain from the street. Thomas could taste the strong and vile air.

Thomas didn't know if he had slept at all during his waiting. He thought of his father and, half-dreaming, he had called out to him. His father had answered, telling him to fear not and that all was well. Thomas had lain back against the pillows and in that complete trust had drifted again into sleep.

Thomas awoke to the *tap, tap* of Galphus's cane. It seemed speedy and urgent and matched his steps. He rattled the green door with a heavy turn of the key and entered quickly.

"Get the boy and shut him up. I have been followed—we have *visitors,*" Galphus shouted at the guard.

From outside in the alleyway came shouting. "Galphus! Galphus! I know you're near!" Crane yelled. "I want the boy, and the boy comes now."

There was a scurry of feet from the stairs outside. The door to Thomas's cell opened quickly, and two Druggles grabbed Thomas from the darkness. They bound his hands and feet, gagged him tightly, and then threw him to the floor.

"Say nothing, and make no sound. We have uninvited guests," one said as he slapped Thomas around the face and left the room. Thomas lay in the darkness and listened as Crane beat upon the factory door.

"Mr. Jacob Crane—I am glad you have come at my wishes," Galphus fawned as Crane pushed his way into the factory. "Did my messenger find you?"

"Don't treat me like a fool, Galphus. You promised to bring the lad back. I've just seen the writ of indenture upon the door of the Salamander—the boy's name is upon it."

"So it might be. A hasty decision on his behalf and one I warned him against. But sign he did, all legal and irreversible, Captain Crane."

"Just like death?" asked Crane.

"Sadly, just like death. And that is the grave matter of why I called you."

"Then I suggest, if you wish to delay yours, that you bring the boy to me now and give me the indenture. I promised him a future,

120

and your sweet ways will suit him not."

"If only that were possible. Were you not told?" Galphus paused. "I sent word to you, Jacob....Life is so cruel." Galphus sat at the desk in the cold room that he used to store his goods. "There has been an accident. A fall from the roof, a stupid mistake, and poor Thomas is—"

"No, Galphus, more lies?" Crane asked.

"Look at me, Jacob, look at me. These are not lies, Jacob. He is dead. Believe me." Galphus looked at Crane as he turned his head to the side.

"Then you killed him, and I will not rest until I have seen him for myself."

"I would advise you as a friend to remember him in life," Galphus said slowly as he breathed deeply. "He fell from the tower, Jacob, and like any Jack has broken his crown."

"You lie. I know you lie," Crane said as he felt for the knife on his belt. "I will see him and speak to any who saw him fall. One hint of treachery and I will split your face from ear to ear."

"And I will willingly allow you to do it. Look at me, Jacob. There is no treachery here. It was an accident. You can speak to anyone."

Crane was taken aback. He looked at the guards and then to Galphus, unsure what to believe.

"He was looking across the city, he slipped, and was gone." Galphus sighed at each word as if he were the grieving father. "Such promise, such a waste of life."

"Then I will see him. Who was he with?" Crane asked.

"It was I." A young Druggle smiled as he slyly doffed his cap. "I will never live with myself. I should have..."

"What we all should have done in life is not to be wept over," Galphus said. "I have taken the steps of providing him a place of rest in our garden. It's the least we can do."

"I should take him back to Whitby—bury him there," Crane said.

"Unless he was salted or waxed, it would not be wise to do such a thing. Better leave him to us. Take Mr. Crane and show Thomas to him," Galphus commanded.

Crane followed on like a broken horse. They stopped at a small door that led into a narrow room. Inside was a table, and upon it a body covered in an old blanket. The light was dim, barely above the gloom.

"Let me see him," Crane said, breathing heavily and squeezing his hands into fists.

"There's not much to see," the guard said as he lifted the blanket from the lad's face.

In the darkened room, Crane looked at the lad he knew so well. The body was draped in a shawl so that all he could see was what remained of the head. He could barely see any of its features; the face was battered beyond recognition. He stepped closer, only to be pulled back by the Druggle.

"Galphus would not want you to touch him," the Druggle said. "He has been prepared for the burial, and the balm would poison you."

Crane wished that for one moment he would be able to see Thomas's smile again. Taking the knife from his coat, he cut a lock of the lad's hair, twisted it into a knot, and buried it deep in his pocket.

Footsteps came from the corridor and Galphus stood by the doorway.

"Look at me, Jacob, look at me. All I can say is sorry." He held out a small bundle wrapped in brown paper and tied with string. "His clothing and all that was his," Galphus said sombrely as his eye twitched and blinked. "We will say good-bye to him at dawn. Join us, Jacob, and bring Pallium and the girl—you were his family; you should be there."

Crane nodded, his hand clutching the lock of hair. "I've seen many die and killed a few myself. Never thought I would ever feel this way. He was a good lad. Doesn't feel like he's dead." Crane tried to smile at Galphus.

"Sadly, it is Thomas. Look at me, Jacob. Grief makes the mind bleary; after the funeral it will all make sense."

"I had you for a different man, Mr. Galphus. Could have killed you myself when I came here. Now I know you're a man of good intent. Forgive me," Crane said as if bewitched or mesmerized and finding the words hard to speak.

"Forgiveness is never necessary and too esteemed. This is just life, and we are but men."

17

Irrefragable Mr. Ergott

An hour later, the moon still burnt brightly. Beadle stood in the doorway of the inn as people began to return to their rooms. They all were desperate for sleep, heavy-eyed sluggards wanting to rest but fearful of the night. Two by two they dwindled away, agreeing to share their lodgings to be safe from the beast.

Twenty of the militia had taken to the road and set off on foot to scour the hills in search of the hellhound. They had taken lanterns and muskets and every hound they could find, leaving the inn without defence. Lady Tanville sat by the fire with Barghast to one side, now totally recovered. Raphah walked the courtyard in the moonlight, looking at the stars and thinking of home.

"What was it?" asked Beadle as he came near. "Do you think it was a dog from the hills?"

"Was a creature, but not one that this world knows much of," Raphah said, only half thinking of his reply, his mind caught up with what had happened. "It was the beast that attacked you at the tree. I saw the look of its red eyes and knew."

"Will it come back?" Beadle asked.

"Has it ever gone away?" Raphah replied as he and Beadle strode back into the inn.

"It wanted to kill me, I could tell," Lady Tanville was telling Barghast as she looked anxiously around her for fear of the beast's return. "It came in through the window."

"It left by the window, but I am not sure if it came that way," Raphah announced.

"Then how else did it come?" Barghast asked.

"The door," he replied.

"Opened the door with its clawed hands?" Barghast jested.

"You are one to speak of such things—how would you do it?" Raphah asked, knowing he betrayed the confidence.

"It's not possible even to dream such a thing," Barghast said as he got to his feet. "No one can change from man to beast."

"What?" asked Lady Tanville, unsure as to what was being said.

"The creature could be a changeling, someone who can turn into an animal at will. Someone who wished either to frighten or kill you," Raphah said as Barghast stared at him, not wanting him to say any more.

"I agree with Barghast. No such thing," Lady Tanville said, the thought of a changeling shuddering her mind. "It was a dog from the moor, that's all. Why should it want to kill me?"

"Perhaps it has some interest in this quest of yours to find your sister in London," Raphah said.

"My private affairs are of no concern in this matter," she said, suspicious that Barghast should talk of such a thing. "It was a hound. Something from the fell. There are legends of these creatures throughout the north. This is not an uncommon belief. It is not a man who can change into a wolf—that is for fairy tales." She said this hopefully, as if speaking to convince herself. "It was just the savage hound, nothing more."

"When the hound struck, who in our party didn't you see?" Raphah asked her.

"Mr. Ergott, Mr. Shrume, and Bragg. I never saw them," she said as she thought of who had not been in the passageway. "But the inn is full of people from all parts of the land—why do you ask?"

"Then we visit Mr. Ergott, Mr. Shrume, and Bragg. They're in rooms next to yours, are they not?" Barghast asked, showing more belief that the beast might be a changeling. He got to his feet and ran to the stairs. "Come, Raphah, let us see if one of them is the beast."

Barghast and Raphah ran up the stairs. Lady Tanville prodded Beadle to follow. By the time they had climbed the stairs and crossed the landing, Raphah and Barghast were at the door of a room and were listening intently.

Barghast turned the handle and slowly pushed the door open. It slid silently ajar. Upon a table in the corner was a candle. It flickered as the drapes fluttered in the wind. The room was dark. There was the stench of blood and the faint odour of a dog. Upon the bed lay Mr. Shrume. Barghast took a pace closer, stopped, and then turned to them.

"No further, Lady Tanville. We're an hour too late," he said. Shrume was dead and lay in a pool of blood. "It was the beast."

"How do you know?" Raphah asked, looking about as if the creature still lurked in the room.

"See for yourself. There is no question of it. We must find Mr. Ergott and then Bragg."

"What kind of a beast are we looking for—a fat one?" Beadle asked under his breath.

"A beast that snaps the necks from the living and then makes off into the night, Beadle. A beast that would make a meal of you and take you like a morsel," said Barghast.

Suddenly from the high fell came the crying of a beast that called out to the moon, howling like a lost wolf. It cried as if it searched for others of its kind.

"Black Shuck?" asked Lady Tanville, as the vision of the creature from her room burnt in her mind. Beadle hid behind her, not wanting to see anything.

"The creature is closer than that. We will recognise him by his surprise to see me alive," replied Barghast as they left the room and walked along the corridor.

It was Raphah who was the first to enter the room of Mr. Ergott.

It was empty. All was neat and clean, the bed unruffled. Taking a tinderbox, Raphah lit the candle, shut the open window, and cast the bolt in place. He took a moment to look through the glass, across the moat and towards the fell. The cry of the dog came again.

"It gets nearer," Barghast said softly as he tried to make out the flickering lights upon the moors.

"The militia search the moors," Raphah said.

"And we are alone," said Lady Tanville anxiously as she and Beadle stayed close by each other. Beadle gently held her hand, more for his own comfort than hers.

"All we need to see now is Mr. Bragg. If he is there, then it is Ergott who is our devil-hound," Barghast said.

"Don't like Ergott," Beadle sniffed. "Said I were ugly, as ugly as a dog."

"Then he only sees the condition of his own heart and not how you are truly seen," Lady Tanville said.

"I go first, Raphah," Barghast said as they left the room and went along the passageway.

As they approached the door, they could hear the sound of talking. Bragg was boasting drunkenly to himself.

"Worse than a fool is a drunken fool," Lady Tanville said, following the procession closer to the door.

"But at least it will loosen his tongue. Leave Barghast and me and we'll talk with him. Watch the door and beat upon it should Ergott return," Raphah said.

"You leave us here, alone, with a mad dog roaming the inn?" Beadle asked nervously. "Rather face Demurral," he said, forgetting who was with him.

"It *is* you…" Barghast said, as if he knew of Beadle from long ago. "I have been searching my mind as to when and where I saw you before. A face like yours isn't easily forgotten. My mind must vex me in my dotage." He pointed at Beadle with a long finger. "The servant of the master, of course…"

"Can't say I remember you," Beadle stammered, knowing full well of the night that Barghast spoke of.

It had been ten years before. Demurral had grown in his desires to follow his dark heart. Beadle had grown a beard and long whiskers. He had seen a picture on a rum bottle of an old sea-hawker. The man had a beard and chin-wings, which Beadle thought gave him charm. Beadle had waxed and curled his whiskers until he looked like a mad walrus.

The visitor had called at the vicarage and demanded to see Demurral. Beadle now knew the man to be Barghast. He had called unannounced and entered the house without being made welcome. He had sat in Demurral's own chair. Whilst waiting he had lit the fire and poured himself a glass of wine.

What had then taken place had mystified Beadle since that day. Demurral had gone into the study and had bowed to the man, taking great care not to look him in the eye. The visitor didn't speak but held out his hand as if to receive a gift. In return, Demurral had gone to his safe-chest, taken out a silk bag, and placed it in the man's hand. The man had then finished his wine, nodded to the parson, and walked out without any farewell.

No mention was ever made of the strange transaction. Later that night, as the moon had risen from the sea, Beadle had listened at the chamber door as Demurral had sobbed like a child. He had been troubled for his master, knowing that something was deeply wrong. Even though in his heart he despised the man, it pained him to hear his master blubbering. Beadle had thought of the times when he had been left to cry. Even though Demurral had beaten and scolded him, all that Beadle desired was to open the door and show him some kindness. Yet it had been from that night that Demurral had changed. In giving up the silk bag to Barghast, it was as if he had become like a madman.

"You must remember me?" Barghast asked again quietly as they stood outside Bragg's door.

"I haven't the memory to bring these things to mind," Beadle said as he looked away.

Raphah tapped upon Bragg's door. Not waiting to be summonsed within, he pushed the handle as he and Barghast stepped inside.

"Mr. Bragg," he said loudly. "We thought by your conversation you were entertaining."

Bragg was slumped in the chair by the fire, a flagon of wine by his side. He was slow to look up from the flames.

"Ah, Barghast—fresh from the hunt. What news of the beast that stalks our lives? Is it the one at Galilee Rocks?" Bragg asked as he sipped his wine.

"We are unsure," Barghast replied. "But Shrume is dead. Killed like a farmyard chicken, not fifty feet from this room."

"Dead? How can he be dead? I heard nothing. I have sat by the fire all this time. Since the hound ran from the inn all has been quiet," Bragg said.

"Did you know Mr. Shrume before the journey?" Raphah asked.

Bragg ignored Raphah and looked at Barghast. "You should keep better company, Mr. Barghast. There is a curse on this Ethiopian's head. Remember—he was the one who sat in Ord Vackan's chair. Look what has happened since. You vanished, Lady Tanville attacked, Shrume dead, and Ergott nowhere to be found."

"Ergott? Did I say Ergott?" Barghast asked Bragg. "I only mentioned Mr. Shrume."

"A mistake, a presumption, a conjecture, a…" Bragg flustered and sweated before the fire. "So Shrume is dead—the tragedy. Who will be next?" He gulped his wine eagerly and tore off chunks of bread from a loaf. He swallowed hard as his eyes flicked like a snake from Barghast to Raphah and then to the window.

"Why do you travel to London?" Barghast asked.

"I am a collector of fine objects, and I take something to a customer. He buys many things from me, and I offer a personal service. Why should this concern you?" he asked.

Suddenly from the high fell came the calling of the hound.

"There, that's your hound. Came from the hills, Black Shuck. Got in through Lady Tanville's window and did the deed. You know what you'll have to do. Bury Shrume before dawn, facedown, or he'll be back. Once a hellhound has killed you, then you'll return—you of all people should know that, Mr. Barghast. A man of your travels will have heard every tale," Bragg rambled, his piggy eyes widened to the rims.

"That's all they are, fireside tales," Barghast said.

"Just look at what's happened since the Ethiopian joined us. Hell has come a-calling. We should make him walk to London. Who'd be next? There's too much good eating on me, and whatever is following us has only appeared since *he* arrived."

"Raphah's money is as good as yours," Barghast argued.

"Then he should take it and spend it somewhere else. The man's a Jonah, bad luck, misfortune, death on two legs, that's what he is," Bragg replied as the wine slobbered over his lips and down the front of his nightshirt.

"One thing," Barghast asked as they turned to leave. "Mr. Ergott— are you and he…*friends?*"

"No time for that man—he is a charlatan. Believes he's a diviner and a dowser. Why would I need an acquaintance like that? Who would keep company with a man who plays with a stick? Rather have a dog for a friend, at least the dog can bark." Bragg laughed, pleased with himself. "Listen to me, Mr. Barghast. You'd be better off ditching the Ethiopian and mixing with us. Taints a man, bad company, and corrupts good character—even if he can heal the sick. Think I'd rather be dead than let him touch me." Bragg seethed as he spoke, cringing his shoulders and shuddering at the same time.

"I have that feeling myself," Barghast replied.

"Really?" said Bragg, astonished that someone should share his view.

"Usually for fat old drunks who find their own company *pleasurable,*" Barghast continued as he turned and followed Raphah from the room.

The door of the chamber closed quietly, and Bragg sat in his own company before the fire. The soft light flickered against his face. He waited as he heard the footsteps walk along the corridor and down the stairs.

Bragg broke the bread and dipped it in the wine before taking another bite.

"Safe to come from your hiding place, my dear little hound," Bragg said as the creature crawled from beneath the bed. "They believe you to be Black Shuck…"

The beast curled itself by Bragg's feet, warming against the fire. Its dark fur bristled as it sniffed the air. Bragg stroked its long nose and looked into its red eyes.

"To think that they would want to hurt someone as sweet as you," he said.

The beast grumbled a low growl at the edge of hearing. It sounded as if it purred softly, its large dog ears listening to every word spoken in the hall below.

Funeral

At dawn, as a far clock struck the hour, Smutt's body lay beside a damp grave. The tomb had been hewn from thick clay and dug to three shovels' depth. Like most of Salamander Street, the garden—if that is what it could be called—never saw the sky. It was a bare patch of earth surrounded on all sides by the factory. Upon the dirt lay the body, wrapped in grey rags and tied with hemp cord. Looking down upon it was Galphus. He waited impatiently, tapping the head of the corpse with his cane and listening to the dull thud that it made.

From the door of the factory stepped Jacob Crane. Kate held Pallium's hand and clutched three flowers. She followed him slowly and wept as she walked. Crane kept a hard stare, straining his lips across his teeth to stop them from trembling. He kept his eyes from looking at the body as he nodded to Galphus in welcome and nervously rubbed his hands together. In his heart he felt as if he had come to bury his son. Looking at Kate, he remembered Demurral's house. The garden there was bright and faced the sea. He had fought to keep Thomas from a grave in that garden.

From inside the factory, two of the Druggles came and took hold of the body. Upon a quick stamp of Galphus's cane they picked it up with the straps and clumsily dropped the body into the grave.

Kate could restrain herself no longer. She screamed in pain as if her heart were being torn from within her. Crane held her to him as the harsh shovelling of clay splattered against the carcass. Soon, Thomas was gone, no words said, dust to dust.

"Short life," Galphus chirped as they looked at the pile of earth. "Makes you think of wasted time. Salamander Inn, Jacob?" he asked as he turned to Crane with the offer of a drink. "Never too early to taste a fine wine."

Crane looked to Kate, who held out the flowers. "Let's give her some time alone to say good-bye," he said. He took Galphus by the arm and walked towards the door, and Pallium followed.

"When she has finished her mourning, bring her to my room. We'll wait there," Galphus said to the Druggles who stood in the shadows with their muddied shovels. Crane took a final glance as Kate sank to her knees in the dirt and pressed the flowers into the grave.

Galphus led Crane from the courtyard and into the factory. They walked silently through the workrooms until they came to Galphus's study.

It was a windowless room stacked with shelves and wooden boxes. There was a large desk lit by several candlesticks. To one side was an old skull and several discarded teeth.

"Tell me, Crane," Galphus said, "how much would you need to free your ship?"

"Enough and enough again," he replied.

"On my desk is a bag. Take it and pay off what you owe. Take it from me as a gift, and from you I'll take a third share in all you make from now on," Galphus said.

"What else will you take?" he asked.

"Just a third. Nothing more. Reasonable and honest for the amount in the bag. I know that when you pay the release there will be more than enough."

"Signed for or shaken upon?" Crane asked. He looked at a thousand glass jars neatly placed upon the shelves in tidy rows; each one was precisely labelled with a name and date, and underneath this inscription were words that differed from jar to jar in a tongue he could not comprehend.

"The offer is there and I will not shake or sign. Let us say that it is just for the taking." Galphus saw that Crane was staring at the jars. "They are interesting, are they not?" he asked as he lifted one from the shelf and held it before Crane's face.

"Empty jars—interesting?" Crane asked.

"More than that. They are the finest collection in the world."

"Of what?" said Crane.

"The last breaths of those who have gone before. Aristotle, Caesar, Pythagoras, and there," he said, pointing to a larger jar at the end of the shelf, "King George the First." Galphus smiled and spoke excitedly, all thought of the funeral now a distant memory. "I know it may sound strange, but to me it is an interest and one that not many people may entertain. They are my *pneumamorte...*"

"So why keep them?"

"I believe that they possess a power, that in the last breath the soul jumps from the flesh. This is glass made from the sand beneath an Italian volcano, Capacious Alta. It has the power to trap the soul. That soul can give us vigour. Think of it, Jacob—wouldn't you like to live forever?"

"I would like to die old and in bed," he said.

"I have summonsed a man to bring me an implement so that I can partake of these breaths, hear the last words of those who died, and take on their lives. As we speak I am being brought a cup, and from this I will drink my eternal life. I tell you this as a fascination. I know you have seen much, and now that we are partners I can tell you more." He smiled.

"Kate," Crane said as she stepped into the room with a tearstained face. "Galphus and I were..."

"I heard. Pity his implement was not here to give Thomas life," she said angrily.

"Come, have breakfast with us. We can mourn your friend over a drink," Galphus invited her.

"I have Thomas's things for company—Crane gave me a parcel of clothes. They are all I need." Kate scowled and looked to the floor. Her face was set like stone. "I'll go with Pallium. He said he'd take me back. I need to sleep," she said.

"Jacob and I have some business. I'm sure he'll be along later." Galphus held out his hand. Kate turned without speaking and made off along the corridor to where she had left Mr. Pallium.

Together they made their way from the factory back to Salamander Street and Pallium's home. He offered her chocolate and milk, but Kate refused and asked that she could sleep some more. The door to the stairs opened on its own. Taking quick strides, she climbed up the stairs and turned into her room. The morning fire still burnt warmly.

Kate pulled open the parcel that Crane had given to her. Inside were Thomas's clothes. They were cold and damp and stank of shoe leather and glue. She took the shirt and warmed it by the fire. It soon was soft and warm and smelt of Thomas. She held it to her and smothered herself within as she tried to picture his face.

The room fell cold. Snowflakes flurried across the ceiling and stacked against the far wall. Leaves blew about the boards, and the scent of the forest grew stronger. The magichord began to play softly.

Kate looked to the wall. The picture had gone and the wall began to disappear. There stood the entrance to the forest. The magichord was still in place. She waited and waited as she clutched Thomas's shirt.

"Saw him thrown," a voice from beside her said. "Right from the window of the tower. Looked as if he were already dead."

Kate sat still with fear, not daring to look at the girl. "How would you know that?"

"When you die, your soul jumps from you and goes off. Some disappear and are never seen again. Others, especially the ones who don't know they're dead, hang about. Get up from the body and look around. When your friend hit the ground, there was nothing. So I went looking…"

"And?" Kate asked as she buried her face within his garments and sighed.

"Couldn't find him. Not a trace. Looked everywhere—called out to him and everything. No boy. Just the body. Strange thing is, I found someone else in the cellar, very much alive. Looked like Thomas."

"But I've just buried him. And Jacob Crane saw him not an hour after he was dead." Kate screwed up her eyes and covered them with her hands. "Leave me. You do nothing but torment."

"Typical," said the girl with a tut. "Try to help the living and all they do is complain. When will you realise that death is not the end of life? How many spectres will you have to see before you believe?"

"But I don't believe. You're just a dream, a madness of my mind," Kate shouted.

"Then look at me. Look at me if you're not afraid," the girl said as she touched Kate on the face.

"*No!* Leave me alone."

"But if I am just a figment of your mind, then you are alone, Kate."

The words made Kate drop the hands from her face and stare at the spirit. Like before, she wore the crinoline dress. She looked younger, fresh of face.

"Am I mad?" Kate asked the spectre.

"Why ask me? I'm dead," the girl replied, giggling to herself. "So why did Galphus bring you here? Does he want you in the factory, or will he steal all of the man's money?"

"What?"

"That's what he does. You're not the first and won't be the last. Pallium gets them here and hands them on. That's how he's paid. He'll have you in that factory before the morning. He'll convince your friend to leave you here, and then you'll be snatched, vanish from the face of the earth. Had a parson here, came from the north. He would sell Mr. Galphus children. Not particular, our Mr. Galphus."

"How do you know? I thought you were trapped," Kate said angrily.

"I listen. I never eat or sleep but listen. Walk the street and listen. As they work, I listen. Kate, they won't let you leave this place."

"I'll leave when I want," Kate said.

"Do it now—go, and see how far you get. Follow the street and you'll come to a dead end, a blind alley. Whatever way you choose, you won't get out. Galphus made this place, and he's an alchemist, a magician. Look on a map and it doesn't exist. There is no Salamander Street in the whole of London. I heard them, Kate. Listened to the screams of children trying to escape. They soon find out they'll be stuck here forever."

"I'll go now," Kate stammered.

The spectre bent forward through the leather chair and whispered in Kate's ear. "Mr. Pallium is listening to you from outside. Thinks you're talking to yourself. Thinks you're mad."

There was a gentle knock at the door, then the latch slipped and it opened slowly. "Couldn't help hearing you, Kate," Pallium said kindly as he peered at her. "Must be a great shock." Pallium stepped into the room. It was as if he was unaware of all that was around him. He could see neither the spectre nor the forest that lay beyond the wall.

Kate glanced to where the wall should have been. There was the glen that led to the river. She could see it clearly. A fawn ran through the wood, and in her mind she could hear the sound of birds calling.

Pallium stared at her. "I think you should rest. Galphus will come soon and all will be well."

"I want to see Jacob," she said suddenly.

"How can I say this? What words will suffice to calm you on such a day?"

"Words? I want to see Jacob Crane, and I go now," Kate said as the ghost vanished before her.

"I have bad news—he's gone. Didn't want to say. Left you in my care. Knew I would look after you. Galphus and I will be your guardians. Took the money offered by Galphus and went. He wasn't going to drink in the Salamander; he was going to get the money. He's gone for the *Magenta*." Pallium spoke breathlessly.

"He would have told me," Kate said.

"He couldn't—too hard and too hurtful. That's old Jacob. Like a nut, but crack the shell and he's so sweet."

The girl appeared again by the fireplace and shouted to Kate. "He's gone, Kate. Your friend is neither at the inn nor anywhere in the street. Galphus drinks in the Salamander, but the smuggler is no more."

"Gone?" Kate yelled. "How can he be gone? What have you done to him?"

Pallium reached out a hand to touch her brow.

"Don't trust him," the spectre whispered, Pallium unaware of her presence. "I've seen this before. He has a knife."

"Where?" Kate screamed, not knowing whom to believe.

"You're tired—it's the shock. I have some tea. I'll bring some for you," Pallium said as he hurried from the room.

"Gone for Galphus and his men. That's what he always does," the spectre said as the latch snapped on the door and the lock turned. "See—bolted and kept within, you won't get out."

Kate grabbed the door and rattled the lock. It stuck fast. Below, she heard the door open and Pallium dash into the street. Kate ran to the window and saw him scurrying like a rat into the darkness.

"What will he do?" she asked the ghost.

"He gets Galphus and they'll take you away. Then he..."

"What?" Kate asked.

"Just escape. That's all you have to do. That, or cheat them."

"Cheat them how?" Kate asked.

"Come with me into the forest—we could live there together. I wouldn't be lonely and you'd be free."

"But you're dead."

"So could you be. It's like taking a step from the world to another." The spectre sat on the bed, put her face in her hands, and looked Kate in the eyes. "Just walk into the glade and all will be well. Quickly! Galphus will be here soon, and I can't say what he'll do to you."

"I'll hide."

"They'll find you."

"Run—"

"You're locked in—how will you escape? Come with me, Kate," the spectre pleaded.

"Not my time, not for me to decide. Raphah said there was a time for everything, living and dying, and it wasn't for us to choose. There's always hope—no matter what your circumstance."

There was a cry in the street. Torches came through the darkness as Galphus and three Druggles made their way towards the house and Pallium followed. From the window, Kate could see their approach.

"They come for you," the spectre said as she stepped towards the glade. "Come with me."

Kate hesitated for a moment and looked to the street. Galphus walked quickly, his cane beating out the pace as the Druggles in their grey cloth coats and black boots came closer in the twilight.

"You have but the minute and then you'll be theirs forever. The smuggler won't come back—he'll never find the place again. It's easy this way. Just take a breath, Kate. Trust me."

"I want to stay. I want to live," Kate said as the glade grew in its power and presence. The magichord chimed by itself, dancing notes that came forth from within it and could be seen in the air like tiny moths. As the notes flew by, they sang in chords together, filling the room as the light faded. Kate reached out and gripped her hand upon the bed as her feet were dragged from her. "Let me stay," she shouted as the spectre took hold of her from inside the wood and tried to pull her into the forest.

The Black Shuck

They had spent the night camped by the fire in the hallway, taking turns keeping watch. Raphah had not slept a single wink. He felt alone and helpless in a land where so many people hated him. The inn was like a great ship at sea. It creaked and groaned as timbers rasped against the stones. The cold night air shivered its bones. Raphah thought of Africa and fought the voice within that told him to run and leave these people to their own desires. He had come to their land to find the Keruvim, which had been stolen from his people. It was something so old, so powerful, that in the hands of evil men could change the course of history.

As his companions slept, warmed and lit by the flames of the fire, Raphah looked at their faces. Beadle snored, his jowls flapping as his head lolled from side to side. Raphah thought him to be honest, but was crushed by his fearfulness. Barghast was motionless as if he rested in death. Lady Tanville Chilnam sat serenely in the chair, wrapped in her cloak.

The inn grew silent as the night went on and by the dawn was perfectly still. Barghast woke early and had gone to tell the innkeeper of what he had found during the night. Silently and without fuss, the body of Mr. Shrume was taken from the inn and buried facedown beyond the walls. Barghast returned as the house came to life, his boots still wetted by the dew, the fog hanging from his clothes.

In the great hall, a meal was set. Bragg, smelling the scent of meat and hearing the clanking of plates, appeared from his room. Ergott was still nowhere to be found. Raphah checked Ergott's room and returned with news that the bed had not been disturbed and Ergott had not returned.

Bragg didn't appear surprised as he sat at the table and stuffed his mouth to bursting.

"If he is not here, then where can he be?" Bragg said.

From the courtyard came the cries of the militia. In the still morning air, their voices carried from the gates. The innkeeper flung open the doors as a musket man dragged the carcass of a large black dog up the steps and into the inn.

"See," he said proudly. "The beast is dead."

The inn filled with excitement as all gathered round. From every room came people to gawp at the large dog that lay upon the cold stone floor, staring with dead eyes. The vaulted ceiling of the hall with its panelled staircase and mullioned windows echoed with their excited chatter.

"Caught it upon the fell. Heard it calling and then shot it from the crag," the innkeeper said with a broad smile upon his face.

"It's not the hellhound," Barghast whispered to Raphah. "Not big enough and not enough teeth."

"Say nothing to them," he replied quietly. "Let them think it to be the beast. Our coach leaves at dusk—we have until then to find the animal."

"Or man," Barghast added.

The innkeeper roared with excitement as he looked at the hound. He beat his chest in merriment and gave beer to all, and the inn sang out with the celebration. Beadle took his part, dancing on the table, his face covered in froth as he sang of the dead beast. Raphah looked on as he and Barghast sat by the fire. Bragg had disappeared in the throngs of the glee and was nowhere to be seen. Men danced and jabbered. They kicked the dead creature and beat it with sticks.

"I shall look for Ergott," Raphah said as Lady Tanville came to the fire. "He has to be found."

"Taken by the dog—or *is* the dog," Barghast said.

"But they have the beast—we saw it," Lady Tanville replied.

"That wasn't the creature, Lady Tanville," Barghast whispered to her. "That was a wild dog—a wolf and not a changeling."

"Where do we look?" she asked.

"Somewhere close by, somewhere—"

Tanville quickly interrupted. "The cave—there is an entrance from the inn. I showed Beadle last night when you were on the moor. I have a map. It was stolen from Bragg a year ago. I bought it at great price from the thief." She looked towards the panelling on the far wall.

"Within?" asked Raphah, trying to guess her meaning.

"Deep within. Third panel from the floor, second to the left."

Beadle continued to dance upon the table as the hunters celebrated the kill from the hall and into the courtyard.

"We wait," said Raphah as the merrymaking began to still and each man found a place to rest his drunken head. "They will soon sleep, and then we can search for Ergott."

Barghast nodded in agreement, knowing the hunters had been gone all night. The beer would swell their tiredness and sleep would soon come to them. He had been strangely quiet as he looked about him, his eyes searching each face.

"They've caught it!" exclaimed Beadle as he slumped from the table, his song complete and his belly full of beer. "We can travel in peace, find Kate and Thomas, and Demurral won't find us," he said foolishly.

"So you look for someone and someone looks for you?" Lady Tanville asked.

"Some people we know—that we will visit," Raphah said as he tried to cover Beadle's mistake.

"I know the man who pursues you," Barghast said to Raphah. "I took something from him: a shard of wood touched by the hand of Riathamus. What did you take from Demurral?"

"That which belonged to my family. That which he would have

used for magic. I took the Keruvim."

"So it is true. The Keruvim is real and Demurral had it all along. I heard a rumour that it had come to this land. When I first saw you, I knew," Barghast said. "Lives entwined like hemp rope. You in search of your friends and me a beggar. Find you and find the beggar. Eh, Raphah?"

"You could be from Demurral," Raphah said with narrow eyes.

"On this journey I have to trust you and you, me. There is a creature that since your arrival has begun to kill. Any one of us could be its intended victim. I've made many enemies in many years, and now Bragg is one of them."

"So I just trust you? As simple as that?" Raphah asked.

"Thought trust would come easily to someone like you," Barghast said as he picked the piece of the slain dog's claw from the hearth. "Interesting," he said, looking upon it. "There is little wear upon it—not a beast that travels far. More a house dog than a monster from the fell."

Beadle slumped by the fire. The sleeplessness of the night was brought heavy upon his brow by the light of the day. The hall became quiet. The militia drifted away, leaving only those who had joined the hunt from the inn to sleep by the flames. It became like the nighttime. Peace was on all.

Raphah looked to Barghast. "Time?" he asked.

Barghast looked about him. "Time indeed," he said with a shiver.

"I come with you," Lady Tanville insisted.

"Would be best for you to stay and—" Raphah tried to insist.

"I am coming and you cannot make me stay. I have something that will bring a blessing to our journey," she said as she walked quickly up the stairs to her room. When she reached the landing, she turned and looked at them. "Be here when I return—understand?"

Raphah laughed with Barghast. "Have we any choice?"

Lady Tanville soon returned. In her hands she carried a large black silk bag. She nodded to them both and walked to the far end of the hall.

Barghast pointed to the stone floor. By the wall was a single paw print etched in blood. "We are not the first to go this way," he said quietly. "The beast goes before us."

"This is it," Tanville said as she tapped the panel with her hand. It opened slightly. The door slid quickly to one side and the three entered in. Inside was complete blackness.

"Keep awake—don't close your eyes," she said as she opened the bag and brought out the Glory Hand.

"This is not a good thing you have," Raphah said, sensing its presence but unable to see it.

There was the striking of a flint and the burning of tinder, and a glow filled the stair chamber.

"What a surprise, my dear girl," Barghast said as he chuckled to himself. "A Glory Hand. I took you for a lonely traveller, not a witch. Will you not entice us with the spell?"

"We don't need magic," Raphah insisted. "Leave magic to those who don't know a greater power. If we must suffer this contrivance, then let us have only the light from its fingers, without any so-called *magic*."

"But it will make them all sleep." Lady Tanville said eagerly.

"Sorcery and wickedness are the same word. The drink will be enough. I have known the spirit of this same Hand before. It will bring you no good, Lady Tanville."

"Did you use it to steal Bragg's money?" Barghast asked Tanville.

"And nearly get me hanged?" Raphah added.

"It was not the money I wanted. I was looking for a key—the key to his trunk. Bragg stole a painting that once belonged to my family. Some time ago he sold it to a collector in London. I follow him, for wherever he goes I know I will find what he has stolen. On the day my father died, he commanded me to get the picture and bring it home to our castle. Since it was taken, a curse has come upon us."

"All I hear of in this country is curses," Raphah said as they followed Lady Tanville's light down the steps into the cave. "When will you learn to be free of the curse?"

"When faith vanquishes superstition," Barghast said. "Even in this time of great science, does not the chemist by day become the alchemist by night?"

"Then they are as mad as the lead they work with," Raphah grunted. "The sun shines in their faces and they turn to darkness. They worship the stars and not the one who created them. I met a man aboard a ship who would not get from his bed until he had read the dregs of his teacup.... Fools."

"They take it seriously, Raphah," Barghast said as they walked deeper into the cave.

"Then they should wake from their slumber, and you also, Lady Tanville. Whatever curse is upon your family can be broken."

"Then help me find the picture," she said angrily, her hand shaking the light of the Glory Hand. "Unless it is in the castle, it will cause great harm. It is the prison for a spirit."

"Your great-aunt Lady Isabella?" Barghast asked. "The ghost painting?"

"How did you know?" she asked.

"Let us say I have an interest. I heard the story of how she was painted, a likeness captured from the grave. She haunts wherever the picture hangs. I have heard that she is prone to much trickery for a ghost."

"Isabella has done more than that," Lady Tanville replied as she stopped in the vault of the stairway and looked to the passage below. There in the dust was a further paw mark upon the stone. "My father heard that she had taken to killing those on whose wall her picture hung. Lady Isabella will not be at peace until she is back at Chilnam Castle."

"Then I will help search for her so she will have peace. How can you allow the spirits to walk the world of men?" Raphah asked, at the edge of his temper.

No one replied.

As the glow of the Hand lit the stone about their feet, his words echoed ahead of them. Raphah looked up. High above his head was the glistening roof of a gigantic cave. It shimmered in the light of the Glory

Hand. The steps that had come from the inn had brought them to a vast cavern. A wind blew against their faces like a sea gale. Far away was the sound of rushing water.

"Here," Barghast said, pointing to the shadows that lined the floor. "The creature came this way." There were distinct marks upon the wet sand that lined the floor. "It went further in."

Lady Tanville shuddered. The vast emptiness of the cave reminded her of the castle she had left and the reason for her journey. A vision from her past flashed across her eyes.

It was cold and foggy, the morning of her eighth birthday. The ghost of Lady Isabella had dragged her from the bed. She chased her playfully from the nursery in the spire of the castle. Down the circular stairs, Tanville ran as fast as she could. At first she laughed—a game they had played before. Then something had changed. Lady Isabella grabbed her by the hair and pulled Tanville down each flight, faster and faster.

Tanville had reached out for balance as she screamed for Isabella to stop. Tanville screamed even louder, and Lady Isabella twisted her faster. The castle faded and all around them was the great hill. There stood Isabella on a high cliff, spinning Tanville as if she were a top. Every twist took her closer to the edge.

"Hold out your arms and fly, Tanville," Isabella had laughed. "Then we can play always."

Tanville had done as she had said, and just as she had reached the precipice she slipped. The dream was broken. Tanville stood perilously at the top of the stairs. She looked at Isabella, who laughed.

"Jump!" Isabella said as Tanville stared at the floor far below.

Just then two arms snatched her from the air. She could never forget the smell of her father, holding her close and banishing Isabella.

The next day the priest had scourged the spectre. He had poured holy water upon the picture and nailed iron bars across the frame. With his withered fingers he had laced it with henbane and holly leaves. For many nights the castle was sleepless as Lady Isabella gripped the bars, screaming from inside to be set free. For a year and a day the picture had been turned to face the wall so that she could not escape. When the picture was stolen, Lady Tanville was glad it had gone. But the dying wish of her father had caused her to search for it again. "As I die," he said, "bring Isabella home again to rest with me."

Now as they went further into the cave, Lady Tanville's hands trembled. Barghast, knowing something was wrong, took the Glory Hand from her and held it above his head to cast the light as far as he could.

"What troubles you?" he asked as they walked towards a place where the tunnel narrowed and stalactites hung down like teeth.

"It's the cavern—it presses in upon me, takes my breath," she said.

"We have nothing to fear," he said softly.

"And what of Ergott?" she asked. "Is he not to be feared? You think him a man who can change to a beast."

"Whatever Ergott may be," Raphah said, "I'm certain Barghast will take care of him."

Just then there came a scream—half-man, half-dog. Then the sobbing of a child and the scream again.

"We can't go on," Lady Tanville said. "It's the creature."

"You two must go back—take the Glory Hand, Lady Tanville," Barghast said. "The hellhound, it's here..."

Scrofula

Galphus and his men burst into Pallium's house and ran up the stairs. Kate's screams filled the upper passageway and made their steps even more urgent. In her room, Kate held on to the bedpost as the spectre pulled her towards the forest glade.

"She escapes," Galphus cried as he ran across the landing and unlocked Kate's room. There was Kate, holding fast to the bed, her fingers white-knuckled, gripping the post as she slid across the floor, pulling the bed with her.

Neither Galphus nor the men could see the power that had hold of her. Pallium stumbled into the room and then stood aghast as Kate's feet began to disappear into the solid wall.

"Help me!" Kate screamed as she felt the first chill of death touch the tips of her toes. "She has me and takes me to her world."

"Who has you?" Galphus shouted. He ran towards her, grabbing her hands.

"A spirit takes me. She came from the picture," Kate moaned as she felt the grip on her legs tighten to breaking point.

"Get the picture," Galphus commanded the older Druggle. "Take it and throw it to the floor."

The Druggle grabbed the frame and threw the picture to the floor.

Kate was catapulted back into the room and fell upon Galphus.

"She would have me dead," Kate said.

"And I will have you alive," Galphus muttered to himself as he got to his feet and held her by the arm.

It was then that the ghost appeared to Kate.

"I wanted to save you," she said as she stood by the window with her arms folded and brow vexed. "They'll only kill you. Ask him what happens to all his indentures."

"I don't believe you—you wanted me dead," Kate shouted.

"I want no such thing," barked Galphus, believing Kate spoke to him and not the ghost. "We came to save you."

"You could have set me free, but you wanted to kill me," Kate said to the ghost, who smirked at her maliciously.

"You speak to the ghost or me?" Galphus asked.

"Both of you have the same desire," Kate said as she looked at the bruises upon her wrists. "I want to see Jacob Crane. He will take me from this place."

"Jacob has gone—took the money and went for his ship. Look into my eyes, Kate," Galphus said slowly. "There are ways and means. Some give in willingly. Others need to be *encouraged*." Galphus spoke in a matter-of-fact way as he took a pair of thin black gloves from his pocket and slid them with difficulty onto his fingers.

"He'll poison you," said the ghost. "He'll offer to give you *Gaudium-auctus*."

No sooner had the spirit uttered the words than Galphus brought a silver pyx from his pocket. He nodded to the Druggles, who without further instruction took hold of Kate and held her by the hands and feet. She struggled violently, kicking out in an attempt to break free.

"As good as dead," said the ghost cheerfully. "Should have come with me. At least you would be free."

"Don't think Jacob Crane will like this," Pallium said, backing away to the door. "Liked the girl, he did. If he ever found out, Mr. Galphus..."

Galphus ignored Pallium. He slowly unscrewed the cap of the

pyx and, grabbing Kate by the chin, dribbled several drops into her mouth. "*Gaudium-auctus...,*" he said, smiling at her. "It won't be long before you are begging me for more and will do anything to please me. Still see the ghost?" he asked. "If you do, then please inform her that soon she too will work for me. I have not lived these seven lives just to take capture of the human spirit. I would like to have my very own haunting. My friend Obadiah Demurral often promised me that, but nothing came to pass."

"Demurral's a murderer," Kate screamed. Suddenly she realised who this man was who had her at his mercy. The spectre was still by the window, gazing at her and shaking her head. "I could have escaped—if you had given me the chance," she said to the ghost as the Druggles let go their grip and allowed her to slump to her knees. "Can't you do something?"

"Does she talk to us?" Pallium asked.

The ghost thought for a moment, and then with a sudden twist of her hand sent a fire stick spinning from the grate across the floor towards Kate.

"Take it and fight. You have but a short time," said the spectre. Galphus jumped back as the metal rod spun at his feet and stopped suddenly by Kate's hand.

Without hesitation, she took the rod and smashed it against Galphus's leg. Jumping to her feet, she hit out at the two guards, beating them upon the arms as she ran to the door. Galphus fell to the floor, the sound of the ghost cackling in his ears. He looked up towards the window and for the first time in the candlelight could see the apparition.

"There!" he shouted, pointing to the ghost. "I can see the spirit."

Kate wasted no time. She slipped the lock and ran to the stairs.

In the minute, Kate was at the door. She looked in the direction of the Salamander Inn, then turned away and began to run. She wished Thomas were there—he would know what to do, how to hide. In their mischief they had always been together. Now he was gone, as dead as the ghost that tormented her, and he would never be seen again. From behind she heard the steady footsteps upon the stone and voices calling for her.

She turned into an alleyway and stopped and took her breath. For some reason she found it hard to walk each step. Her feet were an encumbrance, a tiresome burden that slowed her to a snail pace. She leant wearily against the wall, her eyes stinging and wanting to close. The spectre appeared beside her.

"It's the *Gaudium-auctus*. It will make you feel as if you are without blood in your veins."

Kate tried to focus her eyes on the girl. The world became comfortably numb. It was as if her feet had disappeared. Gone were thoughts of Thomas—all she could see was the vivid outline of the ghost as the light faded. "Name," she said dreamily. "I need to know your name..."

"Isabella...Isabella Chilnam..."

"Isabella," Kate said, and then she felt something upon her wrist and jerked from the floor as if to run. The chain that held her hand stopped her. It manacled Kate to the wall. She didn't know if she dreamt what she saw. All of a sudden Kate was in a room, Galphus's room. The wall was lined with glass jars. She was in the corner and she cared not. All she could feel was the smile upon her face that stretched her lips from side to side. Wherever she was and whatever had happened held no importance for her. All that mattered was the glowing smile that filled her with a deep sense of joy and the vibrant light that seemed to flicker all around.

The door opened and Galphus walked in. He looked shorter than before, his head far too big for such a small frame. Kate began to laugh to herself. She couldn't stop. Her belly hurt. Tears trickled down her face. *How could a man go through life with a head the size of a horse?* she wondered.

Galphus smirked as he took a jar from the shelf and examined it carefully. "See," he said. "You are enjoying my *Gaudium-auctus*."

Kate continued to laugh. As Galphus turned to sit at the table, she thought she saw several black slugs make their way across his face. She looked again and they were gone.

"I won't work for you," Kate said. "When Crane hears of what you have done, he will kill you. I know you tricked him. He will look for me."

"And he will never find Salamander Street. Only those I desire to see can ever find its entrance. They do not find me; I find them. Who is to say that Crane himself is not a prisoner just like you?" Galphus paused and looked at her. He could see the *Gaudium-auctus* had turned her veins purple and reddened the tips of her fingers.

"Within the hour, Kate, you will be crawling upon the walls and begging me for another dose. That is the way of *Gaudium-auctus*," Galphus said. "I intend to give it to the world. First it shall be free for everyone, and then, when it takes hold, it shall be like a pearl of great price—impossible to find. Men will sell their children, priests will steal and murder, the Monarch himself will hand over the kingdom. Good will be called evil and evil, good. Look at Pallium—once as fat as a pig. Now his only desire is to count what little money he has left and give me whatever I want. I once found him trying to work out how long he could live and still pay me for the *Gaudium-auctus*. I intend to charge him a penny more each day and see his life shrink even more." Galphus laughed.

"Then I would rather die and be with Thomas," Kate said.

"You shall be with him, but he is not dead. That was a deception for the benefit of Mr. Crane. Thomas is alive. He is my servant, a replacement for young Smutt, who had a terrible *accident*."

"So what the ghost said was right," Kate screamed. She fell to the ground. The floor swiftly crawled with all kinds of creeping insects. "Do something, Galphus!" she screamed in panic as a large beetle appeared from the crack between the floorboards and the wall and walked towards her. As it came closer, it grew in size to that of a small dog.

"What troubles you, Kate?" Galphus asked, as if she had a minor malady.

"Kill it, Galphus, kill it now!" she screamed as it appeared to come closer.

"There is nothing there but your dream—the *Gaudium-auctus* is leaving you."

"Then let it be gone."

Galphus banged his cane upon the floor three times. The door opened and the Druggles entered and without a word took hold of Kate. She had no strength left and hung like a cloth doll in their arms.

"Take her to the upper warehouse and put her in the cell," Galphus said. "She would like to see Thomas, so bring him as well. And leave this outside the door." He handed them the pyx of *Gaudium-auctus*. "She will want to know it is nearby. I am expecting a visitor from the north. An old friend. Tell me when he arrives."

As Kate was being carried out, Galphus whispered to her, "One more thing. Kill Thomas—and I'll let you keep the pyx and the *Gaudium-auctus* for yourself…"

Capacious Alta

eave me," said Lady Tanville Chilnam as Raphah set out to see where Barghast had gone. Ahead was a narrow tunnel through which came the roaring of running water.

"He is just ahead," Raphah said. "Barghast needs our help."

"What is he?" Tanville asked.

"A wandering soul, cursed to live forever."

"Is he human?"

"And something more…" Raphah said as he took her by the hand and led her on.

The sound of the water grew louder, and ahead the light of a travel lamp lit a glow around a pair of feet.

Neither of them spoke as Bragg came into view. He was carrying a shovel and lamp. Strapped around his capacious frame was a linen bag. He muttered as he walked, swinging the lamp back and forth, unaware of their presence.

Bragg walked as if he knew the caves well. He left the chamber and continued on through a narrow passageway that led upwards. Raphah and Tanville walked on, close enough to hear the tap of his step but far enough to whisper to each other without being overheard. They followed the light of Bragg's lantern as it disappeared ahead of them.

"Bragg was the last one to hold the picture of Lady Isabella—sold it to a man named Galphus," Lady Tanville whispered. "I once followed Bragg to Salamander Street. Also, I read a letter when I took the money from him. Galphus wrote to Bragg saying it would be good to meet him in person and not by courier. Bragg has an old goblet that Galphus wants to buy." Lady Tanville held on to Raphah's coat as they stumbled up the dark passageway.

"On the night the dog attacked me," Lady Tanville continued, "I had listened at Ergott's door. I heard him talking to a man. Ergott spoke about the journey. He too spoke of this man, Galphus, and two children. He told the man about Bragg and a chalice. Ergott argued with the man in his room about finding children. Ergott had asked the man what he would do with them and he'd said they had to die— I know these are the companions you seek."

"How did you know?" Raphah asked, sure that she could not have discovered this by mortal means.

"It…it was Beadle. He didn't want to tell me, but—"

"Beadle?" Raphah laughed. "The first sign of friendship and he cannot control his tongue. Beer and good companions. Did he tell you everything?"

"For an hour, as we searched the cellar and the edge of the cavern. Beadle thinks much of you. He told me *you* helped change his heart."

"Beadle changed himself. He had lived under the curse of his master, and when he was free he found himself.

"This way," Raphah said as they stooped through the entrance of another cavern and made their way onwards. From the footprints in the sand he knew it to be where Ergott, Barghast, and now Bragg had trod. A little way ahead they heard the sound of digging, of metal clashing with stone.

In the shadow of the lamp, Bragg sweated as he dug at the earth. When the spade was no use, he got to his knees and dug with his hands. Raphah couldn't make out if Bragg was digging something up or burying an item.

High above him in the arch of the cavern, Raphah crawled to a ledge to gain a better view. Lady Tanville waited in the passageway. She shielded the flickering light of the Glory Hand with her coat.

Raphah watched as Bragg fumbled with a small chalice. Bragg wiped the remnants of dirt from its rim and sniffed the cup. He looked about, as if he was making sure he wasn't being watched. Picking his way through the stones, Raphah climbed higher. Far below at the bottom of the cave, Bragg took the cup and wrapped it in black silk.

Then Bragg took the linen bag that was wrapped around him and put it in the hole. He placed several stones in the hole and then covered them with fine sand. With a fat hand he then scrubbed out any trace of his presence.

Raphah looked on from the shadows as Bragg turned to face the lamp and pick it up from the floor. His face changed: he began to smile, and a word of greeting formed on his lips as if to welcome someone he knew. Bragg's eyes then changed, widening with disbelief as he took a pace backwards. It looked as if he was about to scream or shout out when—

There was a sudden rush. A knife spun through the air. Bragg clutched his chest and staggered forward.

Raphah clambered down the rocks as Lady Tanville dashed from the hiding place, her clothes torn as if a beast had set upon her. She screamed as she ran, looking for Raphah.

Bragg stared at her. The smile came back to his face. "Capacious Alta....Consanguineous," he said as the blood dribbled from his mouth and down his chin.

Bragg fell backwards like a crashing oak, his hands flailing about him as he desperately tried to hold on to life. Upon his face was the grimace of a frightened child.

"Capacious Alta....Consanguineous," Bragg said again as he reached out to Lady Tanville. Without a word, she walked to him and pulled the knife from his chest. Bragg gasped, muttered to himself, and then fell, face to stone.

"He came from the tunnel—I didn't hear him," Lady Tanville said. "He attacked me....then this. I never saw his face, but it was a man—that's what I think he was. He threw the knife."

"I saw no one, just Bragg," Raphah said. "I thought he had seen you and that's why he smiled."

"Smiled at the one who killed him. There are others here. We must leave now," she said as she shivered.

"Not without Barghast," Raphah said.

Lady Tanville held the knife in her hand and watched the blood drip to the floor. "Why did he kill him?"

"For this?" Raphah asked as he picked up the black silk bag that had fallen out of Bragg's coat. He took out the cup. "This is the cup that Galphus wanted."

"A pot mug—why should he want that?" Tanville asked.

"More than that, much more than that," Raphah said. "If I am right, then this has not been seen for many years."

"And should never have been seen at all," Barghast said as he limped into the cold chamber, holding his arm. "Ergott has gone, nowhere to be found," he said wearily.

Raphah held the cup up in the light of the Glory Hand. The Glory Hand dimmed suddenly in the presence of the chalice, as if in reverence. *This is not the time*, Raphah thought to himself as he held the Grail in his hand. *Not in this dark place…* The words were whispered in his ears time and again as if spoken to him by a friend.

Barghast stared at the goblet. It seemed quite ordinary. All that set it apart was the silver rim inlaid into the clay. Years had hardened the clay to stone that felt as strong as metal in Raphah's fingers.

"Do you know of this cup?" Raphah asked.

"I have heard of the Grail Cup," Barghast said in awe as he looked at the simple goblet. He reached out and touched the silver rim. "I met a dandy who dined out on telling the tale. Said it was buried beneath a rose by an abbey wall. The entire world was captured by his ramblings. And to think they have searched the codes yet all the time it was here at Peveril, in a cave below the old castle." Barghast wanted to laugh, but could barely hold up his head. "I'm so weary, Raphah. But it is a good feeling," he sighed. "The beggar is near,

I know it. One more road and then I'll taste the sublime slumber."

"What will you do with the goblet?" Lady Tanville asked Raphah.

"It is a morsel to catch a rat," he said as he lifted the lamp from the floor and stared at Bragg slumped in the dirt.

"What of Bragg?" asked Barghast.

"Killed by a knife," he said.

"Then whoever did this is not far. In fact, they could be in our midst," Barghast replied. "I will tell the innkeeper. He will not want another death. We'll put Bragg in the grave with Mr. Shrume. There is no reason to lament his loss. He shared a carriage with Julius Shrume—now he can share his grave."

From somewhere high above came the moaning of an agonised man. It was quickly followed by the noise of heavy boots scrambling upon the rocks. It got closer and closer by the second.

Raphah looked to Barghast. "Bragg's assassin?"

Barghast listened intently, his eyes searching the cavern. "Ergott," he said slowly.

Holding the lamp higher, Raphah looked towards the pathway that led into the chamber. Like a blundering blind man, Ergott stumbled from the pitch black and into the paltry glow of the lamp.

"Bragg? Is it you?" Ergott asked. His hand covered his face to shield it from the brightness. "I've been lost, man, for many hours. Lamp burnt out and have stumbled my way back. Bragg?" He spoke the last word as he looked down from the path and saw the humped body of Bragg facedown on the dirt. "What have you done to him?" he asked, not daring to come any closer.

"Not us, but another," Raphah said.

"You stand above him like witches at a cauldron and you expect me to believe your lies?" Ergott said. "Look, that *is* a dagger I see before me...and something is rotten in *this* kingdom."

"We didn't do this, Ergott. It was your disappearance from the inn that brought us to this place," Raphah said. "What are you doing in the cavern?"

"I was lost, went for a walk in the fields, and found my way in here.

The lantern burnt out and I couldn't find my way," Ergott said. "But why should I explain myself to you?"

"Because Julius Shrume is dead and Lady Tanville was attacked by a hellhound," Barghast said.

"And you think I am responsible for both?" he replied coldly, looking at Bragg. "Do you take me for the hound?"

"Your excuse is not one that can be easily proved," Raphah said.

"That's choice, coming from a thief," Ergott said, and he began to move away from them. "And how will you explain the demise of Mr. Bragg—self-inflicted wounds? I will have my account to give."

"I trust the magistrate will not take too much notice of a man obsessed by magic and whose habit of smoking, shall we say, *clouds* his understanding. Then we shall see," said Barghast as he searched the pockets of Bragg's coat.

Within them were many things: balls of string, empty shells, and a large monocular spectacle. In one pocket was a silk ribbon and attached to that a thick brass key, like one that would fit in an old chest. Sundry papers and bills of sale lined the other pockets, and nothing to incriminate Ergott or indeed Bragg could be found. As he was finishing his search, Barghast had almost given up when his finger struck upon a small piece of metal. He picked it carefully from the lining of Bragg's coat and pulled it into the light.

At first glance it looked like nothing more than a large button cut with three rectangular holes. It was only when Barghast put it to his mouth and blew sharply that it made a distinctive high-pitched sound just at the reach of human discernment.

Ergott appeared to grow more and more uncomfortable. He scratched his neck and twitched his face as he fumbled with the wand in his pocket. He muttered to himself and rubbed his chin.

"A wolf whistle," Barghast said as he put the metal to his lips again. "What was the rhyme?" he asked, and then went on. "Once to call from mountain range, twice the wolf to man will change, thrice will change him back again, once more for luck and see him then—is that how it should go, Mr. Ergott?"

159

"I have no idea, Barghast. Silly children's riddle and of no meaning. Why Bragg should carry a wolf whistle is beyond me. Perhaps he had a desire to see if there were any such beasts left in the country?" Ergott said uncomfortably. "Now that I have found a light, I will take it and be gone. I have been without sleep and need to rest before the journey."

"It's been a long time and in a different land that I last saw one of these," Barghast said. "Used to call a man-wolf from the hills by its master."

"Master?" Lady Tanville asked, never having heard of the story.

"There is a belief that when a man or woman is charmed by a magician, they can be turned into a creature of their desire by the playing of an instrument. In the case of the wolf it is always a silver whistle. These are highly collectable and very rare. To blow it in the presence of a man-wolf would render it transformed immediately. This is something to keep should we need to find the beast." Barghast placed it in his pocket.

"Then I wish you luck," Ergott said. "I am a dowser and my art is a science, and as I have said, I search for that which is lost—not that which wets against the trees and chases sheep. So if I can be excused?"

"We will walk with you so that the assassin does not strike again," Barghast said.

Raphah knelt upon the floor and, putting his hand upon Bragg's head, closed his eyes. In that moment all were silent.

"One more thing," Barghast asked of Ergott. "Your uncle is Lord Finnesterre, I believe?"

"What of it?" Ergott snapped.

"He sent you on this quest to search for two lost children?"

"That he did. What concern is it of yours?" Ergott asked.

"Your uncle and I share a common acquaintance," Barghast replied.

"And who would that be?"

"Obadiah Demurral."

Ergott did not reply. He stood and stared, the shadows flickering

160

upon his face, his brow twitching with every heartbeat. He swallowed hard, trying to bring a smile to his face.

"Really?" asked Ergott. "Then upon my return I shall seek him out and give him your favour."

No one saw the figure of the man who looked down from a high balcony cut by hands long dead into the rocks above. The man watched intently as they left the cavern, taking the light with them. Once they had gone, he took a silver bowl from the leather sack that was strung around his neck and scooped water from a nearby pool. The man crouched in the darkness and struck a flint against a burnt rag, and then lit the lamp by his feet. Long shadows flickered against the high walls as he took a small knife from his pocket, cut the tip of his finger, and dripped seven drops of blood into the bowl. With the blade of the knife he stirred the water and watched as it turned to solid ice. As the liquid froze, a vision appeared in the ice. The man watched as Raphah, Barghast, and Lady Tanville walked through the cave. It was as if a floating eye followed their every move.

"Never shall they be from my sight," he muttered as he looked upon the vision that danced in the ice. "From the day I first saw him, I knew he was the key to the world. Seven drops of his blood will fill the chalice and bring down the kingdom of heaven."

The Quondam God

In the upper warehouse of the factory, Kate was imprisoned in a large cage. Outside the cage, on a tall stool and set upon a china plate, was the pyx. Inside the pyx was fresh *Gaudium-auctus*. In the hour that she had been imprisoned, she had heard the comings and goings of the factory below. The light of the London skies had faded to afternoon grey.

The only thing that Kate could see from her prison was the pyx sitting tantalisingly upon the plate, two arm's lengths from where she now sat. At first she hadn't thought of it, but with the passing of every second, the desire to hold the pyx had begun to grow and grow.

At first, she thought the feeling was just a desire to quench the burning thirst that cloyed her tongue to her mouth. But as the moments passed, the desire became like the burning sun scorching the ground. It fixed in her mind alongside the memory of her father and the recurring face of Obadiah Demurral that grinned at her. Her thoughts of Obadiah had always been the same. She had known him since she was a young child and had never felt comfortable in his presence. It had been his ranting that had made her believe that if there were a creator, then he had forgotten that the world existed.

From what she could read in Demurral's holy book, this great power loved her. But in her life there was no evidence of this. Her mother had died; her father had turned to smuggling and drink. Until her meeting with Raphah she had only believed in what she saw. Now she wasn't so sure. Over the days since Raphah had gone, she had begun to speak to Riathamus.

She had no idea of what to say or how to say it. *How does one address the Creator?* she asked herself again and again. Within an hour she had decided just to speak and hope He was listening.

Now as she looked through the bars of the chicken shack, she spoke to him again using the lines of a prayer she had learnt as a child. "Give us bread, give us bread," she kept on repeating, the words flowing like a mantra.

The vision of Demurral came and went again and again. The urge to hold the pyx grew stronger with each word she spoke. In the barren room, devoid of any beauty, the silver pyx shone brightly. Kate knew she coveted it, had to have it, had to take it from the chair and possess it forever. It became everything in her world. All her thoughts became focused upon it.

As the last dose of *Gaudium-auctus* left her body, it left a gnawing ache. It was as if she were being dried like a fig and her very essence was evaporating. Her skin felt as if it were becoming crisp; her lips were dry and bruised. Kate looked to her hands: they were thinning before her eyes, and the veins stood from her flesh.

The factory churned beneath her feet. From the floors below she could hear the thud and thump of the felt hammers.

The far door rattled and shook as it was pushed quickly open. A solitary Druggle dragged in a boy, his head covered in a flour sack and tied about the neck.

"Friend for you," the Druggle said. He tugged the rope that held the boy fast, then turned the key, opened the cage door, and in one movement threw the boy inside. "Take off his mask. Here." He handed Kate a small knife with a silver blade and bone handle. "Use this."

With that he locked the door, placed the key on a table by the wall, and left.

The boy didn't speak. He held his head down as if he didn't know which way the world had turned. Kate took the knife and sliced the knot that held the sack to his head.

"Thomas?" Kate asked, unsure if he was real or another delirium.

"Kate..." he said.

"Galphus said you were dead. I went to your funeral—then he said it was Smutt."

"Smutt?" answered Thomas. "Dead?"

"I saw you dead, even put flowers on the grave."

"And Jacob?" Thomas asked.

"Gone..." Kate sagged as she thought of him leaving, unsure if she had been tricked or whether he had deserted them.

"Galphus told me. Said he had sold me to indenture until I was a man. He has them all on indenture, never pays, then they all die."

"He'll come back for us and do the same," Kate said.

"What's that?" Thomas asked, looking towards the stool and the plate with the silver pyx.

"It's mine," Kate said warily. "A remedy...a linctus...for me." She held the knife in her hand, the words of Galphus repeating constantly in her head. "I need it, but he won't let me take it. Left it there to laugh at me."

"We'll get from this place, Kate. If Demurral couldn't keep us locked in his tower, then we can escape this place."

"Demurral," she said nervously. "He's coming for us. I see him when I close my eyes. On horseback. Coming slowly, mile by mile. Nearer by the day. He'll finish what he started. I have to have the silver pot, Thomas, and have it now," she pleaded.

"Give me the knife and I'll force the lock," Thomas said.

"We'll never get from the building, and then he won't let me have the linctus," Kate moaned. "Let's wait. See what happens. I know another way. Sleep on it, Thomas. I'm tired and don't want to run."

"What's wrong, Kate? We can't stay here."

"Wait until the morrow and then we'll be gone. Just let me rest until the middle night—we'll try then. Galphus will be sleeping and the Druggles busy."

Thomas slumped himself into the corner of the cage and looked at Kate. He knew she was stubborn. It would be pointless to argue. He would wait. Sleep first and then escape. If she wanted to stay, she could. But if Galphus could kill Smutt, then he would have no hesitation in killing them.

Kate didn't speak. She wrapped the knife in her coat, a thought crossing her mind as to why the Druggle didn't ask for its return. It was then, as Galphus's voice spoke in her head, that she realized it was for her to kill Thomas. *Kill him and it will be yours,* the voice said.

Kate waited. She counted the seconds in her head and kept her eyes closed for fear of what she would see. Demurral appeared to her. He was smiling, hooded and radiant. Opening one eye, she looked to Thomas. It appeared he slept; his head lolled to his chest.

Kill Thomas and the Gaudium-auctus will be yours, Galphus said again in her mind. She tried not to listen. The pain in her stomach grew to a fever. It spun her guts, knotting them ever tighter as her hands shook. The *Gaudium-auctus* began to radiate upon the stool. The pyx glowed and shone brightly.

"It would be worth his life," a voice said.

Kate looked around her. She could see no one.

"Galphus is right in what he said," the voice spoke again.

Kate looked up. There, hanging from the beam above the cage, was a large spider. It smiled at her and spoke again. "Just take the knife and it will soon be over," it said cheerfully. It spun its web and then descended upon a silver thread that glistened in the moonlight. "I will watch you, tell him how well you've done. Quickly, girl, get it done."

Kate rose to her feet and looked at the spider. "He's my friend, my brother," she said.

"I ate all my sisters," the spider said. "Hard at first, then it gets better."

Kate looked to Thomas. She moved closer and closer, knife in hand. All she had to do was what Galphus had said: kill Thomas and the *Gaudium-auctus* would be hers.

She raised the knife, looking for a place to strike him quickly. There was no sense of fear, no swelling of guilt. Thomas had to die. Gently she stroked his head. Taking the knife, she drew it back, ready to strike.

"*Thomas!*" screamed a voice from outside the cage.

Kate jumped back and let go of him as the spectre of the girl appeared before her.

"*Thomas!*" the ghost screamed again, hoping he would hear. "*She will kill you!*"

Thomas stirred from his sleep and opened his eyes. "Kate," he said as he looked at her. "What were you doing? A voice called me…"

Kate held the dagger in her shaking hand and stared at it.

"He wanted me to," she said awkwardly. "Said he would give it to me if you were dead."

"Give you what?" he asked as he got to his feet.

"The *Gaudium-auctus*. That's all I need," Kate said.

There was a swirling of crinoline as the ghost wafted through the cage. Thomas could see her clearly. "Look, Kate," he said.

"She called you—saved you," Kate said. "She is a ghost."

"Galphus has poisoned Kate," said the spectre. "It will kill her if she has more."

"What do you know?" screamed Kate. "You've never had *Gaudium-auctus!* I want more now…"

In a sudden burst of anger, Kate ran at Thomas with the knife. He grabbed her arm as it thrust towards him and twisted it until she broke her grip. She kicked and punched, not wanting to let go. He threw her to the floor and took the knife.

"Leave it, Kate," he said as he pushed her away. "You're gripped by the madness."

"I want it all—I want it now," she said as she stalked him like a mad cat.

"Stay back and leave me be," Thomas said.

Kate lunged again, trying to claw his face and rip out his eyes. He held her back with one hand and then without hesitation struck her with a single blow. Kate fell to the floor like a corpse dropping from the gallows.

Thomas looked down at her and sobbed. The ghost of Lady Isabella came into the cage and stood by him.

"Look what I have done," he said as he stooped to pick her up from the floor.

"She did it to herself," the ghost said gently. "You must get from this place and bring her to Pallium's house. There is a secret way of escaping from Salamander Street—the only way. I will show you."

"How can we get from this place?" Thomas asked.

"Wait until you hear the clock strike midnight, and then you will be free. I will come for you then."

In a swirl, Lady Isabella vanished from the room. Thomas held Kate in his arms and waited for the clock to strike.

The Green Man

The bugler stood on the roof of the carriage and called the hounds.
The coach had been decked in sprigs of holly and upon the door
had been painted a rough cross inscribed with signs and symbols.

The innkeeper quietly passed words with Barghast, who handed
him a small bag of silver coins. "For the inconvenience," Barghast whispered to him, hoping that the money would ease his conscience and
cover the deaths of his fellow travellers. They both turned and looked
to the freshly dug earth beneath the oak tree.

"I'll keep an eye on them," the innkeeper said. "Make sure they stay
in the grave."

Raphah approached the carriage wrapped in one of Bragg's old
coats. It was far too big but was warm as toast and was just like a huge
blanket. He carried the bag he had found in the cave, and inside was the
chalice. In his mind he had already decided that this would be taken to
his village—a replacement for the loss of the golden Keruvim that now
lay at the bottom of the Oceanus Germanicus. He studied the holly
sprigs and strange signs that adorned the coach. The driver saw him
looking and tutted mournfully.

"Why have you done this?" Raphah asked.

"We go through the great forest," said the driver slowly. "We make one stop to change horses and then we are off again. London by dawn, if we get through."

"And should we not get through?" he asked.

"Sometimes it is difficult," the driver said. "You've seen what is happening. Since the sky-quake and the coming of the comet all kinds of beasts seem to be roaming the world. Only last week a coach was set upon by beasts with red flaming hair dressed in armour." The driver spoke as if he didn't believe his own words. "All that was left was splinters—not one man left alive."

"Filling his head with stories?" Barghast asked as he approached the carriage.

"Only saying what went on," the man replied.

"And we'll be protected by these?" Barghast asked, pointing to the holly sprigs and crude pictures daubed upon the carriage.

"Best not travel without them—then we can say we did what we could." The driver pulled up the collar of his coat and double-charged the blunderbuss. "Will be an *interesting* journey and one I will be glad to end. Billingsgate Dock an hour before eight and I'll be done."

"London," Barghast said with anticipation in his voice. "Not the kindest of places."

"I hope to find my friends before they are found by Demurral," Raphah said.

"Demurral—an old fox and twice as cunning," replied Barghast.

"You are wiser than I thought."

"We are all here for a purpose. I feel as if another hand plays us like a card. None of this has come by chance." Barghast stepped inside the coach. "You travel above?"

"Beadle insists upon it," Raphah replied. "Said he could escape if the beast attacks again. Didn't want to tell him he'd been sharing table with the creature."

"Better to share a table than your mind. I take hope that soon the beast will be dead." Barghast drew close to Raphah so that no one would hear what he would say. "When I put Bragg to the earth, I took a handful of soil and held it to my face. I wanted to know what it would be like. You will never know how I have waited for that time."

"Carriage!" screamed the coachman as he cracked the whip for the off.

The yard burst into sudden life as the gates of the Black Shuck Inn were thrown open. Lady Tanville took her seat, followed by Ergott. He looked even more sour-faced than usual. Beadle clambered up the steps of the coach and onto the roof. He took his place behind the luggage and beckoned Raphah to follow as a large owl flew overhead.

"There is one thing," whispered Barghast before getting into the carriage. "Should Ergott be transformed, he must be killed and killed quickly. I fear that he searches for your friends and that he knows who you are."

Within the minute the coach was under way. The horses jumped and clattered, and around their feet the hounds barked.

Raphah took his place by Beadle's side and pulled the coat around him to keep out the approaching night. The bugler sat with the blunderbuss at the ready and held a sprig of holly in his hand. As they left the inn and made their way to the road to London, all kept silent.

"He's near," Beadle said. "I can always tell when he is near."

"Demurral?" asked Raphah, not surprised by what he heard. "I too can see his work in all that has happened. He will be a day behind. We can get to London, find them, and be on our way. Let us pray that we are protected from what is to come."

In the carriage, Ergott sat quietly and stared at Lady Tanville. He tried to smile and show warmth in his manner. She replied by looking coldly at him. Barghast sat back in his cape and laughed to himself, quite pleased by the entertainment of their mutual anger.

"So how will you search for the lost children?" he asked Ergott.

"I am to meet someone, and together we will seek them out. My dowsing rods will take me to where they are. That shall not be a problem," he said.

"Then what will you do when you find them?" Barghast said as he teased with the wolf whistle, every now and then putting it to his lips.

"They will be returned to their rightful place and all will be well," Ergott said.

"And if they should not want to go?" Barghast asked.

"There will be no doubt of that. I have been asked to recover many things, and never have I failed in my duty." He stopped speaking and looked at Lady Tanville as he thought of something to say. "You look for something, too. I could find it for you—for free, *gratis*, and with no charge."

"I know where to look and I know what I am looking for. I don't need splinters to find it for me."

"You sound as if you are a sceptic, Lady Tanville. Could I give you a demonstration of my abilities?" Ergott asked as he took the pipe from his pocket and stoked it with an even stronger brew.

"Let him entertain us while we journey," Barghast said, raising his eyebrow. "It is a long way to London and the night will soon be upon us. Continue, Mr. Ergott, and I assure you we'll both be enthralled."

"Very well," said Ergott as he sucked upon the pipe and took from his travel bag a small silver cup. "First of all, I take something that belongs to the one I seek and tear from it a small portion." Ergott took a piece of cloth from his pocket and dropped three threads within the cup. "Then we add some fine wine and a powder, the secret of which I am not at liberty to say."

"You said you weren't a magician, Mr. Ergott, and yet you act like one," Lady Tanville sniffed.

"On the contrary, madam. This is a science and not magic," Ergott said as he took a small flask of wine, poured some into the cup, and then sprinkled it with some white powder. "Finally I place this lens upon the cup and concentrate my intention upon it."

"And what happens next?" Barghast asked politely as Ergott took the lens from his pocket and sealed it upon the rim of the cup.

"This!"

There was a fizzing within the cup as Ergott's brew effervesced momentarily and then became still.

"Look!" he said as he held out the cup. "All I need to know will be shown to me."

From within the cup, the deep red of the wine cleared instantly.

It shimmered like a looking glass glazed with snow. They could all see the view of a town as if from the eye of an eagle or other bird that soared high above. Ergott held the cup in one hand and with the other took his wand and held it above.

"Is this the town?" he asked the cup, keeping an eye upon the movement of the wand. In turn the wand bowed to the cup, touching the rim. "Show me more," Ergott said as the vision then changed to that of something looking down from the rooftop. "Is this the street?" he asked. Again the wand responded and touched the rim. "And more," he said to the cup. The scene changed to that of the front door of a house. "Is this the house?" he asked, and before he could even finish the question, the wand had tapped the rim.

"But how do you know which street and in which town?" Tanville asked.

"Simple," he replied. "I ask the wand and it will show me. Right for yes and left for no. It is just a process of elimination. I take a map of the city and hold the wand above and within the hour will have the place where they are hiding." He unfolded a map of London.

They didn't speak for the rest of that evening. Ergott sat in the candlelight, dowsing the map and making notes as he went.

Lady Tanville thought of Isabella and how she would be returned to the castle, her portrait turned to face the wall to be kept from roaming the night.

Barghast kept watch and spied on Ergott, keeping note of where Ergott had marked the map. He saw that in several places he had scored it with a cross, marking where he thought the wand had told them the children were hidden.

The carriage drove on into the night. Leaving Peveril, the road dropped from the hills, and in a few hours they neared the great forest. Branches reached up into the sky and rattled in the wind like sabres. It was as if they were speaking, telling the group to turn back and go another way.

Beadle held on to Raphah's arm, hoping to be reassured that all was well. Raphah slept soundly. The coach slowed to walking pace as the horses became weary and the bugler called the hounds in close.

Beadle could see the moon high above him. It lit many paths through the trees. He stood up and looked ahead. Far in the distance he could see the staging post where the horses would be changed. They would rest for a while and then be off again. The hounds began to bark and chatter, signalling a brief mark of civilisation in the realm of the forest. A spiral of smoke went up into the night air. Beadle could smell burning pine that scented the damp wood as the wind rustled the leaves from tree to tree.

"The Green Man," the coachman shouted as they drew closer. He turned the horses towards a large stable. "Half the hour and then we set pace," he shouted as two men came from the dwelling, torches in hand, to welcome them.

It was only in passing that Beadle noticed the black horse tethered to the door of the barn. He gave it but a fleeting thought as he noted its huge size and deep mane. He pushed Raphah in the ribs, waking him from his sleep, and together they left the carriage and followed Barghast and the others into the house.

They were all welcomed and stood by a warm fire that lit the room. Each was served by a young girl and given a small beer and bread and cheese.

On the hearth wall was the head of a man carved in wood. He had a growth of beard that swept about his face and turned to oak leaves. Within the beard were birds and animals carved to an unbelievable likeness. Beadle stared at the face of the man whose warm eyes looked upon them all.

"Is this the Green Man?" he asked a serving girl as she filled his cup again.

"'Tis he," she said as she turned and went away.

The minutes went quickly by. The fire was warm and took the chill from their bones. Outside, the horses were changed and harnessed and the hounds made ready. It was Lady Tanville who first noticed that Ergott was not with their company. She looked about the room and couldn't see him, nor could she remember him coming from the coach.

"You look troubled," Beadle said.

"Did you see Ergott?" she replied.

"He's not here," Barghast said, and he went outside to look for Ergott.

From the side barn, he could hear voices in conversation and he walked quietly towards them. Ergott stood by the barn door, his back to the night, and mumbled whilst Barghast attempted to hear what was being said.

Ergott stopped and turned suddenly. "Cold night, Barghast," he said, and he stepped from the barn and into the light of the torches that sparkled against the flint and chalk walls.

"You alone?" Barghast asked as he looked into the empty barn.

"Quite. And you?" he asked.

"We make ready. It's time to leave," Barghast said. He looked into the darkness of the barn and then walked towards the coach, expecting Ergott to follow on.

The carriage took on its guests as the bugler called the hounds and the driver made ready. Raphah looked down upon the yard from the top of the carriage and waited for Beadle, wondering what kept him from the journey.

Just another minute, Beadle thought to himself, hearing the baying of the coach hounds.

The fire reminded him of the scullery in the vicarage where he had lived those many years. He would sit by its hearth, drink beer, and dream. He would be alone with his own thoughts, wrapped in a ragged blanket and with a plate of cheese. Snatching that most pleasant of moments when Demurral slept and the house was silent, he would be very happy. He would steal a log from his master just for the occasion. Fire made him feel that way—fire and beer. Beadle pulled the chair closer for a final warm, knowing he would soon have to stand and make ready for the off. It was like the morning, when the bed keeps you to sleeping and begs you not to welcome the world.

"Beadle...Beadle..." whispered a voice from the shadows behind him. Beadle knew it well. It was the voice of Demurral.

For what seemed to be a lifetime, Beadle stood before the fire, unable to move. In his heart he hoped someone would walk in and break whatever spell was over him. Outside he could hear the coachman making the final preparations.

The voice spoke again. "I followed you, Beadle. Told you I would never let you go. My journey is your journey—it's you who has led me to the place. From each other we can never escape," it said darkly.

Beadle took courage from his beer and turned. There in the shadows was the tall hooded figure of Demurral.

"Will you travel with me to the city?" Demurral asked.

"How did you get here?" Beadle replied.

"Followed you. Watched you, and the Ethiopian. Know you too well," he said slowly.

"I travel another way now, master," Beadle replied, knowing in his heart he would have to run. From the yard he heard the bugler call the hounds again and Raphah shouting his name.

"Don't think of running—I'll only follow you wherever you go," Demurral said as he reached out for him. "One day you'll have to face me. I know Raphah has the chalice of the Grail, and it's mine, Beadle. Get the cup and you will live; betray me and you will die."

Without thinking, Beadle threw the dregs of his beer in Demurral's face and ran. He crashed through the door, fell upon the stone steps and into the mud, and scrabbled to his feet. Demurral was close behind, ordering him to stop. The horses bolted at the commotion. The lead mare reared up and then set off in flight as if she knew who was chasing her.

Raphah was thrown from his seat, slipping on the footplate behind the luggage rack and gripping it as the coach bolted forward. The hounds gave chase as Beadle ran behind as fast as he could, Demurral getting ever closer.

Deus Ex Machina

Midnight came with the chiming of a clock. Thomas stood barefoot and sighed desperately as he looked down at the boots he had cut from his feet. Kate had not stirred since she had attacked him. He knew not whether she slept or feared opening her eyes to the world. Since the ghost of Isabella had gone, he had picked at the lock with the knife, desperate to escape. His fingers were sore and bruised, as he repeatedly twisted the knife into the lock.

Upon the final strike of the clock, all was silent. Thomas waited for the coming of the ghost. Kate stirred from her sleep as if she was being called by a voice she knew.

"Beadle!" she screamed, sitting upright. It felt to Kate as if her head were being cleaved in two with an axe. "I saw Beadle...Demurral is going to kill him!"

Thomas didn't reply as he stuck the knife into the lock yet again.

"It was Beadle," she insisted. "He is coming for us—Demurral knows we are here—he knows Galphus—can't you see, Thomas? It was all a trap."

"*Gaudium-auctus*, that's what's speaking. Your ghost said she'd be back at midnight and I'm still waiting."

Kate held her swollen face as the pain throbbed. "You hit me," she said as she looked up at him.

"You would have killed me," he replied.

"I need the *Gaudium-auctus*—you don't understand. It opens your mind to see things and be someone else."

"From what I have seen, it captures your soul and turns you into a murderer," Thomas snarled, prepared to hit her again. "We've been together for years. Thicker than blood—that's what you said. Yet you would have killed me."

"Galphus said..."

"Said many things and told many lies—how do you know the bottles are not empty? Makes you see things, does it? What was Beadle doing, then?"

"He was running through a wood—a dark place, wicked and black. Demurral was there," she said, and then stopped and looked about her as if the dream continued in the air.

There was a sudden chill as a winter breeze blew through the room. The floor, sprinkled with crisp leaves, became like a forest, as if the cage were in the open air. A thick black mist began to swirl.

"It's Isabella..." Kate said nervously.

"She's late," Thomas said as a tumbler slipped within the lock. "Don't need a ghost to set me free."

"But you do need one to show you the way to freedom," Isabella said as she appeared from the whirlwind. The leaves scattered themselves upon the wooden boards. Isabella folded her arms and stared at Thomas. "Galphus has sent his men for you, and they are coming. Be quick—the guards are on the first landing." Isabella vanished from the cage and reappeared suddenly by the door.

Thomas slipped the knife into the lock again and tipped the final lever. The door sprang open. Kate got to her feet and staggered towards him, her wits twisted. She dizzily reached for Thomas to help her, all the time keeping her eye on the pyx. Thomas, knowing her intentions, took the pyx. He snatched it from the table and pushed it into his pocket. "Better I keep it," he said, and he dragged her towards the warehouse door.

Kate shrugged. *As long as the* Gaudium-auctus *was safe,* she thought, *for now anyway.*

"Then how do we get out?" Thomas asked the ghost, expecting some *deus ex machina* to come to their aid and solve an apparently unfathomable complexity.

"You may escape but you will never be free of Salamander Street unless Galphus wants you to be," Isabella said as she began to fade. The scent of the wood began to vanish and she slipped from view.

"Gone...tricked again," Thomas said as he searched the gloom for any sign of her.

"Quickly!" Isabella said as she appeared behind them. "The Druggles are coming for you. This way." She pointed to a painted window much like the one that was in the tower.

"Rather take my chance with the Druggles," Thomas said, thinking this to be a trap and remembering what Smutt had said. He grabbed the warehouse door and pulled it open. A Druggle swung at him with a thick cudgel. It clattered against the frame, splintering the wood.

"*Do something!*" Kate screamed.

Thomas kicked at the Druggle, knocking him back across the landing.

"Bolt the door," Kate shouted as the *Gaudium-auctus* made the whole world tremble and shudder and the face of the Druggle sneered at her like a rat. "Do something!" she shouted again, searching the room for Isabella.

Thomas struggled with the door, pushing it with all his might as the Druggle beat it with the cudgel.

"Isabella!" Kate screamed, hoping to see the ghost.

Isabella appeared beside Thomas, her hands clasped behind her back. "Open the door when I tell you," she shouted above the sound of the beating cudgel.

"Now!" she shouted.

Thomas jumped back from the door just as the Druggle beat at it yet again. It swung violently open, knocking him from his feet and pushing him into the room. The Druggle stepped inside and, seeing Thomas on the floor, began to smile.

"I told you I would see to you later," he said as he stepped towards Thomas and beat the cudgel against his hand. "Now we'll see what will happen to you."

The Druggle had no realisation of the presence of the ghost. Isabella stalked him from behind, only visible to Kate and Thomas. Within a pace he lifted the cudgel to strike Thomas a blow to the legs. Isabella vanished for a second, disappearing through the floor. The warehouse began to shake, struck by a violent tremor. The Druggle stopped and looked as if he couldn't understand what was happening. Thomas smiled; he knew what was to come.

In a lightning crack the floor exploded from beneath, and a gust of wind blew through the boards. Dust and dead mites were scattered into the air, showering all in a thin vapour of dead skin. Another crack of light exploded from the ceiling, instantly dazzling the Druggle. He stumbled back, taking hold of the wall for comfort. It was then that Isabella appeared to them all. Kate cowered to the floor, covering her face for fear this was another hallucination of the *Gaudium-auctus*. Thomas looked upon the sight and hid his eyes with his hands; fear stopped him from staring at the visage of the creature that stood above him. The Druggle didn't move. His eyes opened as wide as his dry mouth, holding his face in a lopsided smile. Terrified, he dropped the cudgel from his limp fingers as he stumbled on weak feet.

The lad gagged as fear gripped his throat.

Isabella had been transformed. Gone the pretty dress with the foxglove flowers. Gone the laced-ruff neck. Now she stood, dark and sinister, a human snake that stared upon her victim through eyes of fire. Instantly she spat out her tongue to catch the lad who stood and trembled. He began to scream.

Isabella coiled through the air as if to strike. The lad ran into the wall trying to flee and hit it so hard that the plaster fell in pools of dust about him.

As the dust settled, they heard the Druggle escape the room and run down the wooden stairs whelping like a pup. Isabella was again transformed and smiled at them.

"How?" asked Thomas as he lowered his hands.

"I did nothing, 'twas all in your minds—you all saw what you wanted. You haunted yourselves," Isabella said as she smoothed her hair and made straight the lace ruff upon her neck.

"But I saw…" Thomas said.

"What you wanted," she replied.

Kate said nothing. She had seen Thomas smile at Isabella. It was a smile he had once given to her. She knew what it meant, and the *Gaudium-auctus* knew her envy all too well.

"There's a way across the roof into the factory and then down to the street. It's the only way—follow me," Isabella said as she made off. Kate stumbled mindlessly behind.

"Wait," Thomas said, and he ran back to the door to the stairs and stacked the wooden boxes against it. "We need more time."

Isabella waved urgently for him to follow. Thomas watched as she went to the window. There was no sign of any physical movement; it was as if she had no feet but just glided without friction. She beckoned him again as she stood by the window. "This is the one," she said. "There is a stairway on the other side; it'll take you across the roof."

"And you?"

"I'll see where they are and come back to you," Isabella said in her shrill voice.

"And tell Galphus?" he asked, still not sure of the ghost's heart.

"It's a chance you take. I'll come and find you. There is your escape—take it," she said with a smile. With that she was gone, vanished like a spring mist. "Come on, Kate. You'll have to go faster," Thomas said as he kicked open the window and stood high above the roofs of Salamander Street. He could see the lights of the city going on forever, glistening against the cold.

Far away, Thomas could see the masts of ships. He thought of Crane and the *Magenta*—he would be there. They turned the corner and the scaffold took them to another window. Isabella stood graciously waiting.

"This way. They look for you in the factory. The guards have gone to wake Galphus," she said as the window opened by itself.

Once inside, Thomas knew where they were. To the right was a flight of stairs. Two floors below he knew would be the front door, and by its side was the room Galphus used as his laboratory.

"Kate, you have to keep up," Thomas said. "We'll get to the door and I'll get the key. Galphus keeps it in the desk in the room at the side. Then we'll be gone."

Isabella glided ahead, and Kate struggled to keep up. The *Gaudium-auctus* whispered to her again, telling her it was almost the moment to steal it from Thomas.

The way was clear. The Druggles could be heard far away as they beat the Dragon's Heart. Thomas looked to his bare feet, thankful he had cut the boots from them before he escaped.

At the turn of the landing, just before the entrance to the factory, was the door to Galphus's laboratory. It stood slightly open. A shaft of amber light came through the crack from a candle upon his desk. Thomas looked to Isabella. Again she disappeared in the blink of an eye and then manifested again.

"He's not there; the room is empty," she said as she smiled at Thomas.

Kate shook with a tremor of disdain and sniffed the air as Thomas pushed the door slowly open and peered inside.

"I'll get the key," he said confidently, nodding to Isabella.

Stepping inside the room, he went to the desk by the wall. For the first time he noticed the thousands of glass jars that lined the shelves to the ceiling. The higher he looked the more he saw. Isabella appeared beside him as Kate stood in the hallway, arms folded and frowning.

"Look," said Isabella. "What are they?"

"Got nothing in them. Just empty jars with writing on," he said.

"Open that one," Isabella said pointing to the highest one as if giving a command.

Thomas obeyed. Climbing the shelves like a ladder, he took the jar from the shelf and read the name that was written upon it. "Andreas Lib…av…ius," he said, stumbling upon the last name. With that he jumped to the floor and began to slowly prise open the cork. The jar spun in his hands as if it were alive. It burnt his fingers and flew from his grip. The stopper popped from the jar and an earsplitting scream filled the room.

"*Comenius—lux—en—tenebris—ereptor—occisor!*" The strange voice bellowed from the jar, as an effervescence of green mist oozed from the lid.

The ghost of Isabella recoiled, dimming in colour and shrinking before his eyes. She was like a fading candle out of wax, the wick burnt to the end.

"Spirit," she gasped as the mist rolled about their feet like an ebbing tide. "*Last words—held in death!*" she grunted. "Go to Pallium's room— I will see you there. This is too much for me—too much death, too much sorrow." The ghost looked to the floor as inch by inch she unwillingly vanished. "They take my portrait—it is gone from the wall.…They trap me again…"

Flibbertigibbet

Beadle gripped the back of the carriage with his fingers. He hopped, skipped, and jumped upon the mud as the carriage gained pace. Raphah grasped his wrist, holding tightly so his friend wouldn't fall, then quickly plucked him from the mud and dragged him onto the coach.

"Where were you?" Raphah asked.

"Demurral," Beadle said, eyes wide, as he rubbed his face with dirty hands. "The Green Man—Demurral was waiting."

"You saw him?" he asked.

"More than that, he spoke to me," Beadle said, unable to comprehend what had happened to him. "He follows us, Raphah—has done all this time. Said that I had led him to you. Everywhere we have been, Demurral has been a step behind. He speaks of a cup, the chalice of the Grail—said we have it."

Raphah looked to the bag that was strung about his neck. "That we do," he said as he opened the bag and gave Beadle a glimpse of the chalice. "It's a beggar's cup."

"Magic?" Beadle asked, quietened by its presence.

"Deep magic. Without the need to cast a spell or kill a chicken. Magic that was won by blood and nail." Raphah carefully rewrapped the vessel and placed it within the bag. He looked behind to the dark trail. Forest creatures moaned and howled.

They said no more. Both knew that Demurral wasn't far behind. Beadle begged the wheels to keep turning. *Faster, faster,* he urged them on in his mind, fearful they would stop.

Raphah looked to the sky and counted the stars as they travelled on. He had spent many nights as a boy looking at the stars and wondering how they hung upon the firmament. Now, far to the north, he was thankful that they reminded him of home.

"He's near," Beadle said to Raphah as the coach rolled from side to side. "I can feel him. He's watching us."

"Then we shall give him the fight he so desires," Raphah said.

"Can't we just give him the chalice and be done with it?" Beadle asked.

"If he wants it, then he will have to snatch it from my dead fingers," Raphah said. "It should not be kept in the world of men."

The carriage went on as the hours passed. The moon set behind the hills and the night became even darker. Stride by stride the horses slowed their pace until the carriage crawled on.

"Can't see," said the coachman as with one hand he held the lamp above him. "You'll have to go ahead," he said to the bugler reluctantly as he shivered in the cold.

The bugler leapt from the driving plate to the ground and summonsed his hounds. Taking hold of the collar of the lead horse, he walked ahead, blunderbuss in hand.

"All's well," he said every few yards until they had gone half the mile. One by one the hounds began to moan. Their growls began softly, tenderly, like the calling to a young pup. Then as they went further down the lane, their voices changed, each hound joining the chorus as their fear grew. The bugler tried to calm them, calling them by name until they clustered tightly around him.

A large, lean dog with a severed ear came to him and nuzzled its head into his leg. It growled a guttural growl and then, reaching up on its hind legs, wailed like a dying child.

"What can you see, Hugo?" the bugler asked the hound as it continued to cry.

The coachman kept a tight rein. He could feel the horses pulling. They snorted wildly, wanting to break free of their bridles and run off into the night.

The road dipped towards a bridge. Though the driver couldn't see this, he knew it to be there. From then on the trees and hedgerows would vanish and there would be open heath for twenty miles. At the ridge of the next hill they would see the distant lights and smell the fragrance of the city—London.

The bugler walked on and his hounds stayed near.

It was then that a sudden blast of light, brighter than the sun, exploded before the carriage. High to the right, a large sycamore was blown from the ground. Its branches scattered across the road as it ripped itself from the mud and crushed the earth beneath it. Several hounds were thrown through the air and strewn across the road. The bugler was knocked from his feet and fell to the mud, and the horses stood petrified.

Raphah pulled the blanket from his face and gouged the splinters from the back of his neck. Beadle cowered, not daring to move as a burning torch was held before the coach.

Lady Tanville held on to Barghast, who peered through the wooden shutter to see a man on horseback approaching through the gloom.

"*Stand!*" shouted the man. He held a lamp and pointed a pistol at the coachman's head. "*Deliver your money or I'll take your lives!*

"*One move and more gunpowder!*" he shouted again.

The bugler clumsily picked himself up and fumbled with the blunderbuss.

"We have no money—we are just travellers," cried the driver.

"No one journeys without the fare," said the highwayman. "I'll take all you have and be gone. No one will get hurt—just cooperate."

There was a yelp of a hound as Hugo leapt from beneath the carriage and took hold of the man by the leg. The hound pulled at his boots as he bit and twisted.

"Curse the dog!" the highwayman shouted.

There was a click, then a flash and a sudden crack. The dog fell to the ground, dead. The highwayman calmly slid the gun into a saddle holster and pulled another from his belt.

"No need to kill my Hugo," the bugler cried as he touched his hand from stone to stone to find his pet.

Raphah looked down from the carriage. In the lamplight he could make out the shape of a large-framed man upon a jet-black horse. He wore a riding cape, and his face was obscured by a silk scarf that covered his mouth.

"Blagdan?" asked the coachman, as if he knew the highwayman's voice.

"Who asks me that?" the highwayman said, pointing his gun at the bugler who grovelled beneath him. "It is I, and I am proud to say that I will take every penny you carry and make your journey lighter— Blagdan, the most wanted man in England, has nothing to lose and all the world to gain." He laughed as he spoke. "Who or what are *you?*" he said as he looked up at Raphah.

"He's a traveller. He's got no money and is on his way to London," interrupted the driver, who held his callused hands to his face.

"Then I'll have him do me a trick," the man said as he kicked the coach door. "Get yourself down and let me see you dance. In fact, I would have you sing me a song. Sing well or I'll shoot you dead, and doubtless no one will ever mourn your passing." Blagdan looked to the driver. "Better you be going—I'll spare your life this time, but be sure to tell the magistrate it was me." The coachman leapt from his seat and ran across the bridge as the bugler stumbled on, half-blind.

Raphah stepped down from the carriage and stood on the ground before Blagden. "I'm not a puppet or a jester, and I won't dance for you," he said calmly.

"Leave him be," said Lady Tanville from inside the carriage. "I have something you can take that is worth more than watching the lad dance."

The highwayman stopped and turned as if to listen intently to the voice. "A woman?" he asked merrily.

"I'll dance and sing for you," said Raphah, "but leave her alone."

"You had your chance. I'd rather dance with the woman. Hold my horse. If it's not here when I've finished, I'll cut off your ears." Blagdan spat the words as he got down from the horse and went to the carriage door.

"Don't do it. Don't open the door," Raphah shouted.

Blagdan laughed as he belted his pistol and took a long, slender knife from inside his coat.

"You little tiger—can't wait to see me?" the highwayman said blithely, gripping the door handle and giving it a slow twist.

It was the last thing he ever said. The door to the carriage was blasted from its hinges. Blagdan fell backwards as the door smashed his face. Barghast leapt from within and grabbed the villain by the throat. He tossed the man back and forth with the strength of ten men until the man breathed no more.

"Leave him," shouted Raphah as Barghast dragged Blagdan along the ground, unwilling to give up his prey.

Lady Tanville screamed as he pulled the body of the man towards the heath. Far in the distance, the screams of the coachman cried out as he ran into the night.

All fell deathly still. Lady Tanville stepped from the coach.

"The explosion knocked Ergott from his seat. He still sleeps," she said.

From out of the darkness, Barghast stumbled back towards the coach. He came quickly from the shadows and into the light of the lamps. His eyes swept from side to side before focusing on Raphah and then on Beadle.

"I couldn't help it," he said as he bent to the ground and picked up Blagdan's pistol from the dirt. "Shoot me now, Raphah—let me taste death."

"It would be no use, Barghast. This is not the time nor the place, and our troubles are not yet over, are they, Beadle?"

Beadle looked to the ground. "Not yet," he whispered, as if he didn't want to speak.

"What does he mean?" Barghast asked.

"Demurral follows us. He was at the Green Man. You are now a part of the mystery, Barghast, and you, too, Lady Tanville."

Lady Tanville looked at Raphah as if she didn't understand. "Demurral?" she asked.

"A magician and a thief. A collector of trinkets that he thinks will bring him power," Barghast said. "I took from him a piece of the true Cross. I heard that he even searched for the Keruvim—it was I who told him of its presence. I had been offered the Keruvim in Paris. It was enough to pay the ransom of a king, and I had no reason to have such a device. I told Demurral in exchange for the true Cross."

"You?" Raphah asked. "I am the guardian of the Keruvim. A guardian who lost it to the sea."

"Then it cannot be charmed by fish and will never be seen again," Barghast said.

"Never," repeated Raphah.

"So why does he still pursue you?" she asked.

"Why do you search for a lost portrait?" Raphah replied.

"Because I have to. It has to be taken home before it does more harm."

"And Demurral seeks that which in his hands will cause harm. It is his intention to kill me. Whilst I am the guardian of the Keruvim, its power is within me. If I am killed, then he will have his desire and the power of God will be his."

"And he wants to kill Thomas and Kate and turn them into begging spirits," Beadle said.

"Then we must travel together. I now know that my quest lies in Salamander Street," Lady Tanville said. "In the carriage, I watched Ergott dowse for the hiding place of the children. I looked upon his map whilst he slept—there is no such place as Salamander Street; it doesn't exist. Yet Bragg had business there."

"Salamander Street is the road for which I search, too," Barghast said. "It is the last road I shall walk, and if it is your destination, then it is mine also." He looked at them and smiled. "I fear that a greater hand plays each one of us. Salamander Street cannot be found easily; only those invited will find the way."

"Bragg was invited," Lady Tanville said. "He was to take that cup to the man called Galphus."

"Galphus?" asked Barghast as Raphah listened. "The man is an alchemist, a dabbler. If he is the key to finding Salamander Street, then a greater force possesses him."

26

Tatterdemalion and Galligaskins

It was only a matter of minutes before Thomas and Kate reached the alleyway that led from the factory to Salamander Street. It appeared to twist and turn less than it had before—no longer a labyrinth in which they would be lost, but an avenue that led them to a destination.

"She's pretty," said Kate as she tramped unhappily.

"Who?" Thomas asked.

"Isabella. I saw the way she looked at you in the factory. She's pretty, even for someone who's been dead a hundred years."

"Doesn't she frighten you?" Thomas asked.

"Frighten?" Kate said in a voice that attempted to be soft and warm. "I'm not sure..." She paused and shook her head. It was as if something was clinging to her skull, something dark, miserable, and black. "Thomas, please, I need to have some *Gaudium-auctus*. Just a drop—let me moisten my lips."

"It'll kill you. It's poison," he replied.

"Not if you've tasted it. It's like honey, and it does things to your head, good things."

"And makes you want more," Thomas replied as he watched her warily. Kate clutched her stomach and moaned as if in pain.

"Thomas, I need some—now." She looked at him pitifully. "Please, Thomas. I will die without it, that's what Galphus said. He said I would die if I didn't have one drop every day."

Kate was interrupted by the sound of running echoing through the passageways like a pack of dogs was pursuing them. Thomas grabbed Kate by the hand and pulled her onwards.

"I can't run," she said as she pulled against him.

"You have to. Galphus will take you," he pleaded, dragging her on.

Kate thought for a moment. "Leave me," she said. "Galphus has more *Gaudium-auctus*—he'll give it to me."

"I can't—won't," Thomas snapped. "Always together—remember?"

"That was then; this is now. Leave me," she said. "You get away, find Crane, and come back."

Thomas thought for a moment as the sound of the beating footsteps came closer still. "Look," he said, pulling the *Gaudium-auctus* from his pocket. "Run with me, and you can have a drop." Then he ran from her.

Kate followed. She ran faster than before, somehow managing to keep pace with him. Thomas pressed on, not knowing which way to flee. He turned every corner and followed his heart. From somewhere in the darkness the voices got closer.

"They'll have us if we don't go faster," he pleaded.

Kate slumped against the wall of the narrow alley and shrugged her shoulders. She stopped and looked around. In the light of the tallow lantern that hung from the stone wall, she saw the cuts to Thomas's bare feet. "Let's not go on. Let's take the *Gaudium-auctus* and die. We'll be with Isabella. This isn't the real world anyway; it's all an illusion. We're already dead, and this is hell. Galphus is the devil, and this is our punishment. That's why you can't get from Salamander Street."

"I'll not believe it. This is life, and we're alive."

"The *Gaudium-auctus* told me: we are dead. Dead as nails in a coffin lid," she said earnestly as she stared at him.

There was a rushing sound from the alleyway as the sound of heavy footsteps beat on the stone. It was as if a thousand feet ran towards them. Thomas snatched Kate from the path, pulled her into a small alley, and held his hand across her mouth to quiet her. She struggled to be free as a herd of Druggles rushed by, staves in hand.

"See?" he whispered. "They know we have escaped. If you want us to be killed, just keep being the knave."

"I want the *Gaudium-auctus*," Kate said, not caring what was heard of her.

From over the wall they could hear the harping of music and the rolling of barrels. Thomas peered from their hiding place and listened for the Druggles. They had gone. Looking up, he saw the light of the inn above the wall. Thomas hoisted himself on top of the wall. He bent down, grabbed Kate by the arm, and began to pull her to him. "Climb, Kate," he whispered as she scrambled towards him.

"Why?" she asked.

"Just do it."

Kate was pulled upwards until she sat with him on the wall. She looked at him and held out her hand. Thomas jumped to the ground on the far side of the wall and landed in a narrow yard of three brick walls and a doorway into the Salamander Inn.

A fiddle played and lilted the music back and forth. The door stood unlocked, releasing the sound of many drunken voices.

"We have to take the chance," Thomas said. "Will you do it?"

"*Gaudium*..." she replied, as if to sign the deal. "Then I'll come."

Thomas hesitated for the moment. He could feel the pyx in his pocket. It burnt against his hand as if he held a hot coal.

"One drop?" he asked, knowing she would drink the lot if given the chance.

"One drop," she replied as a smile lit her face.

He took the pyx, unscrewed the lid, and tipped it upon her hand. A large golden drop dripped out. It fell upon her skin with a hiss. Kate licked it quickly as she closed her eyes and held her hand to her mouth. She said nothing. Every thought she had ever had rushed through her mind, and she slumped to the floor. Her eyes burst with a rainbow of colours as the world around her shimmered.

"Can you see it?" Kate asked.

"What?" replied Thomas as he looked about.

"The music. I can see every note—it dances in the air."

Thomas looked again. He could see nothing and hear nothing but the dull jangling of the violin and the stamping of many feet in time with its rhythm. From the noise within, it was obvious to him that the beer house was full of people and a grand bacchanalia was taking place within its walls. The shouts of drunken men echoed from the doors and windows.

"We need to find Isabella," Thomas said as he listened against the door of the inn.

"You'd like that, wouldn't you?" Kate leered. "Find Isabella. Fancy that—Thomas in love with a ghost."

"She wants to help us escape from this place," Thomas insisted.

"She knows as little as I do," Kate said boldly as she pushed against the door to go in. "She wants to kill us both."

"Galphus..." Thomas said.

"I care not," Kate snorted.

With that, Kate pushed open the door and shielded her eyes as the sharp light beat against her.

The noise was intense. A group of men were gathered around a pair of fighting birds that danced and squawked upon the floor at the centre of the inn. They cared not for the two who stepped in from the cold night.

In the corner was a fire that spat wood sparks from the grate, and a small bench was perched on the hearth. Thomas nodded for Kate to take a seat.

As Thomas sat down, a hand grabbed him by the shoulder.

"Thomas," said Pallium. "I'm glad to see you alive. I heard that you were dead—thought Galphus had killed you."

"What would you care?" Thomas said, pushing Pallium from him. He stepped back, grabbing the fire iron as he stared at Pallium.

"I know you cannot trust me, but I am with you," Pallium said. "Crane needs your help. He is in serious trouble. Galphus betrayed him."

"More lies?" Thomas asked as the bird fight went on about them.

"I can get you from this place. Kate needs to be free from Salamander Street. She will die if she stays here. It is only a matter of time."

Thomas shook his head.

"Trust me," he pleaded. "Galphus has me gripped by the *Gaudium-auctus*—just like Kate. I have to do what he says. But I want to be free. And I am the only hope you have of escaping the Druggles." Pallium looked ashen and drawn.

Kate stared into the fire. Her mind was lost in the embers. Thomas looked at her and in that moment decided what to do.

"Get us from this place, Pallium. Let this not be a trick, or I'll kill you."

Thomas grabbed Kate and pulled her to her feet and from her dream. Pallium turned and ran to the door. They left the Salamander Inn and trotted along the street to Pallium's house. The sound of the Dragon Heart could be heard chiming far away.

The door to the house stood open. Pallium went inside, and Kate and Thomas followed.

"Do you have *Gaudium-auctus?*" she asked Pallium.

"Only enough for the day; only enough for me," he said happily as if he suddenly owned the world. "Quickly—there could be Druggles. They know you have escaped and will be searching for you."

"Why does Galphus keep people here?" Kate asked.

"It isn't Galphus, but Salamander Street. Don't you understand? We are all kept here by who we were before. Victims of our wicked hearts." Pallium laughed.

"Before?" Thomas asked. "What do you mean, *before?*"

"Before I came here I was a businessman. Had many things but wanted happiness. I fell in love, and she brought me here. I thought this would be the perfect place, but it became a prison."

"Then we'll escape," Thomas said.

"Well, I don't want to, after all. You see, this is a prison of my own making. Everyone here in Salamander Street would never want to leave. Our desires are fulfilled. Mine is the desire to hold gold coins in my hand, to count them one by one and never be able to spend them. That is pure joy—*Gaudium-auctus!*" he exclaimed. "Galphus has his own vice. He could no more set Jacob Crane free than I ever could."

"Where is Jacob?" Thomas asked.

"He is closer than you think," Galphus said as the door to the parlour opened and he and three Druggles stepped into the hallway. The Druggles carried two sets of manacles. Galphus looked to Pallium and nodded in thanks.

"Greatly appreciated," Galphus said to the man as he handed him a vial of *Gaudium-auctus*.

"I will kill you," Thomas said as the Druggle wrapped his wrists in the metal straps and twisted the bolt into the lock. "You promised me, Pallium."

"I promised you would see Jacob Crane, and that you will—immediately."

Kate didn't even realise she was being restrained. She looked to Galphus like a begging dog, holding out her hands as her eyes followed the *Gaudium-auctus* into Pallium's pocket.

"For me?" she asked him, her fingers trembling.

"Not yet, my pretty girl," Galphus said, "but there will soon come a time when you can have as much as you want, and in return all you will give me is a breath."

Pallium banged against the wall of the stairs, and as he did the oak panel appeared to split in two and slide open. He took the lamp from the table and lit the way. The Druggles followed, then Kate and Thomas, and finally Galphus.

The stone stairs slipped quickly below ground. The scent of the river ebbed through the sewer as a stiff breeze blew cobwebs about their heads.

"See?" Pallium said. "He hadn't gone far at all." Pallium hammered upon a thick black door that blocked the passageway a yard from the stairs. It was a narrow place, just wide enough for a man to stand shoulder to shoulder with another.

Pallium turned the lock, opened the door, and stepped inside. The cell was larger than they had thought. It was lined with dripping stone, and at the far wall was a wooden bed. On each side of the door was an oil lamp that hung precariously from a wooden spittle rod. They gave a bright light that found every corner of the room.

"More guests," Galphus said as he pushed them inside.

It was then that Thomas saw Jacob Crane.

"Thomas!" Jacob cried.

"You sold us for pieces of silver," Thomas shouted at him. He lashed out at Crane with his feet.

"No, Thomas. I saw you buried and dead, came looking for you. Galphus said you were in the grave—fell from a window. My only sin was believing him and that he would save my ship."

"Very true, Jacob, very true," Galphus said, laughing to himself. "I enjoy lying; it is by far the most exciting thing to do. When you lie you have to remember what you have said, and it is a great test for the memory."

"Crane speaks truth?" Thomas asked.

"What is truth?" Galphus replied. "If you mean he presented the facts, then that would be correct. He never sold you to me. I took you. Took you because I wanted to. It was Smutt who fell from the tower—sent to fly by a Druggle—how exciting."

"Now that you have us, what will be done?" Crane asked.

"Your fate is not yet decided. I know a man who would like to see Thomas again, and someone is on their way to take him to Whitby." Galphus sighed. "As for Kate, they would like her, too, but her fate is sealed with mine and she will stay. Tell me, Jacob. You're a man who always has loved power. How does it feel for it now to be such vainglory? You have the rest of the day to consider."

Blatherskite

hildren? Names?" Ergott complained as Barghast pushed him back in his seat of the carriage. "I don't know their names."

"Then how will you find them?" Raphah asked as the coach rolled slowly on.

"With the dowsing rod—what else?" Ergott grumbled as he folded away the map and slid the wand back into his pocket. "I don't need a name to find a child. I told you all I need is something that belongs to them."

"And who employed you?" Lady Tanville asked.

"A friend of my uncle's." Ergott sank back into the smoke-stained leather and frowned. "I am a dowser. I care not for who employs me."

"And remind us who that would be," Barghast demanded.

"A priest," Ergott said in a matter-of-fact way as he took the pipe from his pocket.

"Demurral?" asked Raphah.

"Could be. The name seems familiar. I am not sure if I can remember."

"Then let me be a lightning bolt to your memory," Barghast said angrily. "Tell us where you look for the children."

"Why such an interest? It is as if you have a stake in my venture." Ergott lit his pipe.

Ergott was silent for a moment and looked at them as he blew purple smoke from the side of his mouth. "I am employed by Demurral, and what of it? He asked me to find two urchins that had escaped his care. I am to bring them to Whitby, and I will be paid. He said they are in the hands of a villain called Jacob Crane. Is that so important?"

"We are satisfied by what you said," Tanville said in a serene voice.

Lady Tanville nodded as she spoke and smiled politely as the carriage rocked from side to side. An uncomfortable silence fell upon the gathering that lasted for several miles.

"Beadle drives well," Ergott said eventually to break the silence. No one replied.

"London will be soon, within the hour at least," he said again, hoping to elicit an answer.

"At least," said Lady Tanville as the carriage slowed upon the hill.

Beadle drove on, the light of dawn breaking upon the Hampstead trees and the road that led across the heath. Ahead was the city that tugged upon the Great North Road, pulling them on. London came suddenly. Fields gave way to houses that soon surrounded one another. Already the streets were full of people making their way to the city. From east and west, those who had fled the sky-quake were returning slowly.

Beadle had never seen anything like this before. He wiped the sweat from his brow as he pulled the horses on a closer rein. For the first time he could see the battered dome of St. Paul's, reaching to the sky like a broken egg. Far away, small fires spiralled columns of smoke into the cold morning air. Above the Thames a November mist clung to the water. Beadle began to sing tunelessly. He quickly forgot the night, and the sight of Demurral faded. Somehow, the day brought no fear.

Beadle allowed the horses to lead them on. He sat, wrapped in the coachman's blanket, and wondered about his fate. Upon the mile, Raphah would call up to him and ask his welfare. Each shared hope. Beadle didn't want the journey to end.

Eventually, as they drove through the beaten streets of Camden and then Holborn, the horses stopped where they had always stopped. Beadle looked up at a cold grey building, its walls drab and scarred. The front of the coaching inn was peppered with marks from the comet, and its torn thatch hung like an old hayrick. No one came to greet them. All was quiet; the street was empty but for the horse dung and several rogues who slept on the steps of the demolished church opposite the inn.

Beadle jumped from the driving plate and opened the carriage door. About his shoulders he had the coachman's jacket. Three sizes too big, it hung like a sack. He didn't care—everyone could see that he had driven the coach. In due course a small woman peered around the door to the inn and looked at him suspiciously. All Beadle could see was her one staring eye. The other was covered in a black patch strapped to her head so tightly that it looked like a ridge in her skin. She didn't speak but examined each of them intently, as if she knew why they had arrived.

Reluctantly she opened the door and gestured for Beadle to step closer. Beadle walked towards her as the others in the carriage watched.

"Where's Mr. Gervais?" she asked.

"Left me in charge. He had urgent business elsewhere," Beadle said proudly as he pulled the man's coat about his shoulders.

"Better come in, and bring them with you," she said, and nodded to someone inside. Raphah and the others stepped from the coach. The inn door opened fully, and a young boy ran to the carriage and led the horses through a narrow gateway at the side.

Ergott clutched his bag as his wand danced in his pocket. Barghast and Lady Tanville followed him inside as Raphah looked down the road to a small park surrounded by tall iron railings.

"Thought there'd be more than this. How can I make a living with just you? No one here but you, the entire place to yourself," she said to Barghast and Ergott.

"Times are difficult since the coming of the comet," Barghast said, trying to answer before she stormed on.

"Don't mention that to me. Madness everywhere. Just look at that dog: quiet as a mouse, and then when the moon comes out becomes like a madman." The woman pointed to a small terrier in the corner of the room and then called it to her. "Ziggie, come here." The dog looked at her from its place by the fire. "Ziggie…" The dog didn't move but rolled over by the fire and roasted its belly.

"Well behaved," Ergott joked as he sat in a dusty chair by the narrow wooden stairway that led from the dark hall to a darker landing.

Ziggie looked at him and sniffed. The hackles on the back of its neck stood rigid. It bared its teeth and gave a guttural growl.

"You have made a friend," Barghast teased as the dog spun to its feet and began to bark.

"That I have," he said as he stood and looked at the woman. "I take it I have a bed and a room of my own?"

"The driver will sleep by the fire. You come with me," the woman ordered them as she walked up the stairs to a landing of rooms above. As they turned the corner from the stairs, they saw a long hall with several doors. She opened one door after another, not giving any sign as to who should sleep in each. Finally she looked at Raphah.

"Do you sleep in a bed?" she asked.

"I sleep wherever you would like me to," he replied.

"The street is a fine place, but then you wouldn't pay me." She looked at him as he smiled at her. In his heart he wanted to laugh at her foolishness. "Do you mind him sleeping here?" she asked Barghast.

"In fact, I would suggest he shares my room," he said. "I have three beds and a fire, and we wouldn't want to overburden you with work."

"Suggest you open the window," she said. With that, she left them alone and disappeared down the stairs to appease her barking dog and find Beadle.

Ergott quickly shut the door to his room without speaking. The bolt was slid swiftly.

"Ergott needs to be guarded. I suspect he knows the way to Salamander Street," Barghast whispered. "I will take the first watch.

We must keep him near at all times. Be ready."

Raphah slept for the hour as Barghast watched through the narrow opening of the door. He could hear Beadle muttering to himself by the fire. Ergott's room was silent. The morning came and went, the afternoon faded, and darkness fell as Barghast waited. By the time the evening came, Barghast, like all the others, had begun to doze. He sat in the chair propped against the wall and rested his head upon his arm. The journey had taken life from them all. In the hallway below, Barghast could hear the sound of Beadle snoring.

On the landing there was a sudden clink of metal as a latch dropped and Lady Tanville entered the room. Like a waiting fox, Barghast was woken from his dreaming. Raphah didn't speak. He signalled for her to sit by the fire as they waited for Ergott.

The wait was quickly over. In the hallway below, an old clock chimed nine times. The dog gave a sudden yelp as if woken from a dream of chasing rats. The door to Ergott's room opened.

Ergott entered the corridor, arms outstretched, divining rod in hand. The rod bobbed and danced in his fingers as if it had a life of its own, and Ergott obediently followed. He gave no notice to the narrow opening of the door to Barghast's room. His mind was focused on the dowser in his hand. The wand led him onwards as if it were a hound that pursued its prey in the dark of the night.

Ergott scurried down the stairs, jumping them three at a time, and skipped across the hall.

"The chase is on," Barghast said as he and Raphah sprang to their feet and dashed downstairs, with Lady Tanville running behind. "When we get to the streets, keep to the shadows. I will go ahead— he won't see me."

As they watched Ergott run across the hall, all that clothed him began to disappear. Thick black fur sprung from his shoulders, and what were once hands became black paws. He fell to the floor by the fireplace and writhed in agony. Beadle woke from his sleep. The dog began to bark frantically as the man contorted before him. Ergott screamed as if in severe pain.

"Blatherskite!" Beadle exclaimed as the sight of the transformation sent him hiding in the shadows.

The changing Ergott looked up, his face contorted. He growled and seethed painfully. The transformation from man to beast was quickly over. The wand vanished from sight.

Beadle hid behind a large potted plant, not daring to step from the shadows. Then the scullery door creaked open, and there was a shriek and a scream as the innkeeper saw what she thought was a lion by the fire.

"*Slabberdegullion!*" she shrieked, as if it were the last word she would ever say. With much ceremony the innkeeper fainted.

Ergott growled loudly and leapt towards the door. He smashed against the wood as the door came open, and he slithered into the street, vanishing in the darkness.

Raphah and Tanville followed quickly. "Stay and see to her, Beadle," Raphah said as they left the inn for the cold of the night. Once outside, they caught a fleeting glimpse of the creature.

They set off on the chase, keeping to the shadows. Ahead they could hear Ergott growling as he ran back and forth through the empty streets.

Slowly they managed to track Ergott from a closer distance. He kept to the wide streets and walked in the middle, away from the shadows.

The streets narrowed and Ergott suddenly transformed, the dowsing wand appearing in his hand. He walked backwards and forwards along a row of doorways. The dowsing rod danced in his hands, and it took all of his power to control it.

"Lubberly louts and flouting milksops," he shouted, his words of frustration echoing around the square. "It has to be here. They have to be here..."

Then he stopped and spotted a small arched door the size of half a man. The dowsing wand led him closer. Raphah and Tanville watched as he walked towards it and turned the handle. Before he entered, he read the sign that was embedded in the plaster. They heard him laugh as he stooped through the entrance and quietly closed it behind him.

Barghast appeared from the shadows. He panted, out of breath, a broad smile on his face. "It is behind the wall—Salamander Street. I have been up on the roofs and it is here, though it cannot be seen with the eye. My journey is done, Raphah. Can you believe it?"

"It comes to us all. I pray we will find Thomas and Kate."

There was a clatter of horses' hooves as a black mare cantered along the road and into the square. The rider wore a long black cloak; his long white hair was tied back. He wore a parson's collared shirt and seaboots. The man jumped from the horse and looked about him.

He surveyed the square and waited, as if making sure he had not been followed.

Raphah was not surprised by whom he now stared at from the shadows. He turned to Barghast, who nodded to him as if he too had seen the man and knew who he was.

The man left the horse and slipped through the door.

"*Demurral*," Raphah said. "He has followed us all the way."

"Then they are all in this together," Barghast said.

"So why send Ergott if he knew where they would be?" Raphah asked.

"To make sure the job would be done. He couldn't leave it to chance. Every step of our journey has been followed intently. We are expected to follow and the door will be open to us," Barghast said.

"What business does he have here?" Tanville asked.

"Kate and Thomas. He said he would never let them go. Something binds him to them. If they are here, then their fate is sealed."

"Not if we take them from him," Tanville said, and she pulled a dandy gun from her pocket. "We shall each endure our fate in Salamander Street, and I shall have an advantage when I meet with Galphus."

One by one, they crept across the square to the small wooden door. Raphah looked at the plaque above it. He read the scrawled letters plastered into the wall: *The Eye of the Needle*.

Barghast smiled as he stooped through the entrance. "I know I will not see this place again, Raphah. You have been a good companion. Whatever comes to pass, I pray that we will stand together when the sun rises in the east."

"A sure and certain hope," Raphah said quietly as he closed the door behind him.

The Jobbernol Goosecap

A thick slime trickled across the ceiling before it dripped to the floor by Crane's feet. Thomas and Kate huddled in the corner to keep warm. Thomas thought how unnaturally cold Kate was—it was as if she were made of ice, or that death itself had already taken hold of her and the heart that warmed had stopped beating.

"I let you down," Crane said, his shoulders drooped and head lowered. "Should have known things were not that easy. All the time, I could think of nothing but Salamander Street. Even on the ship I could hear the word in my head. When the priests seized the ship, this was the first place I thought of to run to. We were tricked, well deceived."

"We can escape," Thomas said, his breath a cold vapour.

"It's gone from me, Thomas. Something has taken the will." Crane's voice sounded strained.

"I won't wait to die, Jacob. And I won't let them kill you and Kate. That's what Galphus will do: kill us all. I've seen what the man does. He takes the moment of death and puts it in a jar. He'll not take us."

Crane laughed. He rattled the manacles that held his wrists to the long metal chain that was coiled about his feet and braced to a metal ring wedged in the cobbled floor. "Think we could take 'em?" he asked.

"We could die trying," Thomas replied.

"Wait until I say the word, and then…" Crane paused and looked at Kate. "He's killed her with the *Gaudium-auctus*, Thomas. I've seen it before. If all else fails, run and leave us both. Take the *Magenta*. There is a drinking house by the river, the Devil's Inn, and close by is *The Prospect of Whitby*. If I have counted the days rightly, then tonight is the Feast of Saint Sola the Hermit. All my men will gather at the inn. Tell them my fate and take sail. With me dead, the revenue men will auction the ship. Steal it before it can be sold and head for France. Will you do this for me?"

"I won't leave you," Thomas replied.

"You'll do what I say and have done with it. Would be stupid for us all to die, and Galphus will get what he deserves before he takes me. Whatever happens, I promise he will not kill her. Even if I have—"

Crane's words were cut short. There was a jangling of a key in the lock, and Pallium and several Druggles stepped into the cell.

"Galphus requests your company," Pallium said. "I am to take you to him, all of you."

Thomas thought Pallium looked even thinner than before. It was as if he were being eaten from inside and something consumed him by the minute.

They were taken without fuss. Crane was held by a long chain, and a metal hoop on a long pole was placed around his neck as he was walked ahead of the rest. A Druggle carried Kate. Unaware of her condition, in her blissful slumber she lolled from side to side. Through several tunnels and then out across a cold yard they were taken into the back of a large house that stood near to the factory, just away from the Salamander Inn. Thomas could hear the constant singing just like the time before. He thought of the warm fire and Pallium's deceitful words.

Inside the house, they were taken into what was once a drawing room. In the centre of the room was a long, narrow table. By its side were a bell jar and other primitive equipment, and near to the table was a wooden chair fitted with wristlocks and strands of copper wire. Above the ornate fireplace was Isabella's picture.

The grime of a hundred years had been cleaned from the paint. Within the frame, Isabella stood proudly, looking down upon them. About the frame was wrapped more copper wire and hanging from it were pieces of teeth and bone. A small writ dangled from the frame; Thomas could make out an inscription on the parchment and could see the red wax seal that bound the spell.

Kate was taken and placed in the chair. Her head was strapped to the high back and her hands and feet to the wood. Crane was tethered like an old horse to the door; what was left of the chain was wrapped around him and tied to the large chair that he had been forced to sit upon. Thomas stood by the door, a Druggle holding him with the chain of the manacle.

No one spoke. Pallium stood by the raging fire and waited. The clock on the mantel chimed the half, the quarter, and then the hour. They still waited.

From the far end of the house the *tap, tap, tap* of cane and footsteps could be heard. Galphus entered the room.

Thomas held back his laughter as he looked at him. Galphus had changed his attire. Gone were the day clothes of a dandy. Now the man was dressed in a black silk gown that billowed as he walked. On his head he wore a tiger skull with silver teeth and emerald eyes; his hands were covered in red silk gloves, and on his feet were Persian shoes that curled at the toes.

Galphus smiled at Kate. He tapped the cane several times on the floor and then looked into the crystal ball.

"All is well," he said smugly. "The doors to Salamander Street have been opened and the trap is set." Galphus looked at Pallium before he spoke again. "We have visitors, Mr. Pallium. You know what to do."

Pallium turned and was gone. A Druggle followed him from the room.

"I feel I must explain," Galphus said as he looked at Thomas. "This has all been an elaborate hoax on my behalf. Please do not feel let down, but I have to say that I actually work in concert with an old friend,

Obadiah Demurral. I believe you are familiar with him?"

Thomas nodded, keeping tight-lipped.

"Obadiah and I are brothers in a fraternity. We are bound by sworn oaths. My life has been set on the discovery of the soul and capturing its essence on death. His has been to find the nature of God and tame it for our use. If it hadn't been for you, we would have succeeded earlier in our task and the world would be a better place. When you escaped Whitby, we first thought our task would never be complete. Then my crystal showed me that someone you knew well was still alive, and it gave us hope. The Ethiopian has travelled far to find you all, and as we speak he is just about to walk on Salamander Street—look for yourself."

Galphus thrust the crystal towards Thomas. Thomas was shocked to see the face of Raphah edged in the darkness. Quickly it changed to the face of Demurral and then, just as it was about to fade, Thomas saw the head of a black dog. Its eyes glowed red; its teeth were bared and white as it spat and growled.

Galphus laughed. "That is another of our companions—a man who can change from man to hellhound in the twinkling of an eye. He was the bait to bring your friend to us. With every day he gave him another clue as to who he was. Calmly and cleverly he waited his time. Every night he met with Obadiah and told him the good news. Every day, he brought them another step closer to us."

"He won't be cheated by you," shouted Crane. "Raphah knows Riathamus—he can speak to him."

"Then Riathamus can sit and listen to his screams as we steal the Ethiopian's last breath and capture his final words. Not mortal words, Thomas, but the words of an angel. Your friend has lied to you. He is not a man but a Keruvim. That Ethiopian is the keeper of secrets that would explode our mortal minds like a spiked cannon if we knew. Soon, Obadiah and I will have all of his power and more. When I take his last breath from him, he is bound by eternal oath to utter a name so powerful that it is the key that will open time and heaven forever."

"And what of us?" Crane asked.

"What do you think, my pirate friend? Shall I set you free or take you to your ship and burn you upon it?"

"Do what you want with me, but let the children go," Crane shouted.

"Never. Spoil my enjoyment? Since I was a child that picked the wings from a butterfly, I have delighted in times such as this. I would no more set them free than cut off my right hand."

"Set them free or, as Riathamus is my witness, I will sever your hand and dip it in wax, and it will light my way to bed," Crane said.

"Spirit," Galphus said as he banged his cane against Isabella's portrait. "How much room do you have in that world of yours?"

"Don't torment me, Galphus," a shrill girl's voice replied. "Let me from this prison."

"I would invite Captain Crane to keep you company." Galphus laughed.

"Then let me from this place and I will take him to be with me," the ghost of Isabella replied. The picture rattled upon the wall.

"Did you hear that? She would take you with her, and my problems would be solved. Sadly, that will not be so. I must await Obadiah. But first I shall prepare my dearest Kate. She is the screaming bait that will lead the Keruvim rushing to bring her salvation."

Galphus looked at Kate as he spoke. Behind her was a handle connected to a large wooden box. He saw Crane stare at the device. "If you are wondering what this machine can do, it takes a charge like lightning and forces it to travel along the copper threads and then into the metal bracelets upon her wrist."

Galphus took a hat made of goose feathers from the mantel and threaded more copper wire within each quill. "A Jobbernol Goosecap," he said pleasingly. "Placing this on the head adds to the charge and takes her life. Her screams should be enough to bring him here. When he comes to this place, he shall find his own death. Living and dying becomes a matter of turning the handle."

Galphus signalled for the Druggles to hide themselves and make ready. Thomas frantically eyed Crane, as if to ask him what to do.

"Hurt her, Galphus, and I will give you thrice the pain, and it will pleasure me to do so," Crane said as he rattled the chains that held him fast.

"You sound like an old ghost, a bard's king, dead and futile. How can you hurt me, chained like that?" Galphus asked, taunting the man.

With that, Galphus thrust his cane into the floorboards. A sudden bright light shone from the crystal and cast a vision upon the high ceiling. There, played out before them, was the scene of Raphah's approach. It looked as if the whole of Salamander Street was cast on the plaster above their heads. Raphah walked side by side with two others, whilst stalking them in the shadows was a red-eyed beast, a dog so terrible that Thomas turned his face from the sight of the creature.

Along the cobbled road they walked, the creature always a few feet behind them, lurking in the thick black shadows. Thomas saw Raphah turn as if he realised that something followed.

Isabella began to scream as she rattled the bars of her prison, desperate to be free of the picture and walk in the world of men. As Galphus played his scenes on the ceiling, she saw there, dressed as a man, Tanville. Isabella shrieked Tanville's name again and again and shouted out a warning to her.

Lady Tanville looked about her, as if she could hear the calling of her name from far away. Galphus smiled, knowing that the screams of the spectre would draw them quickly. He took the handle of the machine and slowly began to turn it. The copper threads began to spark. Kate was pricked from her dozing as the first jolts of lightning shot through her fingers. She twitched in spasm and her back arched. Galphus turned the device even faster.

Kate began to howl as sparks burst from her forehead and the blue essence of her departing soul shimmered above her. Thomas jumped to his feet to intervene but a Druggle stepped from the shadows and with a blow from his cudgel knocked Thomas to the floor.

Crane shouted and Galphus laughed.

In the vision from the crystal, they saw Raphah begin to run towards the house, following Kate's cries.

From outside the house they could hear Pallium shouting. He hollered like a Judas, calling Raphah by name, in words that betrayed them more than a kiss. It was then that the crystal eye turned to reveal the thoughts of the beast, shining through its eyes and seeing what it saw.

There in the street behind Raphah was an older man. With every step he aged a day, as if the centuries chased him from afar. What was once vital and alive was now crumbling and aged. Barghast was transforming as the dirt of the street sullied his boots and the air he breathed speeded his death.

He fell behind, slowing to a walking pace, unable to keep up with the lad. The beast made ready, tracking him from the shadows. It waited as he took several faltering steps and then stopped for breath.

In the light of the tallow lamps they saw the man smile and wave for the other to go on. Barghast sat upon an empty barrel, his hair turning bright white and falling to the floor strand by strand.

As he had walked Salamander Street, the curse upon him was broken.

He bent slowly and picked a handful of dirt from the ground and held it in his hand. He was delighted as the frailty of age took hold of his bones, and he gave thanks.

Then, giving no warning, the dog leapt for him. The hellhound took Barghast by the throat. Upon the ceiling Thomas thought that he could see two beasts fighting. He could hear their cries as they battled each other. For the briefest of moments he thought he saw a lion's head and then, from just outside the house, came the sound of a single shot.

The aura upon the ceiling faded as a shadowed figure stepped into the room. Even Galphus himself gasped in its presence.

"Just in time," he said with a hint of nervousness as he let go of the machine. "I am so glad that you could make it, Parson Demurral."

29

A Republic of Heathens

In a dazzling moment, as if the sun had exploded, the street echoed with the shot from the pistol. Lady Tanville stood perfectly still, her eye still gazing along the line of the barrel. The dog fell down dead, blood seeping from its ears and from the small bullet hole through what had been its eye. Before her eyes the corpse began to change to that of Ergott.

Raphah turned as he ran, taking a final glimpse of Barghast as he lay in the mud. He rushed up the flight of stone steps, and as he passed Pallium, he stared at him eye to eye. It was as if a friend were greeting him. Pallium held open his arms and welcomed him to the house, ushering him onwards towards Kate's cries. It was then, as Raphah took his first steps into the long hallway, that he felt an intense sense of foreboding.

Ahead, Kate's screams and the whirring of the electrometer billowed from the room. Without hesitation or concern for himself, Raphah dashed into the room. A thin hand grabbed him by the throat and threw him with the strength of a hundred men towards the fireplace.

"Raphah," the voice said.

"Demurral?"

Raphah looked about the room. Thomas and Crane sat against the wall, and Kate was strapped into the chair by the fire. Galphus nodded and the Druggles stepped from the shadows as Thomas jumped to his feet to welcome his friend.

"How things change," said Demurral. "I knew that Riathamus would not have you dead so quickly. It was easy to bring you all here. I had Ergott follow Beadle from the day he left Whitby. Does anyone ever notice a dog? Beadle did well for me."

"Beadle?" Raphah asked. "Did well for you?"

"Not that he knew it, but I knew he would find Thomas and Kate. I wasn't sure if the magic would work on Crane and that my suggestions to bring them to Salamander Street would be heard. Obviously all was well. New friends always impress Beadle. He would have searched them out no matter what. Meeting you was a bonus. And all I had to do was follow on behind. Ergott kept me informed. As for Beadle, when I have done with you I will make sure whatever ounce of life he has left will become a misery."

"So it *was* you. And we walked into your trap," Raphah said.

"It was me on the road *and* it was me in the cave. Bragg knew too much and had to die. He found out that Ergott had devoured Mr. Shrume and wanted him for his own. Promised him the Grail—which I believe is carried in your bag. The others were just food for dear Ergott. His appetites are insatiable…"

"But it's over—the sky-quake—Raphah told us…" Thomas said.

"You were lied to. It is never *over*, Thomas. It is not just I who seek the desires of our hearts—there are many people who would like to see heaven overthrown. It is time for a new nation and old order to take power. A republic of heathens. Goodness and mercy are things of the past. Our desires are all that matter. Think of it, Thomas—think of you and Kate as the key to a better future for the whole world."

"Don't think you'll be killing them, Demurral," Crane shouted.

"Jacob Crane, how peculiar. Is that a chain I see around your neck? I thought you were a man of action, one who would never be caught, and here you are trussed like a Christmas turkey."

"A matter of coincidence," Crane replied. "But should I ever be free from these chains, I shall cut the gizzard from your throat and serve it for breakfast."

"And hell shall freeze over," Demurral replied. "Do we have the *Magenta?*" he asked.

"Still in the dock," Galphus replied. "Taken without a fuss."

"Ready to sail?" Demurral asked. "So you believed the priest and the scoundrels we had paid to take your ship, Jacob? Taken in by a fallen cleric, how quaint."

Galphus paused and looked around him. "I...only have the Druggles, and they have never sailed such a ship."

"Why do you only have Druggles? Is there not a man who can sail amongst them?" Demurral asked.

"The people think the *Magenta* to be carrying the plague," Galphus replied. "But," he said quickly, "it is prepared to sail and everything is ready at Dog Island."

Crane cast a look to Thomas and gave him a sly wink and half a smile. "The ship, wait until we are on the ship," he said in a whisper.

Demurral turned, his stare telling them to be silent. "Did you think you had won? Escaped? Free to live your life as you desired?" he shouted. "I could not rest in the grave until I have seen this day."

"What will you do to us?" Thomas asked.

"What I should have done days ago, if an angel hadn't interfered with things. Meddling wingless wonder, fit for hell. Take the manacles from them and bind them, Galphus. Bind them tightly, for we take them all to Dog Island. Then our work will be complete. Pallium," Demurral shouted, "go and find Mr. Ergott; he should have made a feast of Raphah's companions."

Demurral looked at Kate, who stared at him through eyes that bulged with the pain of the electrodes. "This is not the place to take Kate's life. That shall be kept for Dog Island."

They heard the door open and Pallium step into the street. This was followed quickly by a scream, and moments later Pallium rushed back into the room.

"The man Ergott is dead," he said, shuddering at the sight he had witnessed. "Shot in the eye ... and ..."

He did not say another word. Lady Tanville pushed Pallium into the study, while holding a pistol to his back. She looked about the room. There was Galphus dressed in his finery. There was Kate strapped in a chair with a goose wing hat upon her head. Crane sat chained to the door, and Thomas skulked nervously by his side.

"I've come for Isabella," she said as she pointed the gun at Galphus's head. "The picture was stolen from my family and I seek its return."

Demurral looked at her and laughed. "My dear girl," he said, "the picture is all a part of what I seek to do. But once I am finished I will gladly give it to you."

"But he'll kill them first," Raphah said, pointing to the children.

"The picture *and* your guests," she demanded, knowing in an instant that they had to be set free.

"A request too far," Demurral replied. "I would suggest that you do the honourable thing and shoot me as you shot Mr. Ergott—for I will not let them go."

Lady Tanville clicked the hammer of the pistol and took aim. All that Demurral could do was smile, and Galphus gulped nervously.

Thomas noticed the woman's eyes flicker from Demurral to the picture of Isabella. The ghost hung to the bars, staring out like a lost child.

"Kill him, Tanville!" she screamed from within the confines of her prison.

"No!" shouted Crane. "Leave that to my men—they wait this night for *The Prospect of Whitby*—let them kill him. Remember, tell Beadle—*The Prospect of Whitby*."

For a brief instant she looked at him. Lady Tanville licked her lips and then, as her hand slightly trembled, she pulled the trigger. Again the gun exploded. The shot hit Demurral in the chest, sending flecks of blood and linen cloth across the room. He reeled backwards, clutching the wound. Then with his right hand he thrust his fingers into the skin, burrowing them deeper.

Demurral gave a sudden and sharp cough as if he cleared his throat of a fishbone. He shook his head, pulled his fingers from the wound and dropped the lead bullet to the floor.

"I am beyond dying," he said like a man tired of the day. "It will heal. I am a curser of God and cannot be destroyed until He Himself comes for me."

"Take her," Galphus shouted to the Druggles, who appeared from the shadows. "See that she causes no more trouble. Our plan has to be carried out tonight. In the morning, I will test her to see if she has a soul."

"And so you shall," Demurral said, looking closely at Kate. "To the ship and then to Dog Island. Nothing shall end this day until I command it."

Like a forlorn caravan of wastrels, Raphah, his companions, and Isabella's portrait were marched from the house and into the street. An old carriage was drawn up by the door. It was as wide as Salamander Street, and its black-lacquered doors could barely open to allow them inside. Thomas was pushed to the roof and tied to the luggage rail. When all were gathered in, the carriage took flight.

Four horses charged on, rolling the coach from side to side as it scraped against the houses. They were garbed in funeral black, and each was plumed about the head with the blackened tail of a cockatrice. The coachman whipped the horses to go faster. Ahead was a solid wall.

Thomas covered his face as they drew closer. "Stop!" he screamed to the coachman, who turned to him and grinned as the coach sped towards the wall. "No!" Thomas screamed again as the first horse vanished through the solid stones as if it were a ghost.

Suddenly there was a whooshing of the breeze as the night sky blazed above. People stopped and stared as the coach was driven madly towards the dock. Soon it turned towards the Thames. Salamander Street was left far behind. Far in the distance, Thomas could see the masts of several ships rising from the water. Then there was the *Magenta*, tall and bare, still tied to the quayside.

The horses slowed. The coach stopped, and the doors opened. On the *Magenta*, a crew of grey Druggles waited for their master.

Galphus led the procession from the quayside and onto the ship. A crowd of people gathered and looked on.

"Prisoners of the King," shouted Demurral as he strode behind, kicking out at Thomas. "Stop your staring and be about your business."

"We can't be late," he shouted to Galphus, who married himself with his cane. "She will not wait for us—not tonight."

The many eyes gave no heed to what he said. They stared and stared as Thomas and the others were quickly taken below deck and the ship made ready. Three small boats, each with oars and a small mast, pulled the ship into the tide. It creaked and groaned as the fingers of the current took hold and pulled it against the breeze.

Crane felt the ship begin to move beneath his feet and smiled. He looked around his cabin. All seemed strangely familiar. The door was locked. Galphus sat in Crane's chair and glared, his eyes bloodred. Propped against the wall by his desk was the picture of Isabella. The spirit was nowhere to be seen. All that was present was her outline against the canvas. On the deck above, they could hear Demurral shouting to the Druggles as they attempted to steer the ship to Dog Island.

Salamander Street was deathly still. Lady Tanville Chilnam looked out of the upper-floor window of Galphus's house. The room was bare but for a leather-backed chair placed close to the fire. A single candle burnt on the mantel. Outside the door a Druggle waited. Lady Tanville stood with the empty pistol in her hand. No one had thought to take it from her when they had pushed her from the room and bundled her up the stairs. She had heard the carriage take flight as the horses sped from the street. Now that she was alone, she thought of what she had done and what she could do.

Lady Tanville could picture Ergott's body lying in the mud. She felt no compassion or concern for what she had done. Her mind was numb. And all she could feel was the irritation of being locked in the room.

For several seconds she searched the street to see where Barghast had fallen, but couldn't find him. In the last minutes of his life she had watched him age, the curse on his life broken by the dust on which he walked.

Wrinkle crept upon wrinkle as he had withered before her eyes. She had tried to save him from Ergott. She hoped he had died peacefully.

She could see the shadow of the Druggle that crept in under the door, lit by the storm lantern he held in his hand. The house was silent and as quiet as the street outside. From somewhere very near she heard the creaking of an old door. There came a sudden rush of footsteps that pounded against the stairs. The Druggle had not the time to even shout out. He gave a muffled scream, and Lady Tanville heard him drop the lantern.

A bloodied, frail hand slowly appeared around the door's edge and then the face of Barghast. He was old and near to death. "Quickly," he said breathlessly. "You have to leave this place and find Raphah."

Tanville took hold of him as she led him step by step along the landing and down the steps. Flames from the broken lamp licked against the walls. They passed quickly, listening to the creaking of the house as the fire took hold.

"You'll have to leave me," Barghast said, his face now that of an old, old man without teeth or hair. "I die a happy man."

"But not here," she demanded. "Not in this place."

Tanville pulled him out the door. His pace was slow, laboured, and painful. She looked back to the flames that now grew brighter. High above she could hear the beams spit and crackle as the roof burst into bright red flame and lit the sky.

Lady Tanville dragged Barghast into the narrow alleyway that led to the factory. From far away they could hear the clanging of the Dragon's Heart as the Druggles beat out the warning of the fire.

"I die here," Barghast said calmly as his flesh began to fall from his bones. "This shall be my resting place." With that, he held out his hand to reach for someone Lady Tanville could not see. Barghast smiled as if he stared into the face of a long-lost companion. "I will not turn you away. I know who you really are," he said to whoever stood before him. Then he turned to Lady Tanville, opened his eyes, and whispered his final words. "Tell Raphah…not a beggar…but a King…he will know what you mean…"

Barghast slumped to the floor, his flesh crumbling. Lady Tanville held his hand as it became a jumble of bones.

From the factory the sound of a human stampede drew closer. After saying a final good-bye to Barghast, Tanville began to run. A voice inside her seemed to be telling her which way to turn on the road ahead.

In the distance she could see the Eye of the Needle. The door diminished in size with her every step. Behind, she could now hear Druggles chasing her.

The doorway had shrunk to the size of a small window by the time she reached it. Lady Tanville grabbed the now tiny handle and pushed open the door. She dove through the fading aperture and smelt the London street. Just after she managed to squeeze herself through, the portal finally disappeared.

Dog Island

Taking Demurral's tethered horse, Lady Tanville Chilnam made her way back to the lodging house. Beadle slept by the fire, the innkeeper's dog by his feet. Tanville woke Beadle gently.

"Raphah?" he asked, rubbing his eyes wearily.

"Taken," she replied, "by ship to Dog Island with Thomas and Kate *and* Jacob Crane."

"And Barghast?"

"Dead." She spoke the word softly, unable to tell him all that had happened. "So is Ergott. He was the beast. Demurral was also there. It has all been a trap. It was his desire to capture the children, and in that he has succeeded."

"Never," Beadle exclaimed angrily as he threw a lump of wood into the fire. "We should go and bring them back. We can't give up on them, Lady Tanville."

"Crane had a message for you. He said, 'Tell Beadle—*The Prospect of Whitby*.' I have no idea what the man meant."

"I know," Beadle said excitedly. "He meant to tell you that his men were at the Devil's Inn, a pub by the Thames at Wapping—that is the place where *The Prospect* is always birthed. It's a collier brig, a ship, full of smugglers, murderers, and hob-smackers. A landmark if ever there was one. His men will be there—that's what he meant. He knew I would understand—the old dog knew..."

Beadle could not contain himself. He danced a jig upon the hearth and kicked the embers of the fire about the stone tiles.

"Dog Island is just at the turn of the river. It'll be quicker by land. I have heard so many stories of the place, I could take you there blindfolded," Beadle said eagerly. "Let's steal a horse and make for it. Keep your gob shut and let me speak and then we'll keep our throats. Dog Island!"

They left the inn immediately and set off into the night. Demurral's horse took them through the darkened streets. Beadle held on to Lady Tanville's waist as the horse trotted on by the river until the streets became narrow and dank.

Lady Tanville lowered her face as they passed the gangs of seafarers huddled by the torches that lit the street. To her right, she could hear the tide beating against the walls as the river ran quickly to Dog Island. She twisted the wet leather of the horses' reins in her fingers and thought of how the providence of her family was held in her young hands.

"Wapping," Beadle said after they had gone another mile. "Soon be at the Devil's Inn."

The Devil's Inn was a small dark building with a mass of people in front. Some drank from flagons of beer whilst others drew on clay pipes.

"How will we find Crane's men?" she asked Beadle as they got down from the horse and started to walk.

"No need to look any further," a voice said from the doorway of the inn. "If it's Crane you want, then you can talk to me."

Lady Tanville looked at the man. He filled the frame of the door with his gigantic hulk. The man had a small beard and dark eyes. Wrapped in a thick coat, he looked out of place, almost from another time.

"And why do you want Crane?" the man continued.

"I have to find the crew of the *Magenta*," she replied as Beadle hid behind her.

"That vessel has gone for good," the man said. "Why does a young lass like you want to see a rascal like Crane?"

"Because he's in danger. As we speak the *Magenta* sails down the river to Dog Island, and tonight he is not captain of the ship."

The man snatched her by the arm and brought her inside the inn. Without a single word, he took her through the inn and onto a large wooden balcony that overlooked the river. A long bench ran the length of the wall and to one side were steps down to the water. Three iron braziers lit the balcony and by each were huddled a group of tattered and forlorn men.

"This one's after Crane," the man said, and he laughed. "Says the captain is in danger and that the *Magenta* sails down the river."

"Who do we talk to, Mr. Abel?" a voice asked.

"Lady Tanville Chilnam," she replied.

"Who let you out, my *lady?*" asked another man.

"No one did. My family are dead and I the last one. It was I who decided to come—what did I have to lose?"

Before she had finished speaking, Beadle was dragged from where he had stayed behind, hiding in the pub. He was gripped by the ear and squealing like a pig.

"Look what I have found," said a smuggler as he threw Beadle onto the gallery. "If I am right, then this is Beadle of Baytown, Demurral's pet lamb. Seen him many times licking around his master's rump..."

"Strange you two should come together," a voice said.

"We *are* together, Mr. Martin," Beadle said, knowing the voice well. "Travelled from Whitby and met in the carriage."

"And Demurral?" he asked.

"He has the Captain, Thomas, and Kate," Beadle said.

"It's a trick," said another.

"Kill them," said yet another as dark swirls of mist blew across the balcony.

"Truth," Tanville shouted as she stepped towards Martin. "Your master is captured by Demurral and is being taken to Dog Island. You can let him be killed or help us find them. He sent us here to find you."

"Crane told us to come here tonight—the night of the Feast of Saint Sola the Hermit. Strange you should appear in his place," Martin said as he rubbed his chin.

"And he told me where all of you would be found," Lady Tanville insisted. "'The Prospect of Whitby,' Crane said. 'Remember The Prospect of Whitby.'"

"And there she is as always," Martin replied, pointing to an old ship tied onto the landing rail at the bottom of the flight of wooden steps. "Not much of a ship—but with the Magenta gone, it might be our only way home."

Martin stopped and looked up the river. His eyes peered through the gloom. In the distance were the billowing white sails of a brig. It sailed slowly and somewhat cumbersomely.

"Look," he shouted in amazement as he pointed for them all to see. "She's right—the Magenta."

Like a floating gallows, the Magenta came closer and closer.

"I told you it was the truth. Believe me. Crane is being taken to Dog Island by Demurral and will surely be killed."

"Then it will be our business to be catching them," Martin said as he drew a small telescope from his pocket and looked through it. "Quickly—six of you take the rowboat, the rest come with me by land."

His words went unquestioned. Six of them ran down the flight of wooden steps to a long rowboat that was tied at the water's edge. They raised the oars and pushed from the land into the river.

"You two can stay here," Martin said as he looked at Lady Tanville and Beadle. "This is our business."

"It's also mine," Tanville said as she pushed Martin away. "If I don't go with you, then I shall make my own way and Beadle will be with me. Demurral has something that belongs to me, and I want it back." Tanville wanted to say more, to tell them about the portrait and the misery it had brought to so many. She wanted to tell them of her father's dying wish, and the castle that once rang out with laughter.

Instead, she stared at Mr. Martin, her eyes angry and bright, her face

223

set like stone. He thought for a moment as he looked her up and down.

"Very well—so mote it be. And if you die—don't blame me…"

Obadiah Demurral stood on the bridge of the *Magenta*, watching the lights on either side of the river. They moved with the tilting of the ship and reminded him of the harbour at Whitby. On the near shore was the Devil's Inn; its lights shone brightly, set against the walls of the warehouses that flanked each side. He shivered in the cold of the night and, looking around once more to see all was well, went below deck.

The steps led to the door of what was once Crane's cabin. Demurral knocked, and Galphus smiled to welcome him. Demurral thought the man looked nervous again. *Strange for an alchemist*, he thought, as he nodded and looked at Crane and then to Raphah.

"Boy," he said politely to Raphah. "In the time I have known you, I have never told you why all this has come to pass. I am troubled that I should even think such a thought, but something in my mind tells me I should at least inform you as to why your life will be taken."

Crane moved uncomfortably. The leather bands were tight around his wrists; his chains had been exchanged for horse bonds that burnt his hands.

"Why do you have to kill any of us?" Raphah asked.

"Was it not Riathamus who took the first life in the Garden? Did he not kill an animal to clothe the man who ate from the Tree of Life? Did he not want blood and desire sacrifice at all times? If those are the ways of Riathamus, then why cannot we demand the same? It began with blood and shall end with blood—your blood. You three are the divine proportion—each of you chosen for this purpose. A Keruvim for the angels, a boy for Adam, and a girl for Eve. In all creation there is a meaning, even in your dying."

"Take of me what you want," Raphah replied as he smiled at him. "I don't fear death or what is beyond. And as for Riathamus, his demands are mercy, not sacrifices."

"We shall see. Your redemption is in my hands. I will be your judge and your jury."

"And Thomas and Kate—what of them?" Raphah asked.

"I will fill the chalice with seven drops of blood from each of you. Not one of you are spoiled or tarnished by life—that is the way it must be. The Grail has more power within it than the Keruvim. It has the force of heaven—and to think you brought it to me."

"Then do it now, here and now, Demurral, but let me die fighting and not hog-tied," Crane shouted and spat.

"Patience, Jacob, patience," Demurral said as he smirked. "I have waited many years for this moment and will not have it taken from me so quickly. Since the beginning of time mankind has waited to overturn the reign of the Almighty. Think it a privilege that you should witness this at firsthand. You are a guest at the destruction of Riathamus. It is my second chance," he snarled at Raphah. "He should have killed me when he had the chance. Doesn't it sicken you that He allowed me to bring you here? Don't you feel abandoned by Him? And yet you still give Him glory?"

There was a sudden rustling of wind that rattled the windows of the cabin and blew the papers across the chart stand. All felt strangely cold as Raphah raised his eyes from the floor and talked slowly. "I tell you this, Obadiah Demurral. Before the crowing of the cockerel, you shall be gone from this world. Your flesh shall hang like rags from your bones, for it is a foolish man who falls into the grip of a jealous God."

A Pocketful of Stones

The water lapped against the side of the *Magenta* as it made its way into the broken-down quayside of Dog Island. The motley procession were dragged one by one from the ship along the quay and towards a small mound surrounded by a circle of densely planted silver birch. A shale path led like a long white finger through the tall reeds to drier land.

Demurral led the way, dancing like a small child, skipping every other step. Behind, the weary Galphus walked on, followed by twelve Druggles who hemmed in their guests. Thomas was bound like the others. Around his wrists were leather straps that he rubbed back and forth in an attempt to loosen them as he walked.

For most of the mile they walked they said nothing. To the west, Thomas could see the city against the bloodred sky. In the distance, far along the path, he could see even more Druggles. They lined the shale walkway, lanterns in hand that shimmered in the growing breeze. Two held an arch of holly branches high above their heads as they walked through.

Demurral bowed serenely, dropping to one knee and nodding his head. In his hand he held the Grail Cup. Soon they all walked up the stone steps, through the trees that surrounded the hill. Once they were at its summit, they were pushed into a circle that was cut into the earth with chalkstone.

Thomas looked at Jacob and then Raphah. Kate was slumped on the ground, her body shaking. She sobbed as two Druggles hung Isabella's portrait on a low bough of a larch tree. It looked out of place, incongruous in the landscape, as Isabella stared from her prison, screaming in vain at her captors.

Demurral and Galphus bowed to each other as they silently walked the circle. Druggles in turn bowed to them as they went by. It was as if they had all become part of some gigantic living clock. When Thomas looked, he realised they had each been placed at points in time: he at the ninth hour, Crane the third, Raphah the sixth and Kate at midnight. In the centre of the circle was an incense pot that blew smoke about them in the changing wind. Demurral walked the circumference and then stopped next to Kate.

Galphus thrust his cane into the earth and called out as Demurral took a knife from his coat and one by one cut the bars and charms from Isabella's picture. Immediately she broke free, jumping from the frame as the doorway to her world opened. Isabella ran to Kate and danced around her as Kate held out her tethered hands as if to be cut free. Galphus watched his crystal as if it might give him some sign of what should happen now.

Demurral cut Kate's cheek with the knife and dribbled seven drops of blood into the Grail Cup. Then he went to Thomas and Raphah, cut each one, and added their blood to the cup.

When Demurral had gathered the twenty-one drops of blood, he stood in the centre of the circle and raised the cup to the sky.

Far to the south there was a crack of thunder. From the river bubbled a silver mist that crawled from the water and up the pathway. They could all see it drawing closer as the wind blew through the branches above their heads.

"She comes," Galphus said, looking deeper into the crystal. "She comes, Demurral."

Demurral looked into the crystal. In the swirling mist he could see a dark figure striding through the mist-laden fields towards the hill.

"Who do you summon now?" Crane shouted above the wind.

"Your fate and my future, Jacob Crane. Cover your eyes and look not on the form of this woman. Soon you will stand in the presence of Hertha, and you will die."

"Fear her not," shouted Raphah. "All that comes is a demon from hell. What you will see in her eyes, Demurral, is the brimstone that will consume you both."

There was a sudden deathly silence. All was still as the wind ebbed from the branches. Isabella walked slowly back to her picture frame and hid within the glade. It was as if she could sense what was to come. She smiled at Thomas from behind a ghostly yew tree.

From around the hill came a pleasant whispering. It was like the call of dawn birds but uttered on the lips of a thousand excited children. From every tree came the hissing of serpents. Then it came.

Gathering speed as it flew, a dark silhouette broke through the branches of the trees that covered the hill. It landed by the outer circle and, taking the form of a large fox, ran to the centre. Without hesitation, it dived through the skin of a Druggle who stood waiting as if he knew this would be his fate and welcomed it gladly. For several moments it vanished completely within him and then appeared again, a heart in its hand.

"Demurral," said the voice of the woman as she transformed from the fox to human form. "Is all prepared?"

"All is well. The blood is in the cup and the divine principle is set. The seconds tick, and our clock is ready."

"Then we shall steal time and the kingdom of heaven," Hertha said, wiping her hands upon her green velvet dress. "The gate is open, I see."

"All is well," Demurral said again, as if they were the only words he dare utter.

"Then let us chime the timepiece and bring an end to this all," Hertha said.

"It will not end here," Raphah said.

228

"Ah, Raphah. My brother has spoken of you many times. A thorn in the flesh born of righteousness. What angel shall you conjure to stop us tonight?" she asked. "I have it on good authority that Raphael shall not appear as he searches for Tegatus in the depths of the sea. Tonight, *Raphah-the-healer*, it is you and I who shall decide the fate of the world. Think of it. What began long ago shall be completed here.

"You thought you had won when Pyratheon was defeated on the hill by the church. I saw you from the shadows and watched your gloating. But now it is my time—or should I say the end of time? What Riathamus started, I will complete. It shall not be left to that old fool any longer. I will see to that, and in your own way you will help me. The vortex will take you all to hell…you and the power of your God."

"You shall be sent to a place from which you will never escape," Raphah shouted.

"And you—you will beg me to let you die. All of you mean nothing to me," Hertha raged as she threw the remnants of the heart into the fire.

"My Queen," Demurral begged. "The time has come. It is an hour from morning."

"The last one ever—how glad will I be to never see a sunrise," she said. She walked towards Kate and, lifting Kate's head, kissed her cheek. "You will be the first to welcome death."

"Not as long as I live," Crane shouted. "I fear no witch from hell."

Crane looked defiantly at Hertha, who spoke to the Druggles.

"Take him from this place," she said, "and drown him in the river. I fear no man."

The Druggles took Crane's bindings from the tree and dragged him across the circle towards the path through the trees. He stumbled and fell as Demurral kicked him for a final time.

"How things change, Jacob," Demurral said as he disappeared into the wood. "How things change…"

Hertha clicked her fingers. Demurral and Galphus turned like two dogs.

"Take his place, Galphus," she commanded. "The plan needs a soul to be in his place, and the timepiece will soon chime. Cut the bindings from the others. They need to stand freely in their death."

With that, a handful of Druggles cut the bindings on Thomas, Raphah, and Kate. Hertha snatched the Grail Cup from Demurral's fingers and began to spin and spin. She whirled like a mad dervish. It was as if with every turn the earth moved with her. The trees began to whirl about them, and Thomas could not stand as the vortex of Isabella's portrait opened up once more and now began to pull them all towards it.

Hertha laughed as she danced around and around, her long red hair trailing like a comet about to smash to the earth. Raphah looked up at the swirl of stars above them and from far away could hear Crane's tormented cries. Galphus gripped his cane and trembled as from all around him the souls of the dead were sucked from the earth towards the golden frame that hung from the tree.

Thomas could see Kate as she got to her feet in the swirling mist. Isabella came to her side. For a moment Kate looked at him and then fell back towards the vortex. From within the chalice blood began to flow, covering the ground beneath them as the hill spun in time and space like the whirring of a clock. The Druggles ran into the dark woods, leaving them alone.

"Raphah," Thomas screamed. He felt the life flow from him as a purple haze surrounded him. "Kill her . . ."

The world stopped as if time had ceased. Hertha stared at Thomas. He looked and saw her feet had changed to those of a ram. She moved towards him and with one hand gripped his throat. When Kate saw this, she ran as fast as she could and grabbed at Hertha. The two began to fight, the girl holding the demon by her hair and beating at her with her fists.

Demurral stood motionless, as if he couldn't believe what was happening. Thomas joined Kate to help hold the creature down. Raphah seized the moment and grasped the Grail from Hertha's fingers. It was then that Galphus lunged at Raphah, hoping to snatch the Grail from his hands. Thomas picked up a stone from the dirt and, throwing it with all his might, struck Galphus on the hand. The man cowered back as if he were stung by a hornet.

From Hertha's back, two small wings began to form.

Demurral finally woke himself from his trance and jumped towards Thomas and Kate. Before he could reach them, Isabella's ghost grabbed Demurral and threw him to the ground. She fought with the magician to protect her friend, not knowing what he would do to her.

Hertha's wings fluttered and beat, and as they grew larger, she broke free of Thomas and lunged for the Grail. Thomas hit her in her face with an extraordinary strength.

Hertha looked at Thomas, stunned by the blow. She turned to Kate, who now stood near the open portal. With a sudden jab she pushed Kate towards the vortex. Kate stumbled and tripped, falling towards the inner glade as the world within sucked her closer. In a second Kate was gone, transformed between worlds and never to return. Thomas rushed to her and tried to reach her hand. He grasped her fingers and saw Kate's last smile. The *Gaudium-auctus* had lost its power. In her dying, Kate was like she had always been—his Kate Coglan and no other.

Raphah lifted the chalice into the air and spoke in his tongue, calling the names of the angels.

Hertha laughed. "I have heard all those names before, boy," she said as she reached for the cup.

In a single breath Raphah uttered the unutterable and screamed the hidden name of God. "*Shaddai-El-Aadonai*," he said again and again. The dirt beneath him began to awaken and the powers and principalities of the earth stirred beneath his feet like the rising of a volcano.

Demurral pushed the bucket of fire and incense from its stand and spilt the hot coals at Raphah's feet. The ground started to burn.

"Die, Ethiopian!" Demurral screamed as a wall of red flames began to encircle him.

Raphah recited the true name again and again. With every word the fire retreated from him as the ground trembled.

Hertha was beaten back by the flames. They burnt brightly, consuming the grass beneath her feet. The uttering of the Name filled the night air and called across the marshes. It was as if a power had been unleashed upon the world. It came in the sound of raindrops that beat against the river and fell from the sky like silver pearls.

Hertha was silenced. She looked up in wonder as she dropped her hands to her side and sighed.

It then happened so quickly that no one saw Thomas as he grabbed the cane from Galphus. With all the anger and pain that he had ever known—all the misery of his heart—he thrust it like a spear through Hertha's chest, piercing her cold, cold heart.

Hertha stood silently, then giggled, as if this could not have happened.

"An angel," she said softly. "Can only, when killed by love…" Hertha turned to Thomas and smiled at him. "You set me free. I take from you and you from me. I have no bitterness…"

Thomas let her speak no more. "Stop it, witch," he said, and he pulled the cane from her and pierced her again, watching her fall to the ground at Raphah's feet and begin to burn in the flames.

Galphus and Demurral began to pace slowly backwards towards the pathway. Raphah could see Galphus looking for the Druggles—they had all to a man vanished and had run away when the fire took hold.

"Now our numbers are more equal," Raphah said.

"Thou shalt not kill," Demurral murmured as he saw Thomas holding the cane in his hand.

"You know not the meaning of the words you say. They roll from your lips like lies and please no one," Raphah said. He held the chalice towards him as if to summon the powers from within. As he watched Raphah, Thomas felt a sense of peace settle over him, a feeling of renewed purpose.

"*Thou shalt not kill!*" shouted Crane as he stumbled, bruised, towards the circle with a pistol in each hand, followed by Lady Tanville Chilnam and Beadle. "*But I can!*"

He gave them not a moment longer as he fired both barrels towards them. Galphus raised his hands and the lead burst through the palm of his hand and into his face. Demurral turned to run and screamed in fear. The lead sped by and smashed against a tree, missing him by an inch.

Startled from his reverie, Thomas knew he could wait no longer. He thrust the cane through the air like a spear, striking Demurral in the leg. Demurral fell to the ground, bleeding from the wound. Thomas walked towards him, not listening to the shouting of his companions. All seemed like a dream. The trees beat against each other as he picked a burning coal from the ground. He felt no pain, no burning of his skin as his hand blistered and bubbled.

"I have known you since the day you were born," Demurral bleated. "I am the keeper of a secret you now must know. Your father didn't drown, Thomas. I am your father. Your mother worked for me; she loved me. Believe me—*I* am your father..."

"You're the third one to use that line on me," Thomas replied sarcastically. "Crane and Galphus have already tried. My father is in heaven, and that you know." Thomas calmly placed the burning ember in Demurral's waistcoat. "If I cannot see you burn in hell, then I shall see you burn upon the earth."

Demurral began to smoke as the flames took hold. He screamed and screamed, consumed by a fire within. Thomas turned from him and walked away. There was another shot as the Shadowmancer was relieved of his misery. Beadle stood on the outer edge of the dark wood, clutching the pistol he had taken from Jacob Crane. He looked at his master, a tear trickling down his cheek, and knew the world would not be the same again.

Beadle put the pistol on the ground and picked seven small round stones from the path. He looked at each one and, without speaking, put them in the pocket of his frock coat.

32

Chilnam Castle

Thomas sat on the bench by the fire. He looked at the stone mantel and the fireplace within. In the grate burnt a holly log. Above the mantel was the portrait of Isabella. It was where it had always been before, the bars now taken from the frame, the canvas bright and full of colour. Since the return of the painting to the castle, Isabella had not been seen. Beadle had said that she would no longer come from within, not now that she had Kate to keep her company.

Thomas thought of all that had gone before, and none of it made the slightest sense. The world had not changed—all that was lost was Kate. His hand was well healed, the skin mended, and his pride restored. The thoughts of that faraway night had almost slipped from his mind as if in the telling they had faded to a dream.

Thomas had spent the month walking in the forest and gardens of the castle. Since the *Magenta* had put in to winter at Berwick, he longed for the summer and the promise of sailing with Jacob Crane to take Raphah to Africa. In the long nights Raphah had told him of what would come as they journeyed south: fish that would fly from the sea, breezes so warm that they would burn the skin, and nights under the stars as the sea rocked them to sleep. All this was far away from the border castle and the Northumbrian gales that blew from the fell.

Lady Tanville Chilnam sat at the long table that ran the length of the Great Hall.

"They said they would be back by Christmas, and that is three days from now," Thomas said as he stacked the fire with more logs.

"Jacob said he had to be with Raphah; it was the only way they would be safe," she reminded Thomas.

"But why did they take Beadle?" he asked.

"To see Whitby for the last time and help dispose of the chalice," she replied.

"I should have gone with them," Thomas said halfheartedly as the door slowly opened and a small face peered within.

Then the door swung open and Beadle, Raphah, and Jacob Crane stepped within.

"Thomas," said Crane, and he opened his arms to be greeted.

"The chalice?" Thomas asked.

"Buried where no one will find it and in the place where it was taken from," Raphah said as he came into the hall and beat the cold from his coat.

"The chapel at Bell Hill?" Thomas asked.

"It's now but a ruin," Crane said. "We found the chamber beneath an old stone where the Templars had placed the Grail Cup. Think of it: a mile from Demurral all that time, and it took Mr. Bragg to find it."

"Why not take it to Africa?" Thomas asked as Raphah warmed by the fire.

"Who would think to look for the cup of the King a mile from the sea in a ruin by an old farm?" Raphah said. "There will come a time in this world when people will run after legends as if it is those that have the meaning of life. Best to keep these things from foolish men who look for comfort in that which is hidden. It will be safe there."

"And what of the power that Demurral sought?" Lady Tanville asked.

"There will be others, and in a time to come another Keruvim will take my place," Raphah said, as if the battle would rage forever in the hearts of men. In the high rafters above them an owl screeched its song as it waited for night.

"Raphah, what will I say when I face the King?" Thomas asked his friend.

"Love will cover a multitude of wrongs, and when you stand before him you will not stand alone. Each of us shall have an Advocate to speak for us. In that you will have no fear and no concern. As summer turns to autumn, we do not grieve the passing."

Thomas walked over to the painting, his eyes searching for some sign of Kate. There, for the first time, he noticed that within the image another face could be seen if he looked carefully. On the canvas, standing to the side of Isabella, was the smiling face of his lost friend.

Raphah saw Thomas looking at the picture. "Have no fear, Thomas," he said, placing a hand upon his shoulder. "Isabella and Kate have gone on to another kingdom."

"Do you believe all of that?" Thomas asked, looking at Raphah and Crane.

"How can you say that after all we have seen?" Crane replied as he pulled the bench closer to the fire and sipped brandy from a cup. "Even I have no excuses. There is more in the land of men than I dare admit."

"Sometimes my heart doubts, but when I hear you speak, I believe again," Thomas said.

"Did you see all what I saw, Thomas?" Raphah asked.

"Yes, everything."

"Then hold that as the truth."

"I will. But tell me—is Demurral really dead?" Thomas asked as he looked to the burn upon his hand.

"Forever..."

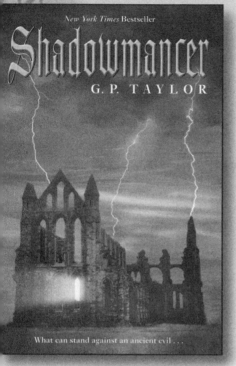